Praise for Laura L. Zimmerman

"Laura L. Zimmerman's YA fantasy *Keen* enthralled me from beginning to end. This present day Faerie story featuring a baffled teenage banshee and her unlikely high school friends has heart, lots of twists and turns, and a great message about using one's gifts for good. *Keen* would be the perfect next read for fans of Holly Black's *Folk of the Air* series and Maggie Stiefvater's *Lament*."

~Carrie Anne Noble, award-winning and bestselling author of *The Mermaid's Sister*

"A banshee tale? So here for it! *Keen* is a powerful story of friendship, love, loyalty, and sacrifice where snappy dialogue and evocative prose paint a vivid backdrop for delightful and dangerous hints of faerie. Snag your copy ASAP!"

~Gillian Bronte Adams, author of the *Songkeeper Chronicles*

"A powerful story of an outcast discovering the beauty of her own voice, filled with memorable characters and vivid twists, Laura L. Zimmerman's spellbinding debut *Keen* will echo in your memory long after you've turned the last page like the eerie final note of a banshee's song."

~Kara Swanson, award-winning author of *The Girl Who Could See*

"I haven't devoured a book this quickly in a long time! Its unique premise, relatable characters, rising stakes, swoony romance, and engaging narrative style make *Keen* a perfect stay-up-all-night kind of read, complete with a beautiful message of healing and self-worth. Laura L. Zimmerman has launched herself right to the top of my list of favorite paranormal fantasy authors!"

~Laurie Lucking, award-winning author of *Common*

"A fantastic debut! Zimmerman draws the reader into the multifaceted world of *Keen*, where nothing is as it seems. I loved the characters and found myself fully invested all the way to the last beautiful page. I can't wait for the sequel!"

~J.M. Hackman, award-winning author of *Spark*

"The lure of the banshee's song is irresistible in life (and death), and it's no different in *Keen*. I was pulled into the story from the first line to the last. Laura L. Zimmerman's debut novel is intriguing, engaging, and hard to put down. I can't wait to see more from her!"

~Pam Halter, award-winning author of *Fairyeater* and the *Willoughby and Friends* Series

"A modern twist of mythical Irish folklore, *Keen* packs a fast-paced punch along with well-developed characters. I couldn't put it down!"

~Missy Kalicicki, co-author of the *Sinners Series*

"The modern faerie tale I've been waiting for! *Keen* grips you from the first page and pulls you into a story you won't want to leave—rife with magic, teaming with incredible characters, and filled with the promise of hope in a dark world."

~Ashley Townsend, author of the *Rising Shadows Trilogy*

"*Keen* weaves such a fantastical mystery, in a sense that your nose will remained glued to the page until you've pulled back every layer and uncovered every hidden clue. Nothing is ever simple for a banshee living through high school."

~Desiree Williams, author of *Illusionary* and *Sun and Moon*

Silence

Also by
Laura L. Zimmerman

Now Available:

Keen: Banshee Song Series, Book One

Lament: Banshee Song Series, Book Two

R.A.D. Detectives: The Case of the Missing Robot

The Curse of Ozpa Springs

Silence

BANSHEE SONG SERIES

LAURA L. ZIMMERMAN

Published by Caffeinated Fiction Publishing

Mont Alto, PA 17237

FIRST EDITION: 2024

Printed in the United States of America

ISBN-13: 979-8-9914958-2-0

Library of Congress Cataloging-in-Publication Data is on file at the Library of Congress, Washington, D.C.

Fiction: Teen and Young Adult Contemporary Fantasy

Fiction: Teen and Young Adult Myths and Legends

Fiction: Teen and Young Adult Coming of Age Fiction

Cover Design by Travis Herdt

❀ Created with Vellum

Chapter One

The dream is always the same. I'm in the same primitive cell I remember from the Unseelie Realm. Miniscule. Claustrophobic.

Eric is beside me. He looks bad. So much worse than when I last saw him.

His smooth brown skin is shredded with cuts, some healed, some healing. Some wounds are fresh. Hands that tremble like an unending earthquake. Hazel eyes that aren't just puffy from crying but tortured. The skin around them is peeling. The whites are no longer white, but instead, the deepest shade of crimson.

His chestnut hair is longer than when I left him. Spots have been ripped from their roots, most likely from those trembling fingers of his. Or maybe it's just falling out from malnutrition.

After all, he's downright gaunt. A shadow of a corpse.

He's lost so much weight that I barely recognize him. Bones stick out at all the wrong angles, the skin along his cheekbones is sunken into atrophied muscle.

But the worst part of the dream isn't how he looks. (He is a traitor, after all.)

No. The worst part is what he says. His words.

The way he begs over and over and over and—

I squeeze my eyes shut and bite my lip until I taste metal. But I can't make the dream stop. I can't stop his cries of agony.

His cries for help.

"Caoine. Please."

Eric's voice is ragged. Childlike.

"Help me."

The syllables run together as if he can't fully close his lips, spittle dripping along his chin.

"I need you. Please."

He needs me? I doubt that. He needed to *trick* me, to *deceive* me into helping his father. That's the only *needing* he's ever had.

"Caoine."

But this is a dream. A projection of my last memories of the boy from when I last saw him. I'm sure of it.

"Caoine."

I'm imagining him. The only way I *can* imagine him, since my brain refuses to acknowledge that he's sitting comfortably by his father's side. Ruling the Unseelie. Without a care for anyone but himself.

"Caoine."

I hate him.

"Caoine."

He betrayed me. *Again.*

"Caoine."

I will never forgive him.

"Caoine."

This is a promise.

"Caoine!"

I gasp and sit up in bed, the periwinkle hued walls and fluffy comforter that cocoon me pulling me from my dream. My dad pushes through my bedroom door, knocking the small rectangular white message board hanging on the front to the floor. He winces, not bothering to pick it up, tossing the kitchen towel in his hand over his shoulder, a goofy grin on his face. "Rise and shine, sleepy head."

"Dad." My voice cracks as I rub the palm of my hands against my eyes and scratch a hand through my rats' nest of stark white hair.

His smile fades, his brown eyes filling with concern. "You okay?" He crosses the plush cream-colored carpet and plops beside me on my bed.

I nod. "Just feeling wonky. My throat hurts and my head feels like it's been hit by a bus." I tug at the collar of my pink and white polka dot PJs, pulling at the damp fabric that's stuck to my skin.

He frowns, making his crooked nose a little bit more off-center. "I'm not feeling great either. Maybe we caught a bug?"

I curl my upper lip. "Not cool. We just got back home. I was sort of hoping I'd get to enjoy my teenagehood now that I'm no longer being hunted by evil faeries."

"Patience, my young Padawan." He chuckles, his smile making him appear boyish, despite the salt that has begun peppering his brown hair. "We've got all the time in the world. You'll get your life back."

He stops, reaching one calloused hand up to curve around my pointed ear.

I swallow against the way my throat closes. *We've got all the time in the world.* A niggle in my spirit tells me that I'm missing something. That time is something we don't have. Not anymore.

My dad's gaze lingers on my hair until my cheeks heat. He drops his hand. "Well, get dressed and run a brush through your hair. There's someone downstairs waiting for you."

"Oliver?" My heart speeds away and the butterflies in my belly fly in a billion different directions simultaneously.

"Oh uh, no. Aubree."

"Ah!" I throw my covers off and jump out of bed. "I forgot I told her we'd grab coffee this morning."

My dad laughs again and shuffles out of my room, shaking his head.

In minutes I'm presentable, dressed in a basic pair of jeans with a fitted top that doesn't make me look quite as waifish as I once did, prior to meeting Aubree. Having fae blood means always looking a bit too much on the thin side. But a simple glamour that doesn't take much work to keep in place gives me a more human appearance.

My hair on the other hand... Sigh. Despite how stark white it is, Aubree encouraged me to remain unique and embrace my differences, along with my fae-ness. I wrangle the mess on top of my head into a bun, lace up my high-top Converses, and race down the steps. I'm more than ready to spend some time with my best friend who I've been separated from for weeks on end—although to her it was only a couple of days.

Time in the Faerie Realms is weird like that.

"Hey, Aub—" Her name dies on my tongue as I pause on the bottom step.

Her appearance is nothing like her norm. She's in plain jeans and a white T, her turquoise hair pulled back in a simple ponytail. My normally happy-go-lucky friend is gone for the moment. Her almond-shaped eyes are hard with determination.

A rock falls into the pit of my stomach. "What's wrong?"

"We've got a little detour to take before breakfast."

My brows stretch to my hairline. "A detour?"

She nods. "Grab those books you stole. It's time you met my mother."

Chapter Two

The morning sun rises above the clouds and warms my skin, a welcome difference compared to what I've faced the last few weeks. The image strikes a memory of honey butter on waffles. My belly gurgles in complaint.

Aubree and I stand in silence a short distance from the high school. Her back is straight, her gaze on the horizon. She appears...nervous?

A breeze of fresh lavender tumbling from a nearby field settles over me. I pay close attention to my surroundings, my heart pounding. I don't want to fall through the Veil again.

A thick patch of trees sits behind us, further down the hill, closer to the school. We're in a clearing, a stretch of grass unbothered by flowers or trees or any other manmade structure. Probably because the invisible Veils hang right in the middle of it. Although unseen to the human eye, these portals to the Faerie Realms will transport anyone to the Seelie or Unseelie Realms when activated. It's one of the few places on earth where both Veils appear together, side by side. Most other locations around the world that host one of the Veils only contain either the Unseelie or Seelie Veil.

I toe through the grass that is beginning to grow over those broken seals embedded in the ground. The same ones we encountered on Halloween night when my life was turned upside down, all those months ago.

Nothing glows now, but maybe that's just because it's daylight. I shove my hands in my pockets, my left hand fitting just a bit off. My missing finger has become a part of me now.

"Caoine." Aubree motions me to join her, her eyes locked on a specific point.

I squint and see nothing at first. But then... The air shimmers and shifts, the form of a body materializing right before us.

I blink, furrowing my brow.

Queen Failenn. She dressed plainly, in a white linen dress that flows to her ankles, a circlet of gold at her waist. She wears no other adornment, her hair twisted on top of her head. I try to focus on the color of it, the shape of her lips, her face, but my vision goes blurry. Once more, I can't grasp exactly what she looks like, her image an ever-changing tide. A secret she's not willing to share.

The queen comes to a stop a dozen feet away. "Hello, lovely Daughters."

I startle. "Daughters?"

She smiles at me. "All fae true to the Creator are my children."

Aubree smiles at me too.

My heart does a strange stumbly thing and my throat closes an inch. *True to the Creator?* I've barely even considered it.

The queen turns to Aubree. "Aubree, my beloved." She ponders Aubree's face with tenderness.

My chest constricts as my mind flutters over thoughts of my own mother. Would she have looked at me in the same way? A mother/daughter relationship is something so foreign to me, yet a strange longing unfolds deep within me.

"Did you bring them?" the queen asks.

Aubree nods and pulls a bag from her shoulder, settling it to the ground. She digs through and reveals the Book of Discernment and Book of Judgment.

Queen Faílenn reaches out. Without moving forward, the books are suddenly in her hands. She cradles them to her chest. "You have done well."

Aubree beams. "Yes, Mother." She gives a small bow to the queen.

I nibble my lip. "So...that's it? If it is, would you be able to tell me how to save my mom?" My mom who I believed to have died the night of my birth to save me from death. A banshee like me who was turned into the mythical *bean-nighe*. A wild banshee.

The queen nods. "There will be time for that soon, my child. First, you must continue the quest to fix the seals. Your chance to save Saoirse will be shown to you when the time is right."

I shake my head. "But you have the books now. Can't you just do the same spell as before?"

"Obtaining the books was merely the first step in a plan that contains many, Caoine Roberts. Repairing the Seven Seals will take all of our efforts to complete the task."

All our efforts?

"But aren't we out of time? The end of the world is coming." I toss Aubree a sheepish look. "Or something like that, right?"

The queen simply smiles. "There is time, child. First, we must gather one fae from each of the *Bunaidh*."

I glance between Aubree and the queen. "The Bunaidh?"

"All fae are connected through bloodlines. However, they all came from a small select group, at the beginning of time when the Creator formed the Realms. We must have one fae to represent each family from the Bunaidh. The original fae who inhabited the Faerie Realms."

I exhale, attempting to wrap my mind around this new information. "So how do we do this?"

"First you must bring me the son of the Unseelie Realm."

"The son." I pretend not to know who she's talking about, but my swallow gives me away.

Aubree leans in, her turquoise ponytail falling over her shoulder. "She means the Unseelie prince."

I clench my jaw. "The Unseelie prince? You mean *Eric*? We need to go back into that desolate nightmare to bring back that... that *traitor*?" I have trouble controlling the volume of my voice.

Queen Faílenn tilts her head. "All will be revealed in time, Caoine. First, complete this task."

"No. We can't. I...*won't*. I don't want to go back there. Ever. And, I hate him."

"This task must be completed or all is lost."

I grind my teeth together. Is this chick for real?

There is zero chance I'm going back to the land that almost claimed my life. *More* than once.

Aubree leans toward me. "Caoine, please. She wouldn't ask us if it wasn't necessary."

My nostrils flare and I stare off into the trees.

The spot where my missing finger used to be throbs. A warning that I should stay in the Mortal Realm and never leave again. Never.

The queen finds my gaze. "Do you agree to do this, my daughter?"

I suck in a lungful of pride and fight for an inch of sanity. "Will you tell me how to save my mom then?"

"That path will become clear as you journey, Caoine. It will be your choice if you save her or not."

Why is she talking in riddles? Can't she just give me a straight answer? "But I'll make the choice to save her, I know I will. That's not even a question. So, does this mean you'll help me find her?"

"That is a question to be answered at another time. For now I must know if you are willing to accept this quest."

"But—"

"Caoine." Aubree's tone is quiet but hard.

I choke on my next words. Why won't she just tell me that she'll help me? My jaw flexes as I bite back my questions. "Fine. I'll help you with this gathering of the Bunaidh and I'll save the jerk who doesn't deserve to be saved. *And* I *will* figure out a way to save my mom along the way."

"You have done well, Caoine Roberts. You have done much for all the Realms. Only time will tell if we will be successful in our quest to bring balance back to them."

Awesome. So encouraging.

I control my urge to ask a million more questions, if only because I care so much for Aubree. "So what's the plan? How do we get back to the Unseelie to save the traitor?"

"Aubree will lead you on your path. Follow her." She turns to Aubree, gently placing her hand on my friend's cheek. "It is lovely to see you, Daughter. Please be safe on your journey. I look forward to seeing you soon." Her smile is so gentle it almost brings me to tears.

Aubree lifts her chin.

I open my mouth to ask the first of a million questions. But the queen is gone.

I turn in a circle. "Hey! Where'd she go?"

Aubree sighs. "She's told us what we need to know."

"So that's it? We don't get any more help?"

She chuckles. "We don't need anymore, Caoine. She's given us what we need. The rest is up to us."

I huff. "Great. Exactly what I was afraid of."

Chapter Three

The coffee shop is crowded, even for a Saturday. Scents of leather and chocolate and yeast float around me. Every table is taken. A chorus of friendly chatter and screaming espresso machines bounces between the walls. Euphoria zips through my inner core at the sight of our old hangout. It feels like months since I've been here. Which, it sort of has been. For me.

We picked Oliver up on the way so we could break the news to him together. Just the thought makes my blood pound through my veins.

The line moves quickly and we're seated at the only open chairs we can find. A set of high-backed reading chairs by the far window, a small table set between them. Oliver and I squeeze together into one seat. Not that either of us mind. I hold his hand —my ultra-white skin in contrast to his dark skin—and settle my head on his shoulder. He's casual, in an over-sized T and jeans, and sporting brand new, very obviously expensive sneakers— probably a graduation present from his parents. I take in his scent of laundry soap and aftershave, my heart doing little somersaults.

He's swiping through social media by the time Aubree joins us. Oliver frowns.

"Something wrong?" I ask.

He shakes his head, turning off his phone. "Nah. Just weird stuff going on in the world." He rolls his eyes at my crinkled forehead of concern. "Earthquakes, tsunamis." He tweaks my nose. " Nothing for you to worry about."

I shrug and turn my attention to Aubree. She places her slender hands in her lap, her face pinched. Her chest rises and falls with every breath she takes. I swallow. Is that my hand that's so clammy or Oliver's?

"I'm ready when you are." Oliver gives a gentle laugh, that crooked front tooth just barely peeking from beneath his perfectly shaped lips.

My heart swoons.

He tilts his head at my faerie friend, clearing his throat. "Your silence is sort of scaring me."

Aubree nods. "I'm just trying to find the words so I won't send you running."

My heart sinks. Way to be dramatic, Aubree.

Oliver leans forward, his elbows on his knees. My hand is still tucked neatly inside one of them. "Okay. Now I am scared. What's going on?"

She closes her eyes as she speaks. "Remember that conversation we had yesterday? About the spell that was done on Halloween night and how when I tried to break it I released something bad?"

Oliver nods, his deep brown eyes intent on my friend.

Aubree draws in a breath. "Well, here's the whole story. I think I told you that I had to borrow magic strong enough to counter the spell Eric used, right? That magic—it was connected to an ancient spell created years ago by my mother and father, King Osín and Queen Faílenn of the Seelie Realm. A spell created in response to the nefarious actions of the Unseelie king.

"To make a long story short, mortals had been at war with one another for hundreds of years. At some point, the fae were ready for it to be over. Although the Mortal Realm may seem separate from the Fae Realms, what happens here still affects those realms.

"A couple hundred years ago, King Raghnall and Queen Mairéad of the Unseelie Realm had the idea to wipe out the human race entirely. They had the idea that this would be the only sure way to end the wars between humans. Plus, they also wanted to use the Mortal Realm in their own way. So, they released seven deadly plagues on the earth, to bring about a global extinction of the human race."

I still. Some of this I already know. But hearing it again still sets my nerves on edge. To know that the king was that evil to eliminate billions of people without a second thought.

"What did your parents think of this?" Oliver shakes his head in disbelief. "Did they even know?"

Aubree sighs. "Not until it was too late. The plagues had been released and destruction in the Mortal Realm had already begun. So they did the only thing they could. They enacted a spell that would contain the plagues and keep them trapped. My mother and father used the strongest magic they could and combined their efforts using the magic of a banshee."

I gasp. This part I definitely didn't know.

"Because there was so much widespread death, they relied on the power of the banshee to complete the spell and make it practically impenetrable." Aubree's gaze connects with mine. "They used your mother."

My jaw drops. "What? Why did you never tell me this?"

Aubree shakes her head. "I didn't know until recently. I've been waiting for the right time to tell you." Her cheeks pink.

"Raspberry mocha with cinnamon?" The barista's voice cuts the tension of the conversation.

I jump in place.

Aubree hides her annoyance and smiles at the employee. "Thanks, Deb. That's mine."

"You're welcome, my dear." Deb gives her a wink. "And the lady gets the mango-peach tea?" I nod and accept my drink.

"Which leaves the large black coffee for the handsome young man."

"Thank you, ma'am," Oliver says, as he takes his cup.

"I like your ears." Aubree gestures towards Deb's pointed slip-on ears.

Deb laughs. "Thanks. I have a thing for faerie lore. My daughters gave me these for fun."

I bite the inside of my cheek. The irony.

"Hope you enjoy your drinks!." Deb skitters off to help the next customer at the register.

We each take a minute to sip our drinks. My mind spirals out of control. My own mother was part of this chain of events hundreds of years before my birth? Maybe there's a reason why I'm part of everything that's happened here in recent months. Why I need to be the one to accompany Aubree on this journey.

"So... you were saying something about my mother?" I ask.

She nods and glances around. "Saoirse was one of the most powerful banshees at the time. In performing the spell, Seven Seals were created. The Seals held each of the plagues, trapping them for eternity."

"Until they were released the night Eric broke your spell." Oliver's voice is low and soft.

"Yes," Aubree whispers.

"And this is why the Seelie queen created the Laws of Necessity." I squeeze Oliver's hand. "To keep Raghnall in check so he wouldn't do something crazy like that again."

"The Laws of what?" Oliver's brown eyes fill with confusion.

"Of Necessity."

Aubree's eyebrows raise as if she's impressed. I learned more in the Unseelie Realm than she probably knows.

"They give full control over the Veils to Queen Failenn. Only those Unseelie with royal blood can move between the Realms. And even then, they must get permission from the queen."

Oliver scowls. "That seems a bit unfair."

Aubree shrugs. "Exactly why the Unseelie have long called

themselves enslaved to the Seelie Realm. But what else could my mother do? Allow Raghnall to release something even more deadly in the Mortal Realm? Or worse, within the Seelie Realm? He had to be kept in check."

"I guess." Oliver nods but doesn't look convinced.

I look at my boyfriend, my eyes skittering over his high cheek-bones. "I think there's a reason you and Eric were best friends."

"Hey now." He tilts his head. "Let's not bring him into this. I'm not sure I'll ever forgive him for holding that knife to my throat."

"I know." My voice is gentle. "I mean, I despise the boy, too. I'll never forgive *myself* for trusting him a second time. But still...I think you two would see eye-to-eye on that point. Maybe your friendship was grounded on more than just a lie. Maybe it wasn't a ruse."

Oliver's mouth twists into a jagged smile. "Ruse? Sometimes you sound nothing like a teenager, you know that?"

I roll my eyes. "Okay." I turn my attention back to Aubree. "Tell him the rest."

Aubree sits up straighter. "My mother can do the spell again."

"Okay." Oliver drags this word out.

I take a long sip of my tea.

"So, she's going to need one of each kind of *Bunaidh* faerie present at the time of the spell. Before you ask, that's a fancy word for *relative of really old fae that have been around since the begin-ning of time.* Each must be in agreement. And we'll need a banshee present, too." She wince-smiles at me. "Which we've already got, so...yay?"

I look down. "And..."

Oliver groans. "Is this the part where we run screaming from the coffee shop?"

Aubree shrugs. "Kind of, yeah. We sort of need someone of royal blood from the Unseelie Realm to be present."

Oliver freezes. "Haha. Come again? It almost sounded like you said you need King Raghnall to agree to be there?"

I nail him with a look. "Or his son."

Oliver shakes his head adamantly. "Eric? Aw, heck no. Nope. No way. I'm not letting that psychopath anywhere near Caoine."

I sigh. "My sentiment exactly. Unfortunately, our hands are tied." And slightly diminished in my case, thanks in part to Eric.

He blows out a breath. "I'm sorry, but no. There has to be another Unseelie prince that can do the job. I don't care if he's worse than Eric. As long as he didn't stab me in the back and attempt to kill me. And kidnap my girlfriend like a madman."

I wince. I knew this would be how the conversation would go. "Do you know any random Unseelie princes hanging around we can tap for the job?"

He pauses. "No, but—"

Aubree nods. "Exactly. And we don't have time to make new friends. These plagues are coming and they're coming fast. Once they begin, massive destruction will rip the Mortal Realm apart."

"And then they will move on to the Seelie Realm. Then the Unseelie?"

Her shoulders sag. "Yes."

"Dude. Not cool." Oliver glances between the two of us. "Why would King Raghnall release destruction that could wipe out his own realm?"

"To be honest?" Aubree shrugs. "He's so self-absorbed, he thinks he'll be able to stop them once they've finished in the Mortal Realm. I'm not even sure he knew for sure they would affect the Fae Realms at first. But he's cocky enough to believe he has everything under control."

Oliver shakes his head. "Dude's got some arrogance issues."

I snort. "Tell me about it."

We sit in silence for a beat.

Why is this thing falling on my shoulders again? I'm only going to mess things up. Per usual. *Sigh.*

"Well, that decides it." Oliver pulls me close to him. "If Eric is going to be anywhere near my girl, then I'm coming along. On whatever suicide mission you two might have schemed up, which I'm guessing you have."

Bile creeps up my throat and I gulp my tea to force it back down. I only end up scorching my throat. I don't want Oliver anywhere near the Unseelie. Or Eric, for that matter.

Tears prick my eyes and I close them. Why do I feel so unworthy of this quest? My instincts are non-existent. I was wrong about Eric six months ago and I was wrong about him again a few weeks back. The first chance he got to deceive me again, it totally worked.

I exhale slowly. Would Aubree go to the Unseelie Realm without me and bring Eric back? I can't shake the feeling I'll be a liability on this journey.

But I say none of this. I swallow my doubts deep inside me where no one will find them, not even me.

Because denial is what I do.

Instead, I say, "How much time do we have before we begin the journey back to the place of nightmares?"

Aubree's voice drops to a whisper. "Two days. Monday morning we leave the Mortal Realm. And then? We steal Eric out from under his father's nose."

Chapter Four

The knock on my bedroom door startles me. I set aside my poetry journal and calligraphy pen. "Come in."

My dad's tired smile is heart-achingly beautiful. The lines along his mouth appear softer, his skin more youthful. Did his time in Faerie mess with the aging process?

"What's up?" I shift closer to the head of my bed so he can take a seat next to me. It smells like he's just showered. His clothes have changed, too, from earlier in the day. Now he's in a light pink polo and tan pants. Since when did he begin dressing so preppy?

He runs a hand down his face. "Just checking on my girl."

I tuck a loose piece of hair behind my ear. "I'm good."

"Are you? You seemed a bit down after your time out with Aubree. Anything I need to know about?" He tilts his head at my silence. "Is this a Faerie Realm thing?"

"It's always a Faerie Realm thing, isn't it?" He pouts at my forced laugh. I clear my throat. "Yeah. Things are...difficult when it comes to that."

My dad raises his brows. "Difficult like, there's something that could affect you? *Us?*"

"Erm, difficult like it could affect the entire world?" My fake smile doesn't amuse him.

"What's going on, Caoine? You're not going back there, are you? I thought we'd put that whole mess behind us."

"Well..." I shrug.

His face grows hard. "No. I won't allow it. You are never going back there. Ever. Neither am I. You and I are both done with the Faerie Realms. There are other fae out there. Let one of them take care of whatever this problem is."

"Dad." Why does my voice sound so whiny? "It's not that simple."

"Sure it is. You're not the only fae in the Mortal Realm. Tell Aubree to find someone else. You are staying home. For good."

I sigh. "Yeah, but—"

"But what? What is there to discuss? Other faeries exist, am I right?"

"Yeah."

"Good. Let one of them do the job. This isn't for you to do, Caoine."

I twist my fingers together in my lap. "Except that it sort of is."

"Come again?"

"I mean...the night that Eric did the spell? The night that you—" I clear my throat again. "That you were taken?" He nods, his posture tense. "Well, Aubree did a counter spell to try to stop Eric. It didn't work but, well, when she did it, something was set in motion."

"*Something*?" My dad crosses his arms.

"Another spell was broken. A protection spell."

"Okay." He draws this word out.

"So...Aubree needs my help to fix things. To stop the consequences of the broken spell."

"But why does she need *you*?"

"Because...because—"

"Let me guess. Because you're a *banshee*, right?" Once more, my silence is his answer. He shakes his head. "I don't get it. Why is your being a banshee so important? Why is it always *you* that needs to save the world?"

Now I do laugh. Because hearing him say it out loud is ridiculous. "I don't know. I was sort of hoping you could tell me why it's always me." I nibble my lip. Do I tell him my mom was a part of the original spell, or will that only break his heart?

He grumbles in response.

"Look, Dad. I'm sorry but I need to go back. There's no way around it. But at least this time I'll have Aubree with me. It will be a quick trip in and out of the Unseelie Realm. Done."

"*Quick* sounds a bit optimistic." The grumpy Dad face comes out.

I shrug. Because I honestly can't say just how long this thing will take. I fiddle with the stump of my missing pinky.

He narrows his gaze. It falls to where I massage my finger. "Then you'll be back for good?"

"Well, then I'll need to head into the Seelie Realm." My voice grows more insistent with his apparent shock. I don't mention that I plan to find a way to bring mom back. No reason to get his hopes up. "But the Seelie Realm is safe. Aubree's mom is the queen. I'll be safe as a kitten there."

"Uh-huh."

"Look, I know you're not in favor of this, but I really will be fine. I need to do this. To save you. To save us."

"What about school?"

"I—" I pause. "I can't promise anything."

"Caoine..." His tone is a warning.

"But I will try my hardest to get back as soon as possible so I can graduate on time." I pause. "Really. Being away isn't any more fun for me than it is for you. I'd much rather be in high school than fighting off whatever darkness the Faerie Realms have to throw at me."

The tension in his shoulders fades. "Does this have anything to do with the fact that we've been home for days and you haven't sung even once?"

He means my banshee song. The thing I was created to sing.

For the first eighteen years of my life, I believed my song was a curse. That people would die when I sang it. Because that's what it was at its core—a beckoning to cross to the other side. It took Oliver, and Aubree, and a lot of heartache for me to realize that the song is a gift. That while singing it, I have the ability to see the outcomes of the hearer of the song. To know whether their death is imminent or something that can be changed.

For some, my song is their final peaceful lullaby here on earth. Their death is inevitable. I am meant to comfort them as they pass.

For others, my song is a warning. A caution to change their ways or make better decisions. An opportunity for them to continue to live.

The one thing that sets me apart from the other fae: banshees only sing in the Mortal Realm. My song is meant for humans, not fae. Which is why I can only sing while in the Mortal Realm, why it's so unusual for it to present itself while in either of the Faerie Realms. Having spent so many weeks in the Unseelie Realm—without my song—has left me missing my true nature.

I sigh. It hasn't come out at all since I've been back. Total silence.

When I first got stuck in the Unseelie Realm, it was alarming that I didn't go through my nightly ritual of releasing my banshee song. Then it became comfortable. But by the end, I missed it. I was actually looking forward to things getting back to normal.

I mean, if a banshee can't sing, is she still a banshee?

I've been through it a thousand times in my head.

I was born to be a banshee. My purpose has always been steeped in my identity as a banshee.

So why can't I convince myself that I still have worth, even though my song hasn't been released in weeks?

I swallow against the sandy grain in my throat. "I'm not sure when that will return."

He rests a hand on my shoulder. "Give it time. Your body probably just needs to adjust to being back in the Mortal Realm."

I bite back against the tears that sting my eyes. "The Mortal Realm? Look at you, sounding fae and all." I smile at him.

He laughs. "Well, I spent enough time there, I guess."

My throat grows tight. "I swear Dad, I'll do whatever it takes to get back to you. As fast as humanly possible. Or, as fast as a faerie can." My laugh sounds off again.

"I know, sweetie." He pulls me into a hug. "I just worry about you."

A tear finally breaks free and finds its way down my cheek. "Look who's talking? Mr. Kidnapped-to-the-Unseelie-Realm for half a year."

He pulls back with a shake of his head. "It still throws me that it wasn't years. It felt like years. Are you sure some sort of mythical creature didn't sneak in and change our calendars or something?"

"I wish it were that simple. But even I don't know. Time between the Faerie Realms and the Mortal Realm works differently."

He glances at my journal tossed to the side. "I'll let you get back to your thing, I guess." My dad stretches an arm overhead as he stands. "When are you leaving?"

My heart races at the very question that's been plaguing my mind for the past twenty-four hours. "Soon."

He nods, his shoulders shaking as he coughs into his arm. "Guess I'll order pizza for supper then. With fries on the side." He throws me a wink before he leaves the room.

I frown. My head has been aching like crazy all day. What are the chances we'd catch a sickness the minute we get back from the Unseelie Realm?

But the idea flits away as quickly as it came. I don't think the Faerie Realms even have sickness. Not unless it's caused by a curse or something.

The pen is light in my fingers as I grab my journal and begin where I left off. The words flow like the delicate fuchsia waters of the Unseelie. Free and winding. Without obstruction.

That's one thing that hasn't been a burden for me since my return. My writing. Every minute I've sat down to reflect on my thoughts has produced an overflow of emotion. The creativity that was once at times difficult to find now leaves my fingertips almost before I can even form the thought in my mind.

I pull in a breath. If only my words could bring an end to this unpredictable curse that's roaming the Realms. A pit forms in my stomach again.

If only I didn't have to go back.

Chapter Five

I'm wandering the castle, the solid stone walls weeping from the chilled air. The stale scent of blood and urine bombards me from all angles. A soft cry echoes from down the hall.

Slam! I'm on my knees, pushed from behind.

Hot tears stream down my face and agony snakes along my left leg in tendrils. Warmth slides along the side of my head.

"Move!"

The gruff voice comes from behind me.

I struggle to my feet, grabbing the wall for balance. That's when I see them. Chains.

They're on my wrists, my ankles. Burns and bruises slice deep into my skin.

Except...

Except it's not mine. The skin. These hands, the clothes. They're not mine. They look like—

A mirror, at the far end of the hallway. I limp my way towards it, the ever-present pinch of something hard in the middle of my back.

Finally, I reach it. Lift my head. Look into familiar hazel eyes, a dark mole sitting just to the right of my eye.

Eric.

"Please, Caoine," he whispers. *Spittle dribbles down his chin as he fights for words.*

"Caoine?"

Wham! *Everything goes black—*

"Caoine!"

I jump.

Aubree frowns. "You okay?"

"Yeah. Sure." I blink away the vision I've just had. This one, more real than any other.

This time I wasn't just seeing Eric. I *was* Eric.

"So what do you think?"

"About what?"

"About the plan?" This comes from Oliver, who sits beside me.

We're grouped in my living room. Oliver and I are on my ancient brown sofa, my head resting on his shoulder. Aubree in the arm-chair my father usually occupies. The TV is off but the antique clock on the mantlepiece of the fireplace *tick tick ticks* our time into oblivion. Oliver's feet are up on the coffee table, those brand new sneakers still on his feet.

He takes my hand in his. "Do you think your dad will be cool with us heading out first thing in the morning?"

"I—" I curl my toes into the shag carpet below me. "Erm, sure. Yeah. We already talked about it. This morning."

"And he's good with you going back in?" Aubree fiddles with a waist-length piece of neon green hair. Her bright pink top with puffed sleeves and matching pink skirt are in perfect contrast.

"Well, he's not happy. Then again, neither am I."

Oliver scowls and sits up, pulling his feet from the coffee table. "My sentiments exactly. That *faerie* dares lay a finger on you, I swear—"

I straighten, too. "Whoa, slow down there, cowboy. You aren't starting a fight with a fae inside the Unseelie Realm. That's just suicide."

He drops my hand. "As if this entire quest isn't suicidal?"

Aubree sighs, clicking her white patent leather high-heels together. "Touché."

"I just wish there were a way...something I could do to keep track of my dad. To keep him safe, ya know? To reassure him that I'm fine, too."

Aubree grins. "You and I are of one mind, sister." She slips her hand into her silver beaded handbag, pulling out identical hand-held mirrors. She holds them up with pride.

"Mirrors? Really, Aubree? You think I'll be concerned with my hair while we're in the Unseelie or something?"

She rolls her eyes, holding one out to me. "Please. Give me more credit."

I accept the gift. It's heavier than it looks, the metal other-worldly. Fine detail is etched along the back. The handle has clearly been carved by a master. "Whoa."

"Oh, you haven't seen the half of it." Aubree holds hers in front of her face. "Look into your mirror."

I glance at Oliver. He's visibly irritated but shrugs and lifts his chin.

"Okay." But I'm not convinced.

At first, I only see myself. The tired eyes, one a gentle shade of faded green, the other so pale it borders on silver. My unwashed hair, alabaster and straight. Those too-thin collar bones that iden-tify me as something other than human.

Then a mist fills the mirror, another image taking my place. Bright red lipstick, heavily mascaraed eyes with sparkling blue eye shadow.

Aubree.

Literally, the Aubree that's sitting right across from me. I can see the antique clock over her shoulder, the one left by my grand-father before he passed.

She smiles and gives a wave. "Hey."

I lift my eyes to look at her, then look back at the mirror. "How did you—you're—" My jaw falls open.

Are there any words when you realize you're holding a magic mirror?

She laughs.

"So cool." Oliver looks over my shoulder, his previous mood forgotten.

I shake my head. "Why am I even surprised by stuff like this?"

"I don't know. Why are you?" Aubree says this to me in the mirror.

"How does it work?" I turn my mirror over and inspect the artistry on the back again. "Do all fae have this kind of stuff?"

"They were made especially for the queen. They're quite rare." She waves me off and hands the other mirror to me. "Let's get your dad in on this."

I nod with a little too much excitement. "Dad. Hey, Dad! Come here."

An affirming grunt comes from the den in the back of the house and my dad's face appears from the hallway a second later, breathless. "Sorry. I was just watching a news segment. There's some weird sleeping sickness out in Asia." When he sees my face he perks up. "What's up?"

I wave him over. "Here." I hold one of the mirrors out to him. "Take this."

His brows yank together, but he takes it, running a hand over the salt and pepper stubble of his chin.

I hold my mirror up and smile.

My dad stands frozen, staring at me, confusion a blanket over his every feature.

I slam a hand on my hip. "Dad. Look at your mirror."

He hesitates but does as I say.

And his jaw drops open. "You. That's…" His eyes bop from the mirror to the real me. "I can see you in the mirror."

My grin is ridiculously big. "Yes, you can. And I can see you, too."

Aubree stands, adjusting her ponytail. "And you will be able to hear each other, once you're no longer together. It's not just visual."

Oliver's eyes go wide. "So cool. I almost want to stay back just so Caoine and I can do the faerie-Facetime-thing."

I brighten. "That's a good idea! You can stay back and take care of my dad."

My dad scowls. "Hey. I'm not that old."

Oliver shoots me a look. "That's out of the question. I was only saying the mirror thing is cool. I'll be glued to your side the entire trip. Just remember that." He kisses my forehead despite his sour expression.

I shrivel, even though my smile still hangs on. He and I have been through this conversation twice before. The minute he heard Aubree and I were headed to the Unseelie Realm to retrieve Eric, he insisted he come along. *No girlfriend of mine is going to a place like that without me.*

I sigh. So overprotective.

He smiles. A thousand butterflies take flight inside my belly.

Okay. Maybe I do want him to come along.

My dad fingers his mirror, his eyes skittering over each of us. "I hate to point out the obvious, but couldn't you just call me using your phone, once you're in the Unseelie Realm?"

"Unfortunately, cell phones don't work in the Faerie Realms," Aubree says. "Besides, we also don't use electricity, so there'd be no way to charge them once they're out of battery, anyway."

My dad gives me a sheepish look. "Oh, right. That makes sense." He clears his throat. "Well, I'll let you three get back to talking." He pauses and looks right at Aubree. "Thanks for this, by the way." He holds the mirror close to his chest and ducks his head as he walks back to the den.

My heart tumbles over indecision. Can I leave my dad after only having him back for a couple of days?

My shoulders grow heavy. I have no choice but to do what Queen Faílenn asks or I'll never get to be a normal teenager. Considering the Mortal Realm will be nonexistent.

"Okay." I shove the mirror in the back pocket of my jeans. "We've got that part taken care of. What's next?"

Aubree smooths out her skirt. "We should leave as early as possible. We have no idea how long it might take to break Eric free. And these plagues won't wait around for us to nab him. Think we can leave by dawn?"

Oliver runs a hand through his cropped hair, nodding in agreement. "What do we bring?"

"We travel light." Aubree sits forward in her seat. "One change of clothes, a handful of snacks, and a water bottle. Oh, and this."

She shifts to grab a couple of small packs that have been sitting at her feet. Tossing one to Oliver and the other to me, I yank on the drawstring and peek inside.

Acorns. Acorns fill the small pouch.

Oliver does the same. "What do we need this for?"

I smile. "It's the only form of currency we can use once we're in Faerie."

Chapter Six

The sun is barely awake by the time we're ready to leave the Mortal Realm.

The three of us stand on my front lawn, a group of misfit teenagers dressed far too warmly for the light breeze that tosses my hair. Jeans, flannel shirts layered under winter coats. A pair of old sneakers for Oliver—his parents would kill him if he got his new ones dirty.

The sky grows lighter by the minute. The soft artificial light from my front porch is swallowed by the natural light of day.

On our backs are packs that hold all we'll need to survive a few days in the Unseelie Realm, as we free Eric from his prison. My own bag holds my silver cloak. The one given to me by the fae who was present when my banshee gift was bestowed upon me, at my birth.

The most precious gift I've owned for so many years. If I don't wear it while delivering my banshee song, it will release as a heart-wrenching scream, unbearable to hear. While wearing the shimmery cape, it releases as the most beautiful lament the hearer has ever listened to.

Since my banshee song isn't to be used within the Faerie Realms, there's no need to bring it. However, my previous trip into the Unseelie Realm proved that plans change. Having to scream my banshee cry without the cloak was dangerous. Terrifying.

So I've packed my cloak just in case. I pray I won't need to use it. I glance down at my missing pinky finger, a shiver pulling goosebumps along my skin.

My heart races as we step out in unison, crossing the grass to Aubree's car. Memories of the conversation with my dad the night before fill my head. He agreed that seeing me off this morning would be too difficult for the both of us. If I see his face this morning, I'm likely not to go at all.

Still, my mind won't stop worrying. By bedtime, he'd looked even sicker than yesterday morning. The bags under his eyes had grown darker and deeper, and his forehead was covered in a layer of sweat.

Not that I'm feeling great, either. My belly is queasy from the whole idea of this trip. My throat closes as I walk away from my house. Away from my only living parent.

Please let him be okay.

I toss another look back. What am I doing? I'm going to lead my friends into more trouble. My heart hitches inside my chest. What if I make a decision that gets someone killed this time?

A vice pinches around my core as I hop in the back seat of Aubree's car, leaving the front seat for Oliver. I don't miss the worried expression Aubree tosses my way as she falls into the driver's seat, nor the way she talks to Oliver with her eyes.

They're concerned for me, which doesn't surprise me. I just need this thing to be over.

As we drive toward the high school, I can't help but notice a large amount of roadkill piled on the side of the road.

Oliver voices the question before I can. "Check out all the dead animals. What's up with that?"

Aubree grips the steering wheel. "It's a sign of the plagues."

. "How so?" I ask.

"The magic used for the plagues isn't natural. So all the things of nature are dying."

"Already? I thought we had more time."

"This is just a side effect of the plagues. More is coming, that's for sure."

Oliver's voice is low. "Like what?"

Aubree waits a beat. She doesn't make eye contact with me in the rearview mirror. "Like, earthquakes?" She bites her lip. "Last night one hit Southeast Asia. It was big."

I worry my hands in my lap. "How big?"

She pauses again. "Almost a 9.7."

Oliver gasps. "That's got to be one of the largest earthquakes ever recorded."

Aubree simply nods.

I swallow. "What else?"

She shakes her head. "Well, if it hasn't happened yet, it will soon. It will begin with natural disasters, impossibly crazy weather, unexplained phenomena. It's possible millions will die before the last plague is even released."

A knot forms in my core but I push it away.

I don't want to go to the Unseelie Realm right now. But we have to. And we need to make this trip a fast one.

The rest of the drive is silent. Aubree parks in the back corner of the high school parking lot under a low-hanging tree. We have no idea how long this journey will take, but hopefully, no one will notice an extra car parked in the same spot for a few days.

Our hike through the woods and up the hill to the clearing behind the school is a quiet one. None of us say a thing. We are all fully aware of what we're about to embark on.

We all know the risk we're taking. Oliver most of all. He will be the lone human among us. The ways he could be tricked or tortured once in the Unseelie Realm are something I can't even consider. He may think he's here to protect me, but it's the other way around.

I don't plan on letting that boy leave my sight.

We find the spot where the Veils hang, like an invisible target. The grass has grown a bit since I was last here, a sign that spring is doing her job. At least *that* part of nature still works.

The marks where the stone Seals are located are only discernible if you know where to look. Two of them now glow a bright red. A clear signal of the impending disasters of the broken Seals.

In a blink I'm taken back to Halloween night, just six months earlier. When Eric lured Aubree and I to this very spot, as he held Oliver captive, a final sacrifice he planned to make at the direction of the Unseelie king. Aubree enacted her own plan to try to free Oliver, instead breaking the hidden Seals that encircle the ground around the Veils.

Breaking the Seals and releasing plagues into the Mortal Realm that will eventually destroy all of humanity.

Little did I know my dad had followed me, that he would jump to Oliver's defense, releasing my boyfriend and himself being stolen into the Unseelie Realm along with Eric.

It was a miracle to discover my dad was actually alive, when Eric came back for me, just a few weeks ago. Or rather, days ago, in Mortal Realm time. But we escaped, my dad and I. Even though the king still wants me for my unusual power that I discovered during my time inside the Unseelie Realm. A power no other fae possesses. The power to bring someone back to life.

A power he plans to use me for, to revive his late queen.

Shivers tingle along my skin as I think on his awful words. On his words as he created a law enslaving my dad and me to the Unseelie Realm. I shake the images from my head.

Aubree stands in front of us, glancing over her shoulder at the two of us. She lifts one hand and waves it in the air before her.

I hold my breath. Sweat has already gathered under my arms and my body is heavily weighed with a double layer plus a winter jacket. My backpack feels like it's filled with bricks. Oliver stills beside me.

The outline of a door appears, the Unseelie Veil glowing with an otherworldly shimmer. Seconds later, the door is fully formed, as if it were waiting for our arrival.

"Ready?" Aubree asks.

"Wait." Oliver holds up a hand. "Mind if I take a bathroom break? I'm not looking forward to relieving myself in the Unseelie Realm." He gives a dramatic shiver as if the thought is revolting.

Aubree scrunches her face up. "Ew. You're going to pee in the woods?"

Oliver lifts a brow. "I'm a guy. If it's convenient, we'll do it."

"Gross. Just make it quick."

I laugh at her overreaction as Oliver disappears into the trees.

She smirks, something I haven't seen much of since returning from my journey into the Unseelie Realm.

"Hey," I say, taking her hand in mine. "You all right?"

My question seems to catch her off guard. She nods unnecessarily quickly. "Yeah, I'm good. Just...tense."

"I can tell. You haven't been you, lately. I feel like the Aubree that met with her mom is totally different from the one I know from school."

She shrugs. "When in Rome, do as the Romans, right? I'm fae royalty. Does it surprise you that I might have to act more formal while around my mother?"

I consider this. "I guess you're right." I squeeze her hand. "But is that all? There's nothing more going on in that head of yours?"

She shakes her head. "Nah." Her smile is genuine. "I'm good. Just want this whole trip into the Unseelie to be over with." Now she's the one to visibly shudder. "That place gives me the heebie-jeebies."

I laugh. "I can confirm that." I abruptly lean in and give her a hug, surprising even me. "I'm glad you're with me this time. I wouldn't want to do this with anyone else by my side."

Mischief fills her eyes. "Even Oliver?"

I giggle. "Well, you *and* Oliver. I'm just happy to have you both back."

"Ditto, girl." She gives me a wink.

"Let's just make sure that all three of us return together. No one gets left behind in the Unseelie."

"Agreed."

We're interrupted by Oliver who is jogging toward us, muttering something about getting the show on the road.

"Now are we ready?" Aubree asks.

We both nod as she steps through the Veil. Her form disappears and Oliver takes in a shuddering breath.

He pauses only for a second before lifting a foot and crossing into a place most humans will never see in their lifetime.

Panic zips through my core for a beat but I push against the desperate feeling and raise a hand to reach through. It disappears at the wrist, my hand in another dimension while the rest of my body remains on earth.

So strange.

I pull in a final gulp of air. Then I step through the Veil and into another world.

Chapter Seven

I step into a Winter Wonderland.

A thick layer of azure snow covers every branch, shrub, and rock. I exhale and a cloud of fog blurs my vision. My nose is immediately aware of just how chilly it is in this world compared to my own.

The sky above is a familiar light lavender. My heart skips a beat. It's likely been weeks since I was last here. But for me, it's still only a matter of days.

The snow beneath my boots crunches with each step I take. Oliver stands to my right, marveling at the mass of trees surrounding us and the vast pastel space overhead.

Trees that resemble mushrooms have white bark and tangerine orange tops. This looks nothing like the spot I arrived in last time but I know that it must be.

Aubree digs through her bag for something.

I slip my hands into my pockets to retrieve the gloves I brought along. I hold them out to Oliver. If I'm feeling the chill then he must be freezing. My fae side kicked in during my last trip, giving me a layer of protection from the ridiculous temperatures in this realm.

"What's the plan?" I cross to stand beside Aubree, keeping an eye on Oliver. There's no chance he gets farther than a yard from me. Period.

Aubree holds a tattered parchment in her hands, her eyes narrowed. "Just trying to get my bearings."

"Is that a map?"

"Of course." She bats her lashes. "Did you expect any less?"

I snort-laugh but lean in to take a look at it.

Seeing the Unseelie Realm on paper is jarring. I recognize specific points, even if just from the drawings. The clearing where the revel was held. The spot where I know the hideout treehouse would be located. Tumblecreek.

The castle.

My palms go sweaty.

Until this moment I hadn't allowed my brain to process the fact that we're actually going after Eric. The guy who betrayed me not once, but *twice*.

My cheeks heat at the memory.

I clear my throat. "So, once we're done with, uh, you-know-who, can we like, arrest him or something? Keep him in the Seelie Realm?"

Aubree shoves the map into her backpack and slings it across her shoulders. The look she gives me holds confusion. "Why would we do that?"

I refrain from crossing my arms in defiance. "Oh, I don't know. Maybe because the guy has betrayed us more times than I'd like to mention. And freeing him for good will likely mean another problem for us down the road."

She shakes her head and begins walking. Oliver silently falls in step beside the two of us.

"I'd imagine he'll flee back here the minute we're done with him," Aubree says with a shrug. "Who knows if he'll even stick around long enough to help us? I'm already prepared to use force to subdue him if need be."

"You think you can take him down?"

"My mother gave me a few tricks to use." She flexes one of her biceps, to which I simply roll my eyes. She chuckles. "As long as he doesn't know we're coming, we should be able to get a lock on him."

"Well, either way, I plan on at least asking your mom if there's something that can be done to make him pay for what he's done. For the betrayal he's shown each of us."

The betrayal he's shown me.

My brain chooses this exact moment to play tricks on me.

A flash of light fills my vision and searing pain lances through my wrists. Eric's face flickers before me, anguish sewn into his every seam.

He opens his mouth to say something but chokes instead. On blood. It dribbles down his chin.

I gasp at the burning that wraps around each of my arms.

I blink. The image disappears.

"Caoine?" Oliver's hand is on my shoulder, gentle as always.

I blow out a breath, masking my expression. "I'm fine."

Aubree glowers in confusion but I've already steadied my agony. My wrists continue to throb. I glance down and stifle a cry. Each of them is an angry scarlet, lines of bubbling skin circling in a never-ending path.

What in the world? None of my visions have ever become physical. *How is it possible that my trauma is manifesting itself like this?*

I tug each of my sleeves down so my wrists are fully covered. Oliver's gaze rests on the spot I just not-so-casually inspected.

I look away. "So, we're walking straight there? To the castle, I mean?"

Aubree steps carefully past a plum-colored bush the size of a dump truck, holding a few of the branches aside for Oliver and me to step around. "For now."

"But your mom gave you instructions, right? On how to capture him, once we're there?"

"Chill. We've got this." But she avoids looking at me.

A knot forms in my throat. "But it was super hard breaking into the castle when I was here last. Do you have an actual plan?"

Aubree gives me a coy smile. "Worried, Caoine?" This is all she can say since she can't lie to me.

My throat closes and my blood races. Oliver slips his arms around my shoulders and pulls me close. I stumble against him but keep walking.

"Caoine's not worried." He kisses the top of my head.

I playfully push away and pretend to be offended.

He laughs. "My girl is hardcore. She's not scared of anything." He attempts to pinch my side but I scramble away. "She's just a planner. Likes to know what's ahead." He looks at me. "You've never been one for surprises."

I shrug. He certainly has me pegged.

The snow suddenly gets deeper. Each step I take sinks until the blue stuff reaches mid-calf. "Whoa. Did your mom prepare for this?"

Aubree tosses me a teasing look. "Oh, come on. We get snow drifts far deeper than this in the Mortal Realm."

"Well, yeah, but there's always an end to the snow. I mean, the weather is predictable. To a point. But this is Faerie. What if the snow keeps getting deeper until it swallows us?"

She looks at Oliver. "What was that you were saying about Caoine not being the type to worry?"

Oliver laughs. I don't.

We walk in silence for a few minutes, a sea of azure rolling in waves before us. No end in sight. I'm just about to ask what the plan is for stopping to rest but I never get the chance.

Without warning a body appears right in front of us. A tiny body that belongs to someone from my past.

He smiles. "Hello, pretty girl."

Chapter Eight

"Nym?" A cloud of fog puffs from my mouth as I struggle for breath.

"Whoa." Oliver places a hand across my torso and pushes me behind him. "Caoine?"

I gently pat his arm and step forward. "It's fine. He's a friend." Oliver's arm remains around my waist though.

The little man looks up at me with his glowing green eyes, his yellowed teeth in a wide grin, barely visible beneath his hooked nose. "Pretty girl has come back."

I shrug out of Oliver's embrace and drop to one knee, pulling the small faen into a hug. He reciprocates with just as strong a show of emotion, his long, thin fingers digging into my back.

"You know him?" Oliver asks.

I stand again. "Oliver, meet Nym. Nym, this is my boyfriend, Oliver." I turn toward Aubree who has gone strangely quiet. "And this is—"

"Daughter of magnanimous queen." Nym's orb-like eyes go even wider and he squats into an awkward bow. His dirty, tattered shirt hangs loosely from his shoulders.

A ghost of a smile touches Aubree's face. "That's right, I am. Are you familiar with her?"

39

Nym straightens, his dark cheeks deepening in color. "Oh, yes! All in Unseelie have heard of unending kindness of Seelie Queen."

I squint at him. "Is that so? I thought all the fae of the Unseelie hated the queen. Because of the Laws of Necessity?"

Nym's mouth turns downward. "Pretty girl speaks truth. Many here do not appreciate wonder of Queen." He brightens. "Also, many do."

"Is this possible?" Aubree steps closer to the man. "Are there Unseelie who are truly allegiant to my mother?"

"Oh, yes, my princess. Nym honored to know many!"

I blink, stunned. Then look at Aubree with a shrug. "This is news to the Seelie Realm?"

"Definitely." She slowly nods.

I turn to Nym. "Welp, your princess happens to be my best friend. Any chance you can get us to the castle? We're here to—"

Nym practically jumps in place, excitement making his overly large ears swing closer to his shoulders. "Pretty girl is here to save my prince. My prince will be free!"

I side-eye my friends. Aubree and Oliver stay quiet. Probably not the time to tell our new-found guide that we plan on kidnapping his favorite faerie in the Realm for our own selfish reasons.

"Right." I give Nym as genuine a smile as I can muster.

Oliver stiffens beside me, his face melting into disapproval.

My heart sputters and I turn my attention back to Nym. "Cool. Think you can do your little teleporting thing and whisk us all to the castle?"

Oliver's bad mood drops. "Teleporting? Sweet."

Aubree glances around, shifting her backpack from one shoulder to the next. "The Faen are quite adept at that, actually."

"Daughter of Seelie Queen honors me with such words." Nym dips into a bow again. He straightens and looks right at me, his face going grave. "Apologies, pretty girl. I cannot do as requested."

I frown. "You can't take us to the castle?"

"Take, yes. Not with magic."

"Why not? You did it before."

"Again, pretty girl speaks truth." Nym's elongated face is drawn with tension. "Many things have come to pass since you left."

"Changed? Like what?" I huff another warm burst of air that disappears into the freezing cold immediately.

"Come. We walk. I talk." Nym turns and toddles in the direction we had been walking before our interruption. He casts an enamored glance toward Aubree as he passes but doesn't stop to wait for us.

Aubree nods. "He's right. We should get moving." She glances around us again. "It's never wise to stay in one place for too long when traveling through the Unseelie."

Oliver holds out an arm, motioning for me to go ahead of him.

"Uh-uh." I shake my head, squeezing the strap of my backpack tight. "You stay in between Aubree and I. There's no chance I'm leaving you to get kidnapped from behind." I place a hand on his back and push him in front of me.

He laughs. "Okay, okay. Got it. My over-protective girl doesn't want to lose sight of me."

"Sure. Whatever it takes to get you to comply."

"Will you two stop bickering back there and get a move on?" Aubree throws this over her shoulder before vanishing around a tree with fire-engine-red, spiky leaves to keep up with Nym.

Oliver gives a salute. "Aye, aye, Captain."

I step carefully, matching my footsteps with Oliver's, just in case we're being tracked. Not that I'd ever be successful in tricking anyone who might be following us. But at least it feels like I'm doing something other than blindly following a faerie.

Again.

I sigh. Images of my last trip to the Unseelie pour through my mind.

Fighting with Eric. Meeting the small band of fae that would come to save my life on multiple occasions. Running from danger with Eric. Getting poisoned by a jealous faerie. Coming to trust Eric as a true friend. Learning my dad was alive, finally breaking him free from his captivity.

Being betrayed by Eric.

A lump forms in my throat. Every memory I have of my time in the land of Faerie includes Eric. The one person I thought had truly changed. That I could trust.

But he's not a person. He's full fae. And nothing about him changed at all. Every word he spoke, every move he made had been calculated. Another way to trick me into giving him what he wanted.

Because that's all it ever comes down to with him. He will do whatever it takes to get what he wants. It's always about him.

Snap.

"What was that?" I say to Aubree, who still walks in front of us.

She and Nym both stop, turning to look back at Oliver and me. Her brow is knitted together.

Pop.

I look down at my feet. "Seriously. What is that? Why does it sound so close?"

"Something amiss." Nym twists his hands together with worry. He looks around. "We should leave."

"Agreed." Aubree visibly tenses. "Let's get moving."

Crack.

"No argument here!" I push against Oliver's back once more and take a single step.

Oliver disappears.

Chapter Nine

Oliver's gone.

One second he was right in front of me, my hands pressing against the warmth of his strong back. The next, he'd fallen through the ground. Completely out of sight.

A hole exactly the size of a person is open just in front of my feet.

"Oliver!" My voice is high-pitched and sounds nothing like me. "Oliver!" I don't even recognize that I'm screaming his name over and over and over again. Nothing about the sound pouring from my body is familiar.

Nothing about the desperate feeling of fear should be familiar. But it is. My throat is practically closed with fear. My brain immediately takes me back a full six months, to Halloween night. The night Eric almost killed Oliver. The night my world changed.

My heart hammers against my ribcage as I throw my pack off and fall to my knees, ripping my fingers into the hard dirt beneath me. The hole is already closing in on him.

"No!" I shriek. "Make it stop!" Bits of blue snow are frantically thrown to the side, crimson blood oozing from my nails as the stiff earth refuses to comply. Dirt and snow continue to slip down the hole, threatening to suffocate him. To bury him alive. *He'll die!*

I gasp and cry at the same time. Spots cloud the edges of my vision.

"Caoine." Aubree breathes this as she tumbles to her knees, her shoulder pressed against mine.

She helps me dig, her breathing just as ragged as mine.

"No, no!" I wail as the ground continues to move together.

I've heard no sound from Oliver. No sign that he's still alive.

Please be alive.

Please be alive. Please be alive. Please—

"Pretty girl, move." Nym's voice is soft and smooth. Void of panic.

Yet he stands above me with all the authority in the Realms. His spindly hands are extended towards the earth, his bulging eyes blinking rapidly as he accesses the situation.

"Nym?" I barely croak this out.

"Caoine," Aubree says, pulling my arm to move back.

Her eyes are locked on the little Faen. Nym tilts his head and curls his fingers inward, flipping his hands upside down.

"Nym?" I ask, even though I know this is not the time to be asking questions.

Aubree's fingers dig into my skin as she pulls me even further away. My cheeks are hot, adrenaline racing up my neck, tears racing down my face.

This can't be happening. Please don't be happening!

Nym spreads his fingers wide. The ground where Oliver disappeared trembles just slightly. Then it shakes like a bowl of jello. With a burst, dirt, rocks, and snow fly into the air, pebbles spitting against my face and hands. An eruption of sound splits the air with a crack.

I duck, along with Aubree, covering my face and head. The cavernous crater opens back up, twice the size it was before. Aubree and I scramble away on our backends to avoid falling in.

Nym twirls his hands as if he were conducting a symphony. Oliver's head appears at the top of the hole, one arm grasping at the dirt around him. He pulls in a ragged breath.

I don't even get his name out before I pounce. Aubree and I each grab a shoulder, helping to pull him to safety. He chokes on something, spitting to the side. Dirt mixed with snow turned to mud cakes his clothes, smears across his face.

With a final grunt, he rolls onto his back, his legs still dangling in the open earth. He groans with a wince.

I don't allow him time to pull himself fully out of the hole. "Oliver." His name is as gentle as a kitten, but my embrace is fierce like a tiger.

He coughs and attempts to roll to his side. But my hug won't let him.

"Hey." Aubree places a hand on my shoulder. "Let the guy breathe."

Oliver coughs again, this time turning into a laugh.

"No." My face is buried into this chest.

His hands cup the back of my head and he leans up to place a single kiss on the top of my head. "I'm okay. Really. I'm fine."

"No," I say again. Seriously. I'm not moving or letting go of him again.

"Caoine." Aubree sings my name, drawn out for added effect.

Oliver pats my back. "Really. I'm good. You can let go now."

"Are you sure?" My eyes rove every inch of his snow and mud-covered body. "What can I do? Are you in pain?"

He coughs again, shaking his head. "I'm fine."

I sit back on my bottom. "Ugh. Fine. But the rules have changed." I stand, reaching down to give him a hand up.

"Changed?" He brushes at the dirt and snow that soak his clothing.

"I'm handcuffing you to my body. You're not allowed to take even a step away from me."

Aubree rolls her eyes. "We don't have handcuffs, dummy."

I stick my bottom lip out. "Can't you just conjure some up? Like an illusion?"

She snorts. "Illusions only work if the human doesn't know it's an illusion." She snags her backpack and throws it back over her shoulders.

Oliver pulls me against him. "I'm good. That won't happen again."

"How can you be sure?" I pout like a child, not even a little embarrassed at my behavior.

"We know what those crazy sounds mean and I'm a thousand percent positive Aubree and Nym will be on high alert now. I'm safe."

I glance at my bloodied fingernails and sigh, closing my eyes. Concentrate. When I open them, my hands are healed. "I'd still rather handcuff you."

He shakes his head and lets me go. "Always the dramatic one."

"And his famous last words were..." Aubree says under her breath.

I clear my throat and cross my arms. "Hey! I can shove you back down that hole."

Oliver laughs, putting an arm around my shoulder as we begin following Nym again. "Okay, okay. I guess a little drama is called for in this case."

"Um, not any better. I'm not the one who dated Jessica, remember?"

He grabs his chest with his other hand in mock pain. "Ouch. That hurt."

"Now who's being dramatic?"

He leans down to kiss me. "Message heard. Don't ever tell a girl she's dramatic."

"Took you long enough." Aubree laughs from the front.

"I'm still a work in progress." Oliver shrugs.

"Pretty girl mad at tall boy?" Nym is genuinely concerned as he looks at us.

Now I'm the one laughing. "No, Nym. I'm not mad. I appreciate what you've done. By the way, how did you do that? I never knew you could do that type of magic?"

The small man nods. "Many things happened since you left."

"Yes. Got that." I blow at a loose bit of hair that has fallen across my eyes. "So? We've got a little bit of walk. Now would be a good time to begin talking."

Chapter Ten

Nym's tinny voice bounces around the rugged terrain, our footsteps the only other sound. This section of the Unseelie forest is much the same as the other, albeit with less snow. Trees knit far too close together attempt to keep us from traversing between them. Trying to trap us.

There is less foliage growing from the ground here, too, probably from the lack of light that trickles through the trees. At least it makes it a bit easier to walk.

"So, why can't you teleport?" I've agreed not to hold my boyfriend hostage while we walk, but I'm still close enough to feel the heat from his body ride along the chilled air.

"Nym has new friends."

Aubree glances over her shoulder at me, her brows cinched together. Nym continues to lead the way, oblivious of our confusion.

I clear my throat. "Um, and your friends don't like you teleporting?"

A child-like chuckle rumbles in his chest. "Friends take teleporting."

"What?"

Now even Oliver looks wary. I rub my hands together, the Winter Realm cold penetrating my faerie skin.

"New friends. Not like us." Nym looks back at me, his yellow teeth in a wide grin. "You know new friends. Remember?"

I blink. "I know them? You don't mean Aibell and those guys, do you?"

He laughs again. "Not those friends. *New* friends. Remember? The day you leave Unseelie?"

New friends? He couldn't be talking about Elan, Eithne, or Einin. They weren't new to me the day I left the Unseelie Realm. And I wouldn't call them friends, either.

I scratch my fingers through my hair. "Uh, refresh my memory?"

His laugh this time is an outright howl. "*Friends*, pretty lady. Ones that help you escape castle."

I jolt at the mental image of who he's referring to. "Those guys? The little ones that created all the damage to the castle?"

Nym nods vigorously. "Friends!"

I huff a breath. "Friends, right. What were they called again? The silence or something?"

"Friends," Nym repeats.

"You had the silence help you escape the Unseelie Realm?" Aubree asks, her voice rising in pitch and volume.

"Erm, yeah?" I shrug.

"That's kind of a big thing to leave out your story, Caoine."

"Is it?"

Oliver gives me a worried look but I shake my head.

I swallow. "Why?"

She throws me another look. "They're unpredictable. No other fae knows what they're capable of. Entire clans have gone missing after a visit from those guys. Whole towns devastated."

Oliver swallows, his gaze bouncing between me and Aubree.

My insides somersault. "Oh. I didn't. Know that, I mean."

"Eric didn't tell you?"

My fingers curl in on themselves as she says the name of my

nemesis. "He mentioned not to be seen by them, to be wary. But he never gave a reason why."

"Well, there's your reason."

"Wait a minute." Oliver holds up a hand. "Are you saying the little silent people are the ones that destroyed the castle? That helped set you and your dad free?"

Aubree snorts at his reference to the silence but she doesn't correct him.

"Well, yeah. I didn't think it was that important to say which fae aided in our escape. The fact that we got away unscathed was enough for me."

"But why would they help you if they're such horrible, menacing, blood-thirsty fae?"

Aubree's tone grows hard. "Hey now, I never went that far."

Oliver reaches out and helps me step over an unusually large limb. "Well, whatever. I don't see why they'd help you and Brent if they have such destructive tendencies."

"Friends not destructive." Nym waves one of his spindly hands in the air. "Friends not horrible, menacing. Friends *friends*."

"How can you be sure?" I ask.

"Nym spends time with them, now that my prince is gone." His voice drifts to sadness at the end of the phrase.

"Okay. So they're nice to you. Maybe they aren't nice to all faeries, though."

He shakes his head. "No. They nice to all."

"Fine." Aubree smacks a branch out of the way. "We'll agree to disagree. This still doesn't explain why you've lost your power of teleporting to them. If they can do something like take another fae's power from them, then it sounds like they're pretty menacing."

"Friends not menacing." Nym speaks as if he's addressing a class of small children. "Friends take magic from fae. But they give magic, too."

I don't bother to hide my astonishment. "They gave you magic?"

Aubree stops in her tracks, bringing the rest of us to a halt. "Oliver. The hole." She turns to Nym. "From what Caoine said about her first trip here, it sounds like that wasn't a power you had. Did the silence give you that power? That's how you did that?"

Nym grins a silly grin. "Friends give magic."

"Okay." Oliver crosses his arms in the analytical way he always does. "So, the silence are now your friends. But by being friends with them, they took your ability to teleport, and gave you a different kind of magic?"

"Like telekinesis?" I add.

Nym hops in place. "Pretty lady's dark friend figured it out!"

Oliver blinks at the way the small faerie references him, but recovers quickly. "Uh, yeah. I guess I did."

Aubree tilts her head. "You still haven't explained how we know we can trust the silence, though."

"Friends," Nym repeats.

"Yes, but—" Aubree never gets to finish her sentence.

A small ball of light zips past my ear. Before I can register what's happening, Oliver has me on the ground, his body covering mine. Aubree and Nym join us, although Nym is unusually jovial about the whole thing. The light flies above us, circling close to our heads this time.

"A wisp!" Aubree attempts to whisper unsuccessfully. "They're dangerous. We've got to hide. Now."

I'm just about to scream at Nym to teleport us out of here when it hits me.

"Shhh!" I hold up a hand for the others to stay still. "We're safe. This wisp means us no harm."

Oliver gives me an incredulous look.

I grin. "This is our welcome party."

Chapter Eleven

I lift my chin and call into the emptiness. "Laoise!"

A laugh from somewhere to our right splits the chilled air.

Aubree nails me with a look. "Please tell me this is a joke."

I roll my eyes. "Oh, it's a joke all right."

"Caoine?" Oliver is reluctant to get back up.

"You can come out now, Laoise. You got us." A spike of adrenaline echoes through my limbs.

This is Laoise, right? What if it's a trick of the fae?

My fears are assuaged when a dark-skinned girl with green hair in a pixie cut steps from the shadows. She wears a broad smile, her silver eyes glimmering in the lavender daylight. She's in a flowing white dress, her bare feet gliding over the snowy ground like liquid.

Laoise comes to stand beside me. Her towering slim form dwarfs me. "I suppose I should not be shocked to see you back." She chuckles. "You seem to appear when there is unrest."

I freeze. "There's unrest in the Unseelie Realm?"

She tilts her head in reply. "Are you going to introduce me to your friends?"

"Oh, right." I shift on my feet. "Friends, meet Laoise, one of

52

the fae who helped me escape the castle. Yes, she's a wisp. But she's a good wisp, so, yeah."

My heart skitters over the thousand words inside my head. Seeing her makes this whole thing real.

I grab Oliver's hand. "This is my boyfriend, Oliver."

He gives her one of his signature smiles and holds out a hand to shake. "Nice to meet you."

Laoise looks at his hand, a giggle bubbling to her lips before she turns her attention to Aubree. Oliver pulls back and wipes his hand on his jeans. I shrug. The fae aren't like us. Well, not like the human half of me. He seems to understand the unspoken meaning and nods.

Aubree and Laoise's eyes connect. Neither speaks for a few seconds, although Laoise looks like she wants to.

I clear my throat. "Um, this is my best friend, Aubree."

Laoise doesn't blink. "Aubree. You are the daughter of the Seelie Queen?"

Aubree flinches minutely. "This is Laoise?" She looks at me. "The one you spoke of?"

Laoise hides a smile. "Expecting someone else?"

Aubree gives a small smile, albeit a strained one. "You're just... familiar. Have we met before?"

"Maybe." Laoise shrugs but doesn't elaborate.

I turn to introduce Nym but stop. He would already know her from the last time I was here. He stands in silence, his orb-like eyes bulging as he stares at Laoise.

"Cool, cool." I bang my hands on my legs to warm them up. "Now the introductions are over, mind telling me what you meant by *unrest*? What's going on?"

Laoise focuses on me. "What hasn't happened, is a better question."

"Ominous," Aubree deadpans.

"After you and your father left the Realm, the attacks on the castle didn't come to an end."

"No." My jaw drops like I've just heard the latest gossip. Which I sort of have.

She nods. "Once the silence engaged King Raghnall in battle, they chose not to retreat. Many other factions of fae opposed to the king's ways have joined in the fight. The call is for him to be dethroned."

Nym makes a squeaky sound from behind the group but shrinks when Laoise looks at him.

I pick at a loose string hanging from the cuff of my coat. "Where is the king?"

She tilts her head. "In the castle. He's barricaded himself in."

"Can't the silence get past his forces? I thought they brought down his magic?"

She nods. "They did. But thus far he has held his ground."

"Whoa." I turn to Aubree and give her a hopeful smile. "Maybe this will make our job a little easier?"

Laoise frowns. "Your job?"

"We're here for Eric."

She jumps, which throws me. She's normally so unnaturally calm in demeanor. "Why would you need the Unseelie prince?"

"Look, I'm not a fan of him right now, either. But we need him for something important, so here we are."

Laoise glances at Nym before looking back at me. "So, you're headed toward the castle?"

"Yep. Do you think that will be a problem? With the fighting and all?"

She shifts on her feet as if gliding across the ice. "I'll get you in."

I look at Aubree, who gives me a concerned glance. I hold up a hand and nod to reassure her that Laoise is legit. We're fortunate to have met up with her since we'll be a hundred times safer now.

"So, does this mean Aibell and Killian have joined the fight along with you?"

Her brow pulls together for a second before she nods. "Ah, yes. Killian is engaged in battle as we speak."

"What about Aibell?"

Laoise shakes her head. "She's otherwise occupied."

"Bummer." I look at Oliver. "I was hoping you could meet them."

"This isn't a meet-and-greet, Caoine." Aubree crosses her arms. "We should get moving."

I turn back to Laoise. "How soon can you get us into the castle?"

She looks me up and down. "First, we will need to do something about the way you look."

"Ouch," Oliver says this under his breath and sniggers.

Laoise glances his way. "That goes for all of you. You attract far too much attention. If we're to be successful, you must blend in. If that is even possible."

Same old Laoise. The fae love to point out the many ways I don't meet their standards.

I flash her a smile. "Lead the way." I hold an arm in the direction we were already headed.

She gives each of us a wary glance before heading to the front of the group and walking. Aubree and Oliver both give me a look that says *seriously?* Nym just appears terrified, for what reason, I have no clue. Laoise was the only one that was ever nice to him.

I sigh and follow the group in the dead quiet, a strange heat gnawing deep in my stomach. A piercing shriek that is all too familiar slices through the frozen air. I gasp.

Scarlet reynards have joined our travels.

Chapter Twelve

Laoise whips around, her silver eyes flashing red for a split second. "Run!"

I don't need to be told twice. The five of us sprint like we're caught in a zombie apocalypse. Which I might prefer, considering death by scarlet reynard sounds much scarier. These unique faerie creatures similar to a Mortal Realm fox will tear any living being to shreds in seconds. I've never actually seen one, nor do I plan to.

Aubree's feet barely touch the ground. No doubt she's aware of exactly what kind of creatures these are. We move as one. The only sound is the awkward crunch of Oliver's shoes as dried leaves and snow are crushed beneath them. The rest of us make no sound. Like, at all.

My heart chills at the realization that my fae side is becoming even stronger. Just a few weeks ago my footfalls were just as noisy, if not more so. But now my movements are soundless, like the other fae's.

I'm not sure if I should rejoice or mourn with Oliver. Being human in this nightmare of a place is no joke. Oliver flashes me a panicked look as we scramble over a fallen tree. Yeah, he'll need an explanation once we're safe.

"Laoise?" I dare to breathe.

She doesn't look back as she practically floats between two large mushrooms. "Just a bit farther."

Which can mean anything in the land of Faerie. Except that this time she's right.

A minute later she grinds to a halt, the lot of us stopping alongside her. Her attention is directed ahead as if she sees something other than the mass of faerie forest.

Oliver catches my attention and I shrug, turning my thoughts back to the nothing in front of us. And then it's no longer nothing. Laoise steps forward and the wall of air around her shimmers, wavers. Floods around her like liquid.

"Whoa," Oliver whispers, his jaw dangling open.

Laoise continues walking ahead without a glance behind.

Aubree is the first of us to follow our new leader. She moves forward without hesitation. Fearless. Once more, the air before us shifts in waves before settling back into place. As soon as Aubree is through whatever invisible door separates us from the unknown, her head rocks back, her eyes darting around her like a deer's.

"Ready?" Oliver takes my hand in his.

I nod and turn to find Nym. He's gone.

I falter. "Where's Nym?"

Oliver looks around, too. "The little guy? I dunno. Guess he found something better to do."

"Huh." I don't bother to hide my irritation.

This again? He spent the majority of the last time I was here disappearing and reappearing at will. Totally annoying.

Oliver shakes my hand to get my attention, then lifts his chin toward the invisible wall. With a deep breath, we both walk towards the strange shimmer that beckons us. The air around us warms, like a sunny day in the middle of summer. It melts over my skin, a bucket of water washing over me, even through my thick layers of clothing.

As soon as the world stops moving, I see it. The town. It's

large, much larger than I would expect. The buildings are made of stone. Majestic, tall. Similar to a castle and its many parts. Fields as long and as wide as the eye can see are dotted along the outskirts to the left of the structures. A broad dirt road runs straight through the groups of structures.

A lengthy set of connected caves line the outer edge of the town to my right. Each of them has a smoke pit, a few articles of clothing that look to be drying on the rocks beside them. Could these be inhabited by those not wealthy enough for one of the homes?

"Sweet," Oliver says.

I glance in the direction he's looking. At the far end of the caves, a fuchsia-hued waterfall pours into a perfectly shaped sphere, orange and yellow grass growing around it. I get the distinct idea that the waterfall is made of something other than water, though. It looks like wine.

Faerie wine.

I shiver, leaning to whisper to Oliver. "Promise me you'll never eat or drink a thing unless you let Aubree check it first."

His laugh is teasing, playful. Until he takes in the way tension paints my expression.

He wavers. "Okay."

I nod and swallow. "Okay."

He squeezes my hand but I don't elaborate. Not now, anyway.

Laoise comes to a stop before an unusually tall, windowless building with dark mahogany double doors.

I clear my throat. "So, um, where exactly are we?"

"I was wondering the same thing," Aubree says as she continues looking around in awe.

Laoise tilts her head, grinning. "Leebury, of course."

Chapter Thirteen

The tavern where we're seated is small and rustic. And completely quiet.

I glance around at the dozen or so fae sitting at surrounding tables. Their eyes are locked on our tiny group as if we just walked in with those scarlet reynards on our heels.

Did we? I literally turn around to be sure we haven't, because really, how would I know? Those creatures left my thoughts the minute we walked into Wonderland.

I attempt to keep my voice low but it's impossible with so many pointed, prying faerie ears with supersonic hearing. "Um, so are we safe now? From the scary reynards?"

Laoise nods. "Leebury has protection around it. Not only is it impossible to find if you do not know where to look, but none of the Unseelie creatures can cross the border. And it's invisible until you've crossed the border, of course."

Oliver visibly relaxes. Although his gaze displays the stress he's feeling over all those staring fae immediately around us.

We wind our way to a table large enough to fit our group and noiselessly take a seat. The table looks heavy, like maybe it was a tree cut down and laid on its side with very little done to it. The chair is solid and hard. Nothing I would want to sit on for very long. I slide my foot through the strap of my pack as I shove it under my chair, just to be safe.

Once we're settled, the rest of the crowd appears to be satisfied, going back to their previous conversations. A soft murmur of chatter fills the space around us.

A plump female faerie no taller than my nine-year-old next-door neighbor sashays over, wiping her hands on the apron she wears over her medieval-style attire.

She flashes a smile, if it can be called that. Most of her teeth are missing and the ones that are left are green. Putrid green.

I bite my cheek. Not the time for a weak stomach, Caoine.

"What can I get ya?" Her accent is different than any I've heard in the Unseelie before.

Aubree brightens. "I'll take a bollenberry nectar." She pulls a few of the acorns from her pouch and places them in the middle of the table.

The server's royal blue colored hair bounces along her shoulders as she flips a wrist. Behind her, a clay mug flies through the air and hovers under a dispenser where pink liquid splashes inside.

I blink.

Someone clears their throat and my attention is drawn back to the server. Her yellow cat eyes are fixed on me, that nefarious grin curling ever deeper.

I grab Oliver's hand. "Oh, uh. Nothing for us." I remember not to thank her, since that's seen as a sign of weakness in the Faerie Realms.

He tenses beside me but remains quiet.

The server's smile drops like dead weight, the floating mug crashing to the floor, shattering into a million shards.

Every eye in the joint is back on us. *Awesome.*

The server flicks her wrist again and a new mug coasts along the air to the bollenberry nectar jug. She looks at Laoise.

The wisp tilts her head. "I do not require nourishment at this time."

Our server nods curtly, tossing her wrist one last time so

Aubree's mug slides before her. As she walks away the acorns on the table disappear.

My best friend eagerly grabs the mug, sucking down the contents. "Mmm. I haven't had this in forever."

I pout and glare after the plump waitress. Why wasn't she mad at Laoise for not ordering anything?

Laoise leans forward. A large silver medallion necklace peeks from beneath her corset. She catches me looking and pulls the fabric to cover it. "So, why do you need the prince?"

Aubree sets her mug down. "My mother needs him, in the Seelie Realm."

The wisp's face falls. "Queen Faílenn? What would she need him for? You delivered the tomes to her, did you not?"

I nod. "Yes. But we're not in the clear yet. She needs Eric to fix those broken Seals we talked about before."

Oliver huffs at the mention of Eric's name, glancing around the room. Sooner or later I'm going to need to address this.

Laoise ignores him, her brows pulling together from this new information. Her eyes fall to my missing pinky finger. Her jaw tightens.

Oliver raps the wooden table with his knuckles. "We know it's a long shot, but think there's a way we can get inside the castle? So we can get out of here?"

He frowns and looks around the tavern again.

"We need to convince Eric to leave his loyalty to his father behind." I agree. "Is this even possible?"

"Loyalty?" Laoise tilts her head. "Do you not know?"

I narrow my gaze. "Know what?"

"The prince. He was never loyal to his father. Not since his most recent return to the realm."

I shake my head. "Wait, what? He stood by his father the night I escaped. He's working for the king again."

Aubree shushes me to lower my voice. Any conversation regarding the king of the Unseelie Realm is a dangerous one.

Laoise rubs her hands together. "You're wrong, Caoine. Eric

was never loyal to his father. Soon after your escape, the king had him arrested and has had him locked away ever since." She pauses. "He's considered a traitor to the king." She side-eyes the room as if she's annoyed.

The breath is stolen from my lungs. My chest aches as if it's been beaten by a two-by-four. My head spins and my belly goes queasy.

Loyal? Eric was always loyal? To *me*?

I grab Oliver's hand again, squeezing it so tightly I'm afraid his fingers might fall off. He's frozen solid.

Breathe.

"Caoine?" Aubree's voice is soft.

Words stick in my throat. "I—I—" He was loyal to me all along? "But in the castle—he helped his father fight against you that night."

Laoise shakes her head. "No. He did not. When he left the king's side he was helping the rest of us enter. After you and Brent crossed into the Mortal Realm, it became apparent that he was against the king."

I can't swallow. It's so hard to swallow. "So he—the whole time he stood by his father, it was an act? He was pretending for—"

My sake?

Another wave of dizziness crashes into my skull.

"You realize what this means, don't you?" Aubree asks. "This isn't just a mission to trick the prince into leaving with us and luring him to the queen. This is a rescue mission. We need to save Eric from a fate worse than death."

Oliver leans back with a grumble.

Aubree's eyes go wide. "You disagree?"

He shakes his head. "I don't buy it. That guy is the best actor I know. Like, Oscar-worthy."

I take in a breath. Exhale. "Look. I know this sounds impossible, but we have to believe them."

His voice is soft. Injured. "Why?"

"Because fae can't lie, Oliver. There's no falsehood behind her words. Don't ask me how I know this. I just do."

His eyes are tortured. "There's no way, Caoine. He can't be good. He—You were there that night. You saw what he did to me. To your *dad*." He grinds his teeth. "We may need to spring him from jail to get him to the Seelie Realm but I'm not looking at this as a rescue mission. No way. He's no hero. He's getting exactly what he deserves if you ask me."

Oliver turns away, the muscles in his shoulders tensed and alert.

I sigh. This emotion, what he's feeling...it's exactly how I reacted the first time I came in contact with Eric. How do I explain weeks worth of interaction with a boy whose soul has been just as tormented as mine? How do I prove that Eric is different?

He has changed. Even if I forgot for a few days.

Of course, Eric is still loyal to me. He promised he was and there's no way he could've lied to me.

How is it that I believed a lie again? That I felt betrayed from poor judgment—only to find that my judgment was light years off course?

Can I ever trust my decisions again?

Laoise tilts her head. "Regardless of what you believe about the prince, if you're to take him from the Unseelie Realm, we'll need to get moving. Breaking into the castle is no easy business."

Yeah. Tell me about it.

Aubree nods. "Have any ideas?"

"I do," Laoise says. "But first we must find a way around the war that rages outside."

Chapter Fourteen

A breeze picks up the loose ends of my hair and tosses them across my face, sending shivers down my spine. The sky is a deep amethyst by the time the four of us are ready to begin our journey.

We stand on the edge of the fields that run behind Leebury. Stretched before us is flat earth pregnant with marmalade-colored grass. Beyond this are rolling hills in shades of lime, scarlet, and alabaster. Patches of baby blue snow dot the horizon. Jagged mountains fill the view in the distance, thick dark blue snow covering every inch of them.

This is where we're headed.

"Ready?" Laoise's voice lilts through the night air.

Aubree and I nod. Oliver swallows, taking in a ragged breath.

My heart skips over invisible faerie toadstools. Nothing about this can be easy for him. I'll never know what it is to walk in his shoes. At least I'm part fae.

Laoise steps towards the magical scene before us. The rest of us fall in line beside her.

My soft boots barely make a sound as we detour around muddy spots and random holes that appear every once in a while. Oliver has similar footwear, along with thick pants and a long tunic that reflects the land of the Unseelie a bit better than his original attire. My clothing isn't as thick, although quite similar to his.

The logic behind why we needed to change outfits escapes me. Plenty of fae adorn themselves in the clothing of the Mortal Realm, some even able to hock their items to those that desire them. Maybe Laoise felt our humanity would stick out less if we weren't dressed in something that could draw a price. Either way, Oliver still wears his puffy down coat, beanie hat, and gloves. There's zero chance I'm allowing him to freeze to death just to convince our fellow faeries that he doesn't have red blood in his veins. Plus, our backpacks give us away as strangers so...*sigh*.

We walk in silence for the first few minutes, Oliver and I taking in the beauty of the realm. The sounds of creatures foreign to our world. Flowers that stand in the distance like the Eiffel Tower. Emerald, coral, sepia. Ruby red bushes that quiver as we pass them.

I shift my backpack to allow circulation through my neck and shoulders again. "So, the castle is beyond that mountain?" I tilt my chin in the direction of the peak farthest to the right.

Laoise glides across the grass. "That's the safest path, yeah."

Aubree's eyes bounce between me and Laoise. "Isn't it a little out of the way?"

I glance at Oliver who just shrugs his shoulders. "Is it?" I ask Laoise.

Her face remains emotionless. "It's not the most direct path."

"Why not?" I attempt to hide my frown.

"The war."

Aubree clears her throat. "The fighting between the castle and those who want to unseat the king? Won't we run into that either way? I mean, it's at the castle. How can we avoid it?"

Laoise stills. "I'd prefer we approach the castle from a safer direction."

"I get that." Aubree nods. "But we're sort of in a time crunch. We don't have time to play it safe."

Oliver shoves his hand in his armpits, to generate heat, I assume. "She's right. I'd like to leave this place as soon as possible."

I make eye contact with Laoise. "Is there another way we can go that will save time?"

She looks away. "There's always another way. The question is, do you want to risk your life?"

Aubree tenses beside me.

"We need to take the most direct route," I say.

Laoise's eyes flash red but she still doesn't look at me. "I must advise against this. I fear it will benefit no one."

Aubree tosses me a look like she's about to throw hands.

I sigh. "I appreciate your concern. But please take us the most direct route, regardless of the danger it may pose."

Laoise stays silent.

Oliver speaks to me through his eyes. *Are we in trouble?*

I shake my head and look at Aubree.

She clears her throat again and pulls out the map. "It shows here that we should aim for the peak in the middle."

The wisp turns her head away from us.

"Okay." Aubree shoves the map away. "Let's take the path to our left."

Oliver and I nod. Laoise follows with hesitation.

"Are you sure about this?" Laoise lilts. "I'm worried you're headed for a trap."

"We'll be fine." Aubree throws this comment over her shoulder. Her patience with the wisp is clearly waning.

"I'm just saying—"

"Laoise," I say, reaching out to touch her arm.

She startles and pulls back.

I smile. "We've got the Queen of the Seelie Realm on our side. Have faith like Killian." I give her a wink.

She shakes her head and follows us.

I don't know how much time passes as we travel. The sky is dark, the shapes of our landmarks slowly being swallowed by the night. I struggle to stay on the path and to keep Oliver from tripping in the dark. My fae side has faded with the daylight.

A thought that's been bugging me since before we left the Mortal Realm plucks at the back of my mind again. I quicken my pace to walk beside Aubree.

"Hey." I tighten my grip on the bag that's slung over my shoulder. "Can I ask you something?"

Aubree nods, glancing around us with her eagle eyes. She's never *not* on alert. "Sure. What's up?"

"Well, I was thinking about what your mother said to us, the day we gave her the books."

"Uh-huh."

"And also about a conversation I had with her while I was last here, in the Unseelie Realm."

She nods again. She doesn't ask how I had a conversation with her mother while I was trapped here, when the queen lives in the Seelie Realm. Does Aubree know her mother can visit people within dreams?

"So..." I swallow. "This Creator she keeps referring to. Can you tell me more about him? Or her, I suppose."

She laughs but keeps walking.

"I mean, when she talks about the Creator, it all sort of makes sense, ya know? Like it's something I've always known, even though I haven't actually known or learned about the Creator."

"Mmm."

"She says I need to trust him, that He is all-knowing and will provide for me. That He has a plan for me and wants to include me in His work."

"Sounds about right." Aubree laughs. "My mother will always bring the conversation back around to the Creator."

"Is that a bad thing?"

She shakes her head. "No. She believes very deeply in the power and love of the Creator. She enjoys encouraging others with the knowledge that they are loved and were created for a purpose. That they aren't alone."

I nod. "That's what she said." I pause. "So, is it true?"

Aubree hesitates and watches the others who walk in front of us for a bit. "Do you believe it to be true?"

"I don't..." I huff. "Yeah, I think I do. It feels...right, somehow."

She nods. "Then you have your answer."

"But, do you believe? In the Creator, the way your mother does?"

Again, she dips her chin in a nod. "I do. I know from first-hand experience that the Creator is real. But just because it's true doesn't mean all will believe. Believing is each being's personal journey."

I'm about to ask her what her first-hand experience was but am cut off by commotion right in front of us.

Oliver trips but rights himself. I jog a few paces to see if he's all right. But he stumbles again, this time grabbing my arm for support. He laughs at his clumsiness.

"Whoa. You okay?" I smile and look into his patient brown eyes, my attention drawn to his crooked tooth that is uniquely Oliver. My heart does funny things inside my chest.

And then that smile changes. Morphs. The teeth are straight, the lips pinker. Cracked. Dried blood at the corners.

Blue blood.

Eric stares back at me.

I gasp.

He looks worse if that's even possible.

Caoine. Help me.

I squeeze my eyes shut. Demand that the picture leave my head.

But it doesn't. In fact, the image grows clearer. Pain laces the skin on my arms and my neck.

I fall to my knees from the agony that slices across my belly.

Please. Caoine.

Tears swim in Eric's eyes. Then the vision hides away.

Caoine.

"Caoine!"

I blink. Oliver holds me in his lap.

Aubree and Laoise stand over his shoulder. All three have concern in their words and comforting touch.

Oliver runs a hand through my hair, pulling what I assume is a stray bit of twig or dirt away. "Are you all right?"

I breathe, and sit up in the spot on the ground where I fell. "Yeah." I look around to gain my bearings. "I'm fine. Just had a... thing, is all."

Oliver helps me stand. "A *thing*?"

"A...vision." I rub my arms even though I'm not that cold.

Aubree squints at me. "You're having visions?"

I nod. "Visions. Dreams. Whatever. I think I've got some trauma from my time in the king's prison."

Laoise draws closer. "What kind of visions?"

I shrug. "Just...Eric. Sometimes I see his face. Sometimes I am him. He talks to me."

Aubree crosses her arms. "He talks to you? How?"

"Like, in here." I point to my head.

Oliver and Aubree exchange a look. Laoise freezes.

"Caoine." Aubree is all business now. "How long has this been going on?"

"Since I got back from here. Just a few days."

"And did he...talk to you like this before you left the Unseelie Realm? Like, while you were both together here?"

I nibble the inside of my cheek, my eyes going to Laoise. Eric hadn't wanted me to tell any of the others about our telepathic abilities when I was here last. The fact that he can talk to me and I can talk to him, in our heads. Or that he can do it with Nym, too.

My eyes lock with Aubree's. "Yes."

"You guys can read each other's minds?" Oliver asks.

I shake my head. "It's not that simple. It's not reading his mind as much as placing a thought into his head. And yes, he can do the same to me."

Aubree huffs. "Why didn't you tell me you two could do this?"

I shrug. "Does it matter?"

Laoise looks at me in disbelief and something else. Frustration?

Aubree grabs my hands in hers. "Caoine, do you realize what this means? Not only is it rare for fae to be able to communicate in this way, but it means that we know without a doubt he absolutely did *not* deceive you. There's no way he could be loyal to the king and still talk to you in this way."

I shake my head. "But isn't this just PTSD? Like, he's not really talking to me, right?"

"I don't think so. I think he has been talking to you this whole time. Which also proves his allegiance to you. To your friendship.

"Eric is truly an ally."

Chapter Fifteen

E ric, an ally?

I linger on the thought. "How so?"

"Because, Caoine." Aubree squeezes my hands. "I have never heard of fae being about to speak to one another in this way across Realms. Ever. If we could, I'd just talk to my mother that way all the time. But I can't. I've had to visit her in the Seelie Realm each time I needed to communicate with her."

My breath hitches. "This...it can't be."

Aubree smiles. "It is possible. And it's good news. This is confirmation, Caoine. Eric is on our side. All we need to do is break him from prison. He shouldn't put up a fight when we ask him to go to the Seelie Realm with us."

I look at Oliver. His expression is flat.

"Thoughts?" I ask.

He lifts a shoulder. "I don't know. This is a lot to process. I mean, the fact that my girlfriend and the guy who tried to kill me are so close they can talk telepathically?" He looks away.

Guilt creeps along my core. I look down at my feet.

He sighs. "I...I need a few minutes to think."

I nod. "That's fair." My mind wanders to the scene I just witnessed, panic rising in my chest. "We've got to get moving. Eric is in real danger. The king is going to kill him!" I scramble to my feet, Oliver rising along with me.

Aubree nods. "Agreed." She looks at Laoise. "Once we get close, can you help us get around the fighting?"

Laoise's face is pinched but she gives a curt nod.

Aubree looks at Oliver. "I know this is a lot to take in, but we're going to need your support. Can you do that?"

He straightens. "Of course. My support was never in question."

I fall against him but he doesn't wrap his arms around me. I tilt my head back. "Oliver?"

His posture remains tight. "Now isn't the time. We'll talk about this later."

An invisible dagger stabs at my heart as I pull back but I don't have time to process his words.

"Pretty girl?" A small voice breaks the tension.

Nym stands at my feet, his large eyes watching my every move.

"Nym! Where'd you go? We missed you."

He avoids my question. "Pretty girl all right?"

I smile. "Pretty girl all right, yes, Nym."

His gaze darts to Laoise, fear filling his eyes. He takes my hand in his and I startle. He's never done this before.

Aubree pulls her pack tighter. "Let's get going. Time is not our friend."

I nod.

Nym looks up at me, his hand still in mine. "Save my prince?"

"Yes, we're headed to the castle. We'll get him out, Nym."

Oliver tenses beside me. Nym looks at Laoise and quickly hides beside me.

I lean down to him as we walk. "You know what he's going through, don't you?"

Nym's shoulders sag. "My prince not well. Help free him?"

A knot forms in my throat. "Yes, we are going to free him. I— I'm sorry I didn't understand before. We'll get him out, Nym. I promise."

He smiles that goofy smile that reminds me of a preschooler who only wants to please his parents.

My chest fills with warmth.

Suddenly I hear my dad's voice.

Literally.

Aubree and Oliver turn and look at me, so I know they hear it, too. We stop as a group.

I spin around looking for the source of the mysterious voice.

The mirror!

I fumble through my pocket until I pull the compact size mirror in front of my face. My dad's beautiful mug looks back at me.

"Dad!" Elation floods my whole body. "How are you?"

Before he can answer, he falls into a fit of coughing. My belly clenches with each hack.

Finally, he says, "I'm fine. Hanging in, anyway."

"It doesn't sound like you're doing okay. Are you getting worse?"

"I'm fine, Caoine. Don't worry about me. How are you doing?"

I exhale. "We're good. We've connected with one of my friends here and are headed to the castle now. We should be there before daybreak."

He wavers. "Daybreak tomorrow?"

"Daybreak like a couple hours."

"But it's not even noon yet."

I laugh. Faerie time! "Right. So we've only been gone a couple hours for you?"

He nods.

"Yeah, it's been almost a whole day for us. No worries. I'll let you know when we arrive and when to expect us home. 'K?"

He manages a feeble smile. "Be safe, Caoine."

"You, too, Dad. With that sickness of yours, I should be the one that's worried."

His face disappears as he reaches down for something. When

he pops back in view he's holding an orange cat. "Don't worry about me. I've got a new friend."

My jaw drops. "Is that a cat? In our *house*?"

He scratches the cat's ears. The cat purrs back. "I found her on the doorstep this morning and she refused to leave until I fed her. She slipped inside and hasn't left my side ever since. She's actually really friendly."

I shake my head. "Wow. I never thought I'd see the day my dad fell in love with a cat."

He chuckles. "Like I said, don't worry. I'll train her to take me to the doctor."

"Haha. Very funny."

"Caoine, we're fine. We've got all the action on the television to keep us entertained."

"Action?" I freeze. He's never been one for TV.

"You know, that huge sinkhole in Europe that swallowed an entire town?"

My belly clenches as a pit opens in my belly. Sinkholes don't get that big. Worry pricks the back of my mind, at the realization that my dad's mental health is failing, too. "Please take care, dad. I'll contact you later."

"Love you, sweetheart."

"Love you, too."

The mirror goes black. I tuck it away as I nod to the others and we begin walking again. Nym grabs my hand like it's a lifeline.

Oliver leans in. "So your dad isn't any better yet?"

I scowl. "No. He's getting worse. Which is super weird since I feel one hundred percent better. Like, way better. I guess my immune system kicked the virus' butt quicker than my dad's."

Aubree gives me a sympathetic look. "No worries, Caoine. We'll get back to him before he's able to miss you."

I shrug. "I think it's too late for that. But yeah, let's focus on getting Eric out and get back home. I'm ready to be done with the snow and cold."

Oliver nods his head vigorously. "I'm on board with that."

I turn to ask Laoise how much farther the castle is. But she's gone.

"Hey," I say a little too loudly. "Where did Laoise go?"

Aubree, Oliver, and Nym all stop and look around with me.

"Guess she got tired of our chatter." Aubree rolls her eyes.

"Yeah but...that's totally not like her. She would never abandon us willingly. What if something's happened to her?"

Aubree's face turns soft. "Caoine, she's a wisp. It's in their nature. She probably ran off to tend to something...wisps do." This is more of a question than statement. "She'll be fine. It's fine. I've got the map."

I huff, tension creeping into my body.

Nym squeezes my hand. "And pretty girl has me." He smiles up at me again and I can't help but feel maternal. "All fine."

"Thanks, Nym. That means a lot."

Especially while lost in the Land of the Fae.

I shake my head but don't voice my opinion. Because really, what's with faeries and their disappearing acts? Somehow, I'll never quite understand them.

Chapter Sixteen

Echoes of death and vengeance bounce between the thick rock of the caves. Below the small hill where we sit stands the oversized depiction of King Raghnall made of stone, the one overlooking his castle. Tough apricot-colored grass digs into my pants from where we're squatted.

Skirting around the battle between the king's fae and the silence wasn't difficult at all. All attention is definitely down by the castle. Nym and Aubree didn't sense any other fae even close to us as we wove our way north of the castle.

The cluster of rocks our group is hidden behind isn't natural. Each one is carved with shapes: a butterfly, lion, wolf, and bunny. At least, that's what they resemble. They also have differences that set them apart from the average animal in the Mortal Realm.

What's the significance of these creatures?

Oliver blows heat into his hands. "What are we looking for?"

A knot forms in my throat. I haven't missed the way he's kept a bit of distance between us as we've walked.

Nym leans closer to me, even though his reply is for Oliver. "We wait."

Aubree looks at me. "Wait for what?"

The little man repeats himself. "We wait."

Right.

The way into the castle still hasn't been made clear to us yet. But we made it in by mere physical force—when I scaled the wall like a crazy woman—and by magic. Sort of. The spell we cast on my last night of freedom here failed but it did get us in the castle. Because we were *caught*.

My cheeks heat at the memory.

This castle isn't impenetrable, no matter what we've been told before. There's got to be a way to save Eric so we can get out of this foreign land.

The space around the castle isn't a traditional battle zone. This fight is done with a bow and arrow, sword and spear. Groups of the king's guards gather along the edge of the castle walls. There's no sight of the silence yet but I know they're there. Just out of sight.

I assume plenty of other fae are fighting in the trees and on the other side of the castle. From Nym's description, it sounds like this is an all-out coup of the Unseelie fae.

Still, hearing the sounds of battle but not seeing any actual combat is a bit unnerving.

This needs to be over. Soon.

I swallow. How much longer will we need to wait?

Before I can ask the question a voice cuts through the early morning air.

"Spying on the king, are we?"

The four of us whip around in tandem.

"Laoise," I breathe. I pull her into a hug. "It's good to have you back." My eyes fall to her clothing, which is different from earlier. "Why did you change? And where is the necklace you had on?"

She frowns. Before she can answer, Nym steps behind me.

Killian gives me a tender smile. "We have missed you, Daughter of Earth."

I step back to look up at my unusually tall fae friend. Killian is an inch taller than Laoise, and just as regal in demeanor.

The tall elf steps back, his hands still on my upper arms. "We've been watching for you. Laoise has been sentinel for the allied group, using her abilities to roam the perimeter and report movements by the king's men. She informed me the minute you all arrived."

He nods his head of white-blond hair in her direction. The long locks are braided and twisted in perfect formation, falling behind his shoulders. His attire is the same as the last time I saw him: shades of green and brown, supple boots, and a bow and arrow slung over his body. That model-worthy square chin of his devoid of hair, his light skin glossy and smooth.

Aubree comes to my side, as she looks at Laoise. "So that's where you went."

Laoise tilts her head, her silver eyes intent on my best friend.

"Thanks for finding us..." Aubree looks at Killian, her brows raised.

I smack my head. "Oh! I forgot. Introductions." I wave in her direction. "Aubree, this is Killian. Killian, Aubree." I step over and take Oliver's hand in mine. "And this is Oliver. Oliver, meet Killian. He's chill. He saved my life and all, although, he's not heavily schooled in sarcasm, so tread carefully."

Killian falters but Oliver just chuckles.

Oliver lifts a hand. "Nice to meet you. Are you here to help us get inside the castle?"

"Get inside?" Killian hesitates.

I glance at Laoise but she makes no move to explain. She must've barely had time to explain to him that we were on our way. Nym tentatively steps around the group, watching our old fae friends with a small smile.

"Yes." I nod. "We've discovered Eric is being held against his will by his father, in the castle. Queen Faílenn has asked us to retrieve him and bring him to the Seelie Realm."

Killian shakes his head. "This is news indeed. How do you plan to accomplish this?"

My gaze flips to Laoise again but she remains silent. "I was sort of hoping maybe you guys would have an idea?"

He considers my words. "Interesting."

The two fae stay quiet. Long enough for things to get uncomfortable.

Finally, Killian speaks. "What assets do we have?"

My shoulders drop. "Assets?" My mind races to my favorite movie, *The Princess Bride*. We certainly don't have a holocaust cloak.

Laoise smiles. "What abilities do we have? So we can work together?"

Oh. I suppose my Gift of Life/healing-others-even-from-the-point-of-death won't be much help.

The wisp tilts her head. "I have invisibility. Little man, can you teleport us in?"

Nym shakes his head, his mouth turning down.

Didn't she already know that, though? Maybe that conversation happened before she joined our group.

I shake my head to refocus my thoughts. "But he does have telekinesis." Killian gives me a strained look, so I elaborate. "He can move things with his mind."

Killian nods. "Splendid. So we can move about the castle in stealth and can surely open the cell in which the prince resides. How do you suppose we cross through the walls?"

I nibble my cheek. Oh yeah. *That.*

Aubree perks up. "I can help with that."

I whip around to look at her. "You can?"

She laughs. "Yes, Caoine."

Oliver narrows his gaze. "How?"

Her smile grows wider. "By walking through walls, of course."

Chapter Seventeen

My brain does a double-take.

Walking through walls? Did I just hear her right?

I blink. "What?"

Aubree laughs. "My Gift, Caoine. Haven't you wondered what mine is? I mean, you told me all about your Gift of Life and how Eric has the Gift of Empathy, how he can absorb others' emotions, their true worth. But I never told you mine."

I open my mouth. Then close it.

Wow.

Oliver holds up a hand. "Whoa, whoa, whoa. When you say you can walk through walls, you mean, like, *walk* through walls? Right through solid matter?"

Aubree crosses her arms. "Yep."

"Whoa." Oliver's eyes are wide, his smile growing bigger by the second.

Killian blinks. "Allow me to riddle this out loud. Laoise uses her Gift to disguise the three of you, Aubree uses hers to traverse the group into the castle, and Nym will open the cell where the prince is being held captive. Am I correct?"

Aubree nods. "Exactly."

My jaw drops. "Genius." I hesitate. "Wait. The king has the

castle spelled. Magic isn't possible within the walls." I turn to Killian. "Is this spell still broken? Have the silence been able to keep the wards down?"

His look is somber. "This is a good question. Yes and no. For the most part, yes, the wards are down. But there have been instances when the king's men have gotten the better of us and the magic has taken hold again."

I look at my best friend, to Laoise, to Nym. "So, we could be sending them straight to a death sentence?"

Oliver tenses.

Laoise nods. "There is always the chance for failure, Daughter of Saoirse. But is saving the realms not worth the cost?"

I exhale, memories of a conversation I had with the Seelie queen just a week ago coming back in full force. Can I really ask my friends to walk into a death trap when I won't even be with them?

Then again, I seem to be a jinx. Maybe my absence will bode well for their mission.

Aubree looks at the wisp. "I am willing. Will you join me?" Laoise nods. Aubree glances at Nym who nods in return. "It's settled then. Let's go save a prince."

Nym smiles for the first time since we've arrived in our hiding spot. "We save my prince."

Killian holds a hand out for Laoise to take, the two clasping just above the wrist. "By the realms, be safe. I believe this plan to be sound. You will return unharmed."

The Gift of Faithfulness. I sigh. If he believes then I believe.

Aubree pulls in a long breath. Finally, she steps toward me, wrapping me in the same fierce hug she gave me just a few days ago when we were reunited.

"When we get home, we're spending the whole day at the coffee shop," she whispers.

My heart skips and tears prick the backs of my eyes but I swallow back the emotion. This isn't a time for mourning. I choose joy. No matter the outcome, I must choose joy.

Oliver pats her shoulder. "There's nothing you can't do, girl. You'll be fine."

She nods. "I know." Then she gives him a wink.

Nym attacks my mid-section with a hug, his long ears bobbing with excitement. "We save my prince!"

Laoise gives me her signature smile as she glides over, falling in step with my best friend and the little man. "We will return soon. With the prince. Be ready to leave the realm as soon as we are back."

Killian nods. "Of course."

Before I can register what my best friend is about to do, Laoise takes each of their hands in hers and they're gone. Here but not here.

A sick sensation bubbles deep in my belly. Why do I feel like this entire situation is my fault?

No. I can't think like that.

I suck in a lungful of air. This *will* work. I must believe that.

I don't look away from the direction they left for minutes. As if my watchful eye can possibly give an extra layer of protection.

"Come, sit, Daughter of Earth." Killian pats the rock where he and Oliver have taken residence.

Right. I sigh and join them.

The sky above is now fully awake, a light lavender with scents of strawberries flitting through the air.

Oliver sits with his elbows propped on his knees. "So, we wait. I guess."

Killian nods, stoically. "We wait."

Why does this seem to be a recurring theme? I fight the urge to growl under my breath.

Instead, I say, "Didn't Laoise tell you anything when she got back? It doesn't seem like you knew what we were doing here."

The elf squints. "When she got back from what?"

"From leading us to the castle. Last night."

He shakes his head. "I know not what you speak of. Laoise

has been by my side for weeks. She hasn't left my sight for even a moment."

I jolt, Oliver doing the same beside me.

"As I said before, Laoise is our sentinel. She uses her wisp form to check the perimeter so we are safe, and to report the movements of the king's men."

"But—" I look to Oliver and back to Killian. "I don't understand. She was with us. Yesterday."

Killian settles his bow beside him on the rock. "I do not know who you were interacting with, but it was assuredly not Laoise."

I reach over and squeeze Oliver's hand.

He swallows, his eyes locked with mine. "Not good."

"My thoughts exactly." I turn to Killian. "I guess that means someone—some *fae*—was pretending to be her then. I did notice she was acting funny but didn't question it too much." Butterflies fill my stomach. "I guess I should have."

Once again, I trusted the wrong person. My ability to make good decisions is so far off. I seriously need to stop making any decisions from now on.

Oliver shakes his head. "Caoine, you couldn't have known. I mean, I believed she was who she said she was. Aubree did, too."

I rub my hands together. "Yeah, but Nym didn't seem to trust her, did he? Now that I think about it, it's like he knew."

Killian leans his elbows on his knees. "You are questioning the wrong thing. The real dilemma is not who was tricking you, but *why*? What motive would he or she have to lead you astray?"

I nibble my lip. "Whoever it was seemed to know Eric was being held against his will. That he wasn't loyal to his father. Is it possible he or she was attempting to stop our success in freeing him?"

Killian nods. "That is a sound reason. I believe you are correct. Laoise and I were not aware of his true allegiance until just now when you told us. I would assume none of the allied fae know this information. Otherwise, there would have been a rescue mission long ago."

I think on his words as we sit in silence for another minute. Who wouldn't want Eric to be saved from torture and probable death at the hands of his father? I gasp and look at Killian.

"Where is Aibell in all this? Is she fighting with the silence below?"

Pain clouds Killian's beautiful features. "Aibell isn't with us. She never has been.

"Aibell deceived us all."

Chapter Eighteen

The woman steps towards me, her smile familiar. Comforting. Life-giving.

She holds a hand out and I take it. But my hand isn't my hand. It's little. A memory from when I was a small girl, pudgy fingers sticky with sweat.

I look up at her because I'm so much shorter than she is.

Her lips move but I don't hear any words. Still, my heart is flooded with the vibrations of her voice, the timbre of it dripping like honey and sunshine.

She speaks kindness and love. I can feel it pulsing against my palm.

We walk into a field of nothing yet it's the only place I want to be. The only thing I need in my life.

I look at her again. Tears prick my eyes.

This is all I've ever wanted.

My mom.

A hand shakes me awake from where I sleep on the ground. I shoot into a sitting position, gasping for air. It was just a dream.

My heart sinks. I would've taken that dream over reality any day. Save for the fact that I also want to have my dad and Oliver in my life, too.

"Caoine," Oliver whispers. "They're back."

I suck in a quick breath and race to pick the dirt and leaves from my hair, rubbing my hands down my face. My back screams at me from the hard ground that was my bed. I stretch my arms overhead to regain feeling in my limbs, as I climb to my feet with Oliver.

We fell asleep soon after the others left on the rescue mission. Having been awake for a full twenty-four hours was enough for my body. My vision goes fuzzy. We maybe got four hours of sleep? It will have to do for now. There's no more time for rest.

I glance around at the rocks but see nothing out of place. "Where are they?"

Killian stands and nods to an outcropping of rocks to our right. "They will be here momentarily."

I rush to brush soil from my clothes in an attempt to look presentable. Killian would know. The supersonic hearing of the fae is the real deal.

Then I hesitate. Something is missing. A pain, a slight discomfort that's laced my wrists since I entered the realm. I frown and look down at them.

Oliver tenses beside me, his hand slapping his thigh in a rhythm. I take his other hand in mine, looking into his eyes. *It will be okay,* I say silently.

And then, there's movement. A flash of color, the rustle of a bush. Four figures stumble into sight.

My heart quakes against my ribcage.

He's here. Eric is here.

Laoise glides across the rugged earth in her mystical manner, Aubree close beside her, looking none the worse for her long journey. Nym practically bounces into the view, his hand tucked neatly inside that of his favorite faerie in the world.

Eric is gaunt, and skeletal. His skin is a sickly jaundiced hue. Clumps of hair have fallen out and his nails are brittle and bloody. Dark burns ring around his wrists.

I glance at my own wrists, a shadow of memory gracing them,

the faint sting that had reminded me of our connection. But I don't feel the pain any longer.

I can hear how he struggles for breath from where I stand. He looks like death.

He's hunched over, one hand on his side, his face barely discernible beneath the bruising and cuts. A limp plagues his gait, the fingers of one hand bent at odd angles.

Shock sticks in my throat. Oliver freezes beside me. I squeeze his hand.

I release my breath. "Eric?" My voice is soft.

His good eye meets mine and spots cloud my vision. My jaw is tight but I manage an almost smile. He collapses onto the ground, a groan tumbling right along with him. I gasp.

"Killian?" Laoise lilts.

The elf walks in his direction.

I hold a hand up. "Wait. Can I try?" I move toward Eric who is no longer moving—his every breath clearly causing him agony —and kneel on the ground beside him. I place a hand on his shoulder and swallow. I haven't had much experience with healing others. But with my Gift of Life, I know it's possible. *More* than possible.

My eyes close and I allow my thoughts to retreat to the emotion that encompassed me days ago, in the moment that I healed my dad, bringing him back to life. The love, grief, determination I experienced in that instant.

Heat pulses through my hands, peace taking residence in my blood. I focus, believe. I envision every scrape, wound, broken part of Eric healing and knitting itself back together. I see his marks turning to scars, turning to new skin. The trickle of the iron poison dissipates from his blood, evaporating into nothingness. I see in my mind's eye that he is whole again. That he is the same Eric I knew from days past. That he is completely healed.

Restored.

He gasps and I open my eyes, falling back onto my bottom.

He looks like a healthy teenage boy. Even better than the first time I saw him in the realm. Not a bruise or scrape remains. He's even gained his weight back. Even his wrists are no longer shadowed.

Before he can speak a word, I place my hand in his, allowing him to pull from my "peace," the emotion he lacks so often. The one he needs to remain sane.

His hazel eyes flutter back and he breathes. His shoulder-length brown hair falls in waves, his light brown skin practically glowing with radiance. I take in the familiar dark mole that graces his right eye. He sighs, the dimple in his left cheek appearing for the first time since I was in the realm.

"Thank you," he whispers.

I startle at his use of the words, the phrase not often offered among the fae. Then I nod and give him a tentative smile. How will he react? My last words to him were callous and harsh.

He sighs again and squeezes my hand. "Thank you."

He focuses over my shoulder and freezes on something behind me. Or someone. He goes still just before he pushes to his feet.

Oliver looks at his old friend in disbelief. His shoulders are stiff.

Awkward.

Eric's chest rises and falls with each breath. "Oliver." The word is neither a question nor a statement. More of a plea.

Oliver jumps at the sound of his name. He pauses. Then, "Eric. You look...different."

His old friend nods. "This is how I prefer to look while in the Unseelie Realm."

The old Eric was a pale-skinned redhead. Eric in his true form sports green skin. I prefer this form of Eric, as well.

Oliver stays quiet. His jaw flexes in an erratic rhythm.

Aubree puts her hands on her hips. "So I know this is super uncomfortable and all, but we really need to get moving. Can you two do your bro-moment thing another time?"

I turn to Killian and Laoise. "Yes, we should get moving. Can you help us find the Veil?"

Laoise tilts her head. "Of course, Daughter of Saoirse. It would be our honor."

The group prepares to head out as I lean in to give Aubree a hug. Along with the news we learned while she was away.

"Hey," I say. "You should know, the faerie who was with us on our journey here wasn't Laoise. It was a fae in glamour."

Aubree balks at this. "Who was it?"

"Aibell. She deceived us all. We'll need to keep an eye out on the way back."

Eric looks at us at the mention of Aibell's name. "I could've told you that. Where do you think I got all those injuries?"

My jaw drops.

"Aibell tricked us all, even me. It turns out, I was never my father's marfóir. It's always been Aibell."

He looks right at me. "She's the king's assassin. And she plans to kill you."

Chapter Nineteen

Dead silence radiates through the nearby trees as the group stands frozen.

Aibell wants to kill me?

I shake my head. "That's impossible. The king needs me, he said so. I have the Gift of Life. He wants to use my gift to bring Queen Mairéad back to life. I can't die."

Why do these words sound hollow even to my own ears?

Eric's eyes land on mine. "But what will he do with you once he no longer needs you?"

I hesitate.

"Aibell has it out for you. I don't know what you did to her, but she hates you almost as she hates me. The king has promised her that you can be her play toy once she returns you to his prison."

Oliver steps forward, his fists clenching. "Over my dead body."

Eric looks to his old friend but doesn't respond.

Instead, Laoise fills the space. "Unfortunately, I believe she would be just fine with that. We have learned much about Aibell and her true intentions since you have been gone, Caoine. You will not like what we have discovered."

Great. Now I've got two adversaries within the Unseelie Realm.

Aubree places a hand on my shoulder, directing her words to the group. "It doesn't matter. Right now we concentrate on getting out of this place." She looks at Killian and Laoise. "Ready to show us the way?"

Killian gives a curt nod. "Of course. First, allow me to suggest we procure a few more weapons, to aid in our journey back."

Eric brushes a hand through his hair. "Good idea."

The elf looks at Eric. "Come." Then at the rest of the group. "We will return momentarily. Be on alert."

"No worries there." My sarcasm is thick.

The fae walk away, deeper into the woods, Nym close on Eric's heels. I have a feeling that little man won't be letting the prince out of his sight again.

As soon as they're gone, Oliver steps over, his arm enclosing around my shoulders. "I don't like this, Caoine. It's one thing to have the big, bad wolf after you, but now someone you thought was a *friend* is out for blood? Looks like you can't trust Granny, either."

I don't speak. I'm just amazed that he's touching me. How long will he be angry with me?

Aubree stands beside us, a gentle hand rubbing my arm. "I agree with Oliver. Our journey has just become infinitely harder. Not only are we crunched for time, but every single one of us will need to do whatever it takes to keep you out of Aibell's hands."

My shoulders slump. Exactly what I didn't want. Why can't things just be straightforward? Why all the complications? All. The. Time?

A buzzing in my pocket makes me jump. My dad must be trying to contact me. I pull the mirror from my pocket, catching Laoise's eye as I do so. Her expression is bleak. She's been unusually quiet through this whole discussion. Maybe she can shed some light on how to shake my new pursuer?

My dad's beautiful brown eyes come into view. "Hey, Caoine." His smile melts my worries away.

"Hey, Dad." I paste a happy face on, refusing to allow him to sense the unrest around me.

"How have you been? Are you at the castle yet?"

Gratefulness floods my body, all the way to my fingers and toes. "Yes! We made it and have Eric with us. We're just about to begin the trek back to the Veil. With any luck, we'll be back to you by nightfall." Pause. "Which will probably only be an hour or two for you." I shrug. "I still haven't figured out faerie time yet."

He chuckles but breaks into a round of coughing. It's in this moment I notice all the used tissues surrounding his head, the scarf that's secured tightly around his neck.

"Are you lying on the sofa?" I squint to see more.

He nods. "It's easier to stay down here where I have access to hot tea and the medicine cabinet. Besides, my new friend prefers to hang out on the sofa, so we've cuddled here most of the day."

The orange cat suddenly makes an appearance, stepping gingerly above his head, her tail wrapping around his forehead before she settles her body into the crook of his arm, her head tucked under his chin.

"She's cute." I try to hide the concern in my voice. "Stay well. We'll be there soon. Then I can take care of you."

His grin is a feeble one. "I know, hon. Be safe." His eyes glaze over and settle behind the mirror. "Maybe when you get back we can take down the Christmas tree."

I wait a beat before speaking. The tree hasn't been up for months. "Did you put it up after we left?"

He blinks back at me. "We put it up at Thanksgiving, remember? We should take it down before the end of the month. We don't want it up at Valentine's Day."

I swallow. "Dad, we did take it down. It's April now. Remember?"

My dad shakes his head. Chuckles. Coughs. "Oh right. I knew that. Not sure why I thought the tree was still up."

A pang of fear blossoms in my belly. Hallucinations are never a good thing.

Conversation erupts around me as Killian and Eric appear again.

"Hey, Dad. I need to go. We're about to leave. Please get some rest. I'll see you soon."

He nods, then drops the mirror.

My chest heaves as I fight for breath. He's going to be fine. *He's going to be fine.*

By the time I turn around, Aubree has a sword in her hand.

I jolt when I see her. "You know how to use that?"

She snorts. "I'm the queen's daughter. Of course, I do."

Right.

Eric holds the other sword, Killian still attached to his bow and arrow. Nym flashes me a huge grin as he shows off the small dagger that's tucked into a leather belt around his waist. He reminds me of a small child, proud of being just like his father.

The prince's voice dips low. "Let's roll."

I nod. Butterflies take residence in my core. We haven't had a moment to talk. I'm not even sure if we need to. I mean, yeah, I totally thought he betrayed us. But I learned the truth before he returned. And we came and rescued him. Maybe he'll never know how angry I was with him.

We grab our packs and the six of us quietly take to the path leading away from the castle. The landscape around us is nothing like what we encountered on our way here. And now that I think about it, it's different from the last time we left the Unseelie Realm.

Does the scenery of the Faerie Realms change in the same way the fae can glamour themselves?

We make our way through the Realm in silence for at least an hour. My feet feel like it's been that long, anyway. The entire time my brain is filled with misery over my dad.

Hallucinations? Can this be real? His sickness seems so much worse than what I experienced.

I'm suddenly hit with an intense urge to sing my banshee song. My insides feel hollow, like I'm missing a limb. I clench my molars together, fighting against the urge to get emotional. Between the weeks spent in the Unseelie Realm, and the fact that my song never returned in the few days I was back in the Mortal Realm, my loss is palpable.

I sigh. A year ago, I'd never have believed I could possibly miss my banshee song like this.

"You okay?"

I clutch my chest at the shock of the voice yanking me from my thoughts. Eric appears out of nowhere. I glance to the other side. Oliver is focused on the both of us, expectedly wary.

Blowing out a breath, I say, "Fine. I'm fine."

Eric narrows his eyes.

I roll mine. "I mean, *I'm* fine. I just...I'm worried about my dad."

Eric's brows pull down. "Your dad is unwell?"

I nod. "Ever since we got back home, yes." He stays quiet so I go on. "In fact, I got sick, too, but I'm better now. I thought it was just a common cold but now I'm not so sure."

"Why?"

I sigh. "Well, I just talked to him—while you were gone? I used this mirror doo-hickey thing that Aubree gave me."

Eric chuckles. "I know about magic mirrors, Caoine."

My heart rejoices at seeing that familiar dimple on his cheek. A wave of nostalgia crashes over me. I've missed this friendship. I really have. Even though it's been such a short time since we were together. It actually felt deeper. Like he's my brother.

Oliver scoffs and looks away but remains beside us as we walk.

"Well, when I talked to him just now, he appeared...worse. Like, really bad." I clear my throat in preparation for what I'm about to admit. "He...I think he might be hallucinating."

Eric stops walking. "Hallucinating?"

Oliver grabs me by the arm and pulls me back as if Eric's sudden stop is suspicious.

The others notice our stall and come to a halt with us.

"Yeah," I say. "I wonder if his fever is high enough if it could be causing them?"

Eric's face falls. "No," he whispers.

He bends at his waist, hands on his knees. "No, no, no, no." He pushes back to a standing position, one hand scratching through his hair again. "Please, no. This can't be happening."

Aubree steps forward. "Eric?"

I dare to breathe. "Seriously, Eric. What's this about?"

He walks in a small circle, both hands clasped behind his head, his eyes tilted to the lavender sky above. His jaw visibly clenches.

After thirty seconds he randomly punches at nothing in the air. "I *knew* it!" He shouts this far too loudly for us to remain visible.

Oliver steps forward, his hands clenched. "Knew what, Eric? What are you not telling us?"

Eric chooses to address me, instead of his old friend. "The *law*, Caoine. The binding decree my father made regarding you and Brent, just before your escape?"

Air stalls in my chest and my throat closes. *No.*

"He forbade you from leaving the realm. But that didn't mean you couldn't *physically* leave. It just meant that if you did, eventually you would grow sicker and sicker until—"

Tears prick my eyes. "Until what, Eric?"

His voice is a whisper. "Until you go insane. Both of you will go crazy until you return to the Unseelie Realm." His attention averted to the ground. "Your dad will continue to get worse until he loses his mind. And then, he'll die."

Chapter Twenty

The remainder of our journey to the Veil is quiet, even though my mind is in full survival mode.

My dad is slowly going crazy? *I* will slowly go crazy? Unless we both return to the Unseelie Realm for good?

There's no way. Just no way this can even be a possibility.

It makes sense that the sickness is connected to the curse the king enacted on my dad and me. I've felt fine ever since I crossed back into the realm. So what does this mean for when I leave again?

How quickly will my sickness return? Will I even be able to accomplish what Queen Faílenn needs me to do?

I swallow the lump in my throat. The bigger question: What if I become a *bean-nighe*, like my mom?

A wild banshee, with a scream that shatters glass. A scream that can drive the most rational people into insanity in seconds. A fae not in her right mind.

My dad might go crazy, might even have to be institutionalized. But I'm fae. What will this do to me?

I blink back tears and nibble my lip until I taste copper.

A warm hand finds its way inside mine. "Caoine." Oliver's voice is like a song in the darkness.

"Hmmm?" I don't dare use my own for fear it will betray me.

"Relax. We'll figure this out just like we've figured everything else out. Right?"

I don't respond.

"Hey. Give yourself grace. Look how much we've accomplished already."

My throat is so far closed I can't even imagine saying words.

Oliver pulls me to a stop, allowing the others to get a few steps in front of us. "Hey." He brushes a lock of hair from my eyes but remains at a distance from me. "We broke Eric out of prison. We're almost to the Veil. That's one step closer to this whole thing being over. As soon as you deliver Eric to the Seelie Realm we can ask Queen Faílenn how to break the curse. You aren't going insane. Neither is your dad."

I suck in a breath, going still. Finally, I nod.

Oliver puts his hands on his hips. "Hey. We've been through a ton of crap already. This will be a walk in the park, right?"

And I laugh. Like, belly laugh.

The conversation isn't that humorous, but something about his words strikes a chord inside me. He's right. How much crazy have we been through already? We will figure a way out of this.

I need to believe that.

Even if I do have terrible judgment in who to trust.

My heart sinks an inch. Why did I trust Aibell again? *She literally told me not to.*

Before I can ask him if he'll ever stop being mad at me, his mouth is on mine and every thought, negative or otherwise, is gone from my head.

All I know is warmth and longing and a desperate gratefulness I didn't know even existed inside me. My arms wrap around his neck as I deepen the kiss and thank the Creator for leading him into my life. This moment would be perfect if it weren't for the fact that we're in the Faerie Realm where anything is possible.

I reluctantly pull back, eager to distance myself from him

before I'm lost forever. "Okay. I'm better now." I can't keep the smile from spreading across my face.

He chuckles and brings one of my hands to his face, the one missing my little finger. He places a kiss on each knuckle, taking special care of my newly healed skin. "I'll always be here for you."

"Are you so eager to be left behind?" Aubree stands a couple dozen feet away with her hand on her hip. "Let's go, lovebirds."

The two of us giggle as we hold hands and run to catch up with the group.

No one addresses the fact that we were missing for a full three minutes. Or that we had a moment totally not appropriate for our life-and-death situation. But whatever.

We walk for a few more minutes in silence. I'm just about to bring up a funny story to lift everyone's spirits but miss the chance.

Before Oliver or I hear or see a thing, every other faerie around us comes to a halt, weapons drawn, positioned in a defensive stance. Eric and Aubree go so far as to drop the packs from their backs.

Eric and Nym stand back-to-back, Aubree just a few paces away, her sword pointed in the opposite direction as theirs. Laoise disappears into a small ball of light. To scout the surrounding area without being seen? Killian backtracks to stand before Oliver and me.

None of us dare to speak. To breathe.

My heart thumps, a locomotive crashing inside my head.

What are they sensing?

Oliver wraps an arm around my torso, pulling me close, the vein in his neck pulsing quickly. Sweat trickles down my back and I fight for air.

Laoise suddenly reappears right beside me, in a defensive position. Every fae in our group becomes statuesque, their senses on high-alert.

Then, we see her.

Aibell.

<h1 style="text-align:center">Chapter Twenty-One</h1>

She steps from the shadows, from behind the tree she's been using as her hiding place. Her signature smirk is in place. The one that says she means trouble and she knows she's already won.

My jaw clenches together involuntarily.

Her skin is almost translucent, dark curls tumbling over her shoulders and halfway down her back. Aibell's the spitting image of her twin—and one of my closest friends—Catherine. The innocence of her heart-shaped face is deceptive. Although, a faint scar that stretches from her right ear and over her brow confirms she's less than pampered.

The main thing that sets her apart from all other fae is her left arm, which is atrophied and smaller than her right arm. The fingers curl in and it's obvious she's unable to achieve very much movement with it unless she manipulates it with magic.

This gift is part of her fate of being a *neamini*—a fae without magic. Her life has been shaped by this unfortunate twist, but she's driven herself to be the best swordsman, archer, and overall fighter of the Unseelie Realm. And the king's right-hand woman.

Her tunic and leggings are tight. Soft brown boots that reach her knee stick to her legs like a second skin. A loose hood hangs from the top of her tunic, one more way to blend in with her surroundings. A bright silver medallion hangs from around her neck.

The necklace! She was Laoise from earlier.

Her good hand rests on her sword, although she hasn't pulled hers out just yet. "What a quaint little group." Her eyes bounce over each of us until they land on me. They flicker red and I can literally see the hunger drip from her lips.

"You," Aubree seethes this through her teeth.

"You've met her?" I ask.

She barely nods. "Although, she went by a different name. I should've known it was you."

That's why she looked familiar to Aubree when she was in Laoise's form. It's much harder to trick fae than it is a human.

Aibell shrugs. "Hello, *princess*. What can I say? I'm tricksy like that." She smirks, as she glares daggers at me.

She wants me dead.

Aibell looks back to Eric "I see you broke the traitor out of his prison."

I almost open my mouth to say he isn't a traitor, something I'd done so many times before when I was in this realm. But it dawns on me that he *is* a traitor. And she's always known it. Her words always meant something other than what I could imagine. He is a traitor to his *father*, the one Aibell herself still remains loyal to.

Did the king always know Eric was betraying him, when we fought so hard to retrieve the Book of Judgment? Had everything been a ruse from the beginning?

My fingers tingle as I watch how she assesses Nym as if she might devour him in a single swallow. She spots Aubree, then Oliver. "I see you've brought new play toys along with you."

Eric grips his sword tighter. "Don't even think about it, Aibell. We outnumber you."

She *tsks* at his threat. "Poor princeling. Unwilling to abide by the rules of war? The fair thing to do would be to choose one among you to fight me. So the better man—or woman—might win." She pauses. "Or are you without integrity?"

"Without integ—" Eric shakes his head, looking to the sky with a mirthless laugh. "Are you even serious? Why would we follow your rules?"

Her face falls. "Because you are your father's son. He taught you the rules of combat. Are you afraid to face the king's true marfóir?"

I see the change in Eric's demeanor instantly and I know she's won. He will take on whatever challenge she gives him.

Their eyes lock together like an unsolvable puzzle. My heart stops.

Without looking away he waves a hand at the rest of us. "Stand back."

Crap. Crap. Crap.

My body goes numb as the air is sucked from my lungs. Not good.

Oliver threads a hand around my waist and pulls me far into the trees. I want to fight him, to resist every step we take.

Eric can't risk his life for me. This is *my* fight. *I* should face her.

But I'm a coward. I could never beat her. Everyone knows this. Which is why I follow Oliver's lead.

Heat blooms deep in my gut from my shame.

Aubree and Killian flank the sides to our front and I swear I sense an odd heat at our backs. Laoise is surely there to give her protection. Only Nym stays close to the opponents. Just out of reach from harm but still close enough to be near his prince if anything were to happen.

What he plans to do, I have no clue. He can't teleport Eric to safety anymore. Besides, I get the feeling Eric wouldn't want to cheat during this fight anyway. He might be talking to Nym in his head but more than likely he's telling him to stand down.

At first the two circle one another. Aibell laughs when she

flicks her sword a couple of times, making Eric jump. He gives no offensive move, possibly sizing up her capabilities?

Then, she attacks. In a flash she leaps forward, striking directly at his chest. He easily deflects the stab, weaving to the side and blocking with his sword. Before he can bring it back around for his own attack she's already charging again.

Swipe.

Aibell's weapon moves smooth as liquid, slicing within an inch of Eric's midsection. I gasp. No doubt her weapon is spelled to cause massive damage, maybe even death.

Eric stumbles but recovers in half a second, his sword swinging from the opposite direction. Aibell easily lifts hers to meet his, pushing him off as if it weighs no more than a feather.

She laughs, dodging another blow and throwing another surprise stab his way. He barely avoids getting cut. His face turns red, sweat now dripping along the sides. Aibell looks like they haven't even started. How is she this good?

Eric grunts as he swings with all his might but she once again deflects his attack. Before he draws another breath, she spins and throws her sword at him with all her force. Right at his face.

A scream lodges in my throat and Oliver squeezes my body like a vice.

Eric is a blink away from facing death but somehow manages to lean far enough away from her weapon that it just misses his nose. This movement causes him to stumble back and fall.

Aibell releases another nefarious laugh, coming to stand above the prince, her sword pointed right at his chest.

I whimper, tears now threatening to flow. Eric can't die! This can't be the end of it. If he dies, it's *my* fault. I move to step forward but Aubree places a hand on my arm.

Aibell spreads her legs apart to exert more power. "Did you truly think you could defeat the king's marfóir? Pitiful that you believed you're better than me." She laughs again. Her attention travels to our group and back again. "Any last words for your friends before I end you, prince?" She looks right at me. "And before I take your best buddy back where she belongs?"

Eric continues to breathe heavily as he leans on his elbows, an unforgiving stare in her direction. "Nice try, but the king's marfóir doesn't know all my tricks. Not even half of them."

Before she can even snarl a reply, he knocks her sword to the side, rolling in the opposite direction at the same time. As the sword plunges downward, all it finds is hard earth. Eric rolls to his feet, slipping a hand into his boot and pulling a spare dagger free.

Aibell struggles to yank her sword from the dirt and turns just in time for his foot to connect with it, throwing it from her hands and into a nearby bush. She growls and spins a back kick at Eric's middle. He spins, swinging his hand around and sinking his dagger into her side.

Oliver gasps.

She cries in pain, her hands finding the blade that hangs from her side, blue blood dribbling down her leg. Eric swipes his sword from the ground, backing her against a tree. Aibell growls, her expression murderous.

He nods at her empty hand. "Now look who's pitiful? Lose something Aibell?" A small smile emerges but nothing about it is cocky.

She grumbles something in the faerie language along with the word *coward* before running in the opposite direction, one hand still staunching the blood flow from her side.

The group of us gives a collective sigh. Eric waltzes over and grabs Aibell's sword from beneath the bush.

I blink, concentrating on not shaking. Oliver squeezes my waist and nods toward Eric. I spot his injuries and I gasp. I cross to Eric's side, checking him over. Assuring this boy who is more of a brother is alive.

His gaze finds mine. All I see is compassion. Relief. "I'm fine, Caoine. Don't worry about me."

Oliver steps beside me, his jaw tense. His hand finds mine,

even though his words are for his old friend. "I'm glad you're safe."

Eric nods, grabs his pack, and tosses it over his shoulder. Then he turns and leads the group toward the Veil.

Chapter Twenty-Two

The mid-afternoon sun has warmed the day to a sweltering spring temperature by the time we arrive in the Mortal Realm. It's nowhere near hot but my skin reacts as if I've just stepped off a plane somewhere near the equator.

I step out of Aubree's car and turn my face toward the sun, a rumble of pleasure tickling my throat. Sigh.

Humid air melts against my skin and my nose tickles from stray pollen that's coated on every vehicle we pass on our way to my house. Birds singing love songs to one another greet my ears as I lean out the unrolled window. Tears well in my eyes. I want to throw my shoes off and shove my toes through the green grass that is just beginning to grow again. But we don't have time.

Fitting seven of us in her not-at-all-big Volkswagen Jetta was tricky but our motivation pushed us to work it out. Laoise and Killian's crash course in the Mortal Realm is still hanging on their faces with each house we pass, the local park, the stoplights that hang overhead. Nym looks like he does this type of thing every day.

"Whoa," I say, stopping Killian as he attempts to open the car trunk. "The swords are fine where they are. Humans aren't accustomed to seeing those types of weapons carried around in broad daylight. It's best if we leave them there for now."

Killian frowns.

Oliver laughs, patting the elf on the back. "We promise to give your bow and arrow back as soon as possible."

Aubree's eyes are on the sky as we approach the house.

"Is there a problem?" I ask.

She side-eyes our surroundings. "Not sure. I've got this...feeling. Like something's off."

I don't hide my panic when my eyes go wide.

"I'm sure it's fine."

Aubree waves off the glare I give her so I choose to drop the subject. For now. Without bothering to welcome any of our guests to my home—let alone a new world—I bound across the grass and up the porch steps, crashing through the door.

My dad is in the same position he was in when I spoke to him through the mirror. He's covered with a blanket and a tissue box sits on the table beside him. Remnants of cold medicine are proof that it's been administered recently. The orange cat sits on the arm of the sofa, above his head. She looks up at me as I enter but doesn't appear bothered in the least.

"Dad?" I whisper.

He doesn't budge and fear spikes through my limbs. Until I see the gentle rise and fall of his chest.

My shoulders fall.

I slide down to my feet and sit on the floor in front of him, my hand on his forehead. He's burning up, sweat covering every inch of exposed skin. As I touch him, he shivers, his teeth chattering.

"Dad," I say louder this time.

He blinks. Blinks again. "Caoine?"

A smile consumes my face. "Yes. We're back."

He moves to sit up but breaks into a fit of coughing.

I push him back down. "Whoa, whoa. Take it easy, Dad."

He waves me away and forces himself to a sitting position. He goes to speak but stops, his attention drawn over my shoulder.

The rest of the group have found their way inside, each standing awkwardly near the front door.

I gesture towards the other chairs. "You can sit if you want." Even though there are only two extra chairs. The sofa is pretty much taken with my dad's makeshift bed.

Aubree directs Killian and Laoise to take the seats and immediately plops down between them on the floor, her legs sprawled out. Eric chooses to remain near the front door, which sort of makes sense since my dad's eyes haven't left him yet. The dude did try to kill him six months ago.

Even though my dad knows the truth, it's still a bit unnerving that the boy is in our house right now.

Nym remains Eric's shadow, bouncing between his spindly feet and grinning like this is all one big adventure. Which I guess it is, for him.

Oliver sits on the floor beside the sofa. "How do you feel, Mr. Roberts?"

My dad chokes on some phlegm, shaking his head until he can talk. Then he chuckles. "I've seen better days. But I'm hanging in there."

"Of course you are." Oliver smiles. "Brent Roberts is indestructible." He lifts a fist and my dad laughs as he mimics the gesture, air-bumping Oliver's hand.

Dad coughs. "Where's your mother?"

Panic slices across my core. My gaze falls from Aubree to Oliver to Eric. *Not good.* I don't bother to answer his question.

Aubree leans forward and pulls his attention from me. "We came as soon as we could, Mr. Roberts. We're working on a way to get you better."

My dad weighs her words. "What does that mean? I've just got a cold. It'll pass in a couple of days."

I glance around at the others. "That's actually something we need to discuss." I nod to the other fae. "First, let's get the introductions over with."

I point to each faerie as I go around the circle. "Do you

remember Killian and Laoise from the last time we were in the castle?"

My dad nods. "We weren't formally introduced, but yes."

"They're on our side. Part of the A-Team." I chuckle at my dated TV show reference but only Oliver laughs along with me.

Killian's forehead crinkles. "You two *are* the good guys. Am I mistaken?"

Laoise smiles and giggles, shaking her head.

I swallow. "And you remember Eric?"

My dad sucks in a breath.

"Which means," I add, "that you'll also remember how his father brainwashed him? Tricking him into trying to—uh," I clear my throat. "Into trying to kill you?"

Eric shifts on his feet. I've never seen him so nervous before.

My dad's face darkens. "Isn't he also the one that betrayed you just a few days ago?"

I shake my head. "Actually, no. I was..." I glance at Eric. "I was mistaken about that. It's impossible he was working for the king. He helped us escape."

"How can you be sure?" My dad's fists are clenched.

I swallow back my insecurities. Ignore the ever-gnawing dialogue in my head that tells me I'll never be a good judge of character. That my every decision is destined to be the wrong one.

"Uh..." I clear my throat. "That's a story for another time. Right now we need to talk about something important. Concerning you."

"Me?" His face twists in confusion as he looks around the group.

I nod. "It's about your sickness. *Our* sickness."

"But you're better."

I snag a loose string on my shirt and pull at it. "Not exactly."

"What?"

"We believe I'll begin growing sick again, now that I'm back in the Mortal Realm. I only got better because I was back in the Unseelie Realm for a time."

My dad sneezes, grabbing a tissue from the box. "What does that have to do with anything?"

Eric lifts his chest, as if ready to take a punch. "It's connected to the law my father made just before you and Caoine escaped the Unseelie Realm."

My dad's head whips around to look at the prince.

"The law is binding." Eric swallows. "This means it cannot be undone. You and Caoine must remain in the Unseelie Realm or..." His gaze meets mine. "Or you'll both go insane."

With his words, an invisible force around my wrists tingles, sending shivers along my arms and across my chest.

My dad winces and I know he feels the same thing. "So, what do we do about it?"

Laoise tilts her head. "We are trying to figure that out, now, husband of Saoirse."

With the mention of my mother's name, my dad startles.

I place a hand on his, a nonverbal promise to fill him in later.

Aubree runs a hand through her hair. "What we do know is we need to get Eric to the Seelie Realm so the queen can perform the spell to fix the Seven Seals immediately. Every minute we delay, the more destruction will sweep the Earth."

My dad's jaw drops. "You mean, this thing isn't over yet? You still need to go to the Seelie Realm? What if Caoine and I...don't last?"

Eric steps forward, confidence pulling at his features. "I've got an idea for that."

This is news to me. I sit up straighter. Has he figured out a solution to our insanity problem?

He pulls in a breath. "This is just a theory, but it seems logical that it will work."

Oliver lifts his chin at his old friend. "Spit it out, then. Or is the idea as slow as your backkick on the field?"

Eric slowly smiles at Oliver's teasing. Oliver nods back but doesn't smile.

I swallow.

The prince steps fully into the circle now. "What if the Seelie Realm slows down the process of the sickness, or possibly even stops it for a time?"

Killian pauses. "How so?"

"Think about it," Eric says. "The Faerie Realms have always been connected. There's a thread that ties them together in a different way than to the Mortal Realm, right? What if the curse —or the law—inside Caoine and Brent is recognized in the same way?"

Aubree shakes her head. "That's not possible. A law within a Realm is subject to that Realm."

He shrugs. "Maybe. But what if I'm right? What if we can slow the sickness down enough to help the queen finish her spell so we can figure out how to break the law on Caoine and Brent?"

Oliver brightens. "She's the queen. She's got to have some answers concerning the law."

Eric points at his friend. "Exactly. Even if the Seelie Realm doesn't slow the sickness, at least we'll be with the queen who might be able to fix it."

I nibble my cheek. *Is this our path, Creator? Are you there?* "Okay, I hear you. So, what exactly did we just decide?"

"We go to the Seelie Realm." The prince looks at my dad. "All of us."

Chapter Twenty-Three

An hour later I'm showered and back in my beloved jeans and graphic T-shirt. Standing in the hot water was a stark reminder of the last time I got back from the Unseelie Realm. Each time I go, I bring someone back with me.

Or in this case, *someones*.

My house is filled with fae. Literally. Which shouldn't be so odd to me, since I am half-fae. But having so many strangers in my personal space leaves me with a level of discomfort I'm unaccustomed to. A year ago it was only my dad and I.

Now my life is filled with friends, a boyfriend, and inhuman beings, all of whom I'd give my life to save.

I scratch a hand through my wet hair, lean back on my bed, and sigh.

Aubree sits at my desk, sifting through my trinkets and forgotten treasures in the top drawer. Because that's what best friends do.

Oliver was the first to shower, then immediately snagged the spare room to sleep. Eric currently occupies the bath, Nym most likely somewhere close. Killian has found things in common with my dad, where they sit on the sofa in deep discussion. The last I saw, Laoise was playing with the cat.

Aubree wrinkles her nose. "You've got a lot of junk in here."

I look at her. "I like junk."

"Well, you hoard it well."

She ignores the fact that I stick my tongue out at her. A rumble from outside hides my sarcastic retort, probably a storm approaching.

I should be sleeping. But too many things weigh on my mind, seeping deep. Every time I succeed in fixing something wrong, another problem rears its ugly head.

"What's got your panties in a wad, Grumpy?" Aubree doesn't bother to look at me, as she inspects an unknown object that may have been a crocheted bracelet, at one time.

I glare at her. "My panties aren't wadded. I'm just...restless."

"Right." She picks up a broken piece of pottery that was at one time a ring holder I made in art class in fifth grade. "Ever thought of getting rid of some of this junk?"

"No."

She rolls her eyes but continues to dig.

I lay in silence, staring up at the ceiling. Finally, I turn my head back to her. "So, what's the deal with these Bunaidh, anyway? The faeries your mother needs for the spell?"

Aubree shrugs. "Not much else to tell other than what she said. There were only a handful of fae created in the beginning. All other faeries come from them. It's important we have someone from each bloodline present for the spell to work."

"Yeah, but how do you know who is part of what bloodline? Like, what if one dies out or something?"

"I don't know exactly. I mean, my mother keeps track somehow. Maybe it's part of the magic of the Bunaidh? Maybe it's possible that only the king and queen of a Realm will have this knowledge?" She shrugs. "Regardless, the queen knows every single fae that belongs to that direct bloodline."

I nod. "Who are the others that will be there? Besides Eric?"

She opens her mouth but doesn't speak.

I squint at her. "What aren't you telling me?"

"It's not important." She shakes her head.

"Uh-huh." The fae can't lie. But Aubree's a master avoider. "I'd love to hear the unimportant information you're withholding from me." My smile is icy.

Her hands freeze mid-air, a forgotten stuffed animal in them. "There is...one other Bunaidh that I'm aware of. *Was* aware of."

I sit up, scooting to the end of the bed now. No words are needed. My stern look forces her to continue.

She slumps back in her chair, her hands suddenly more interesting to look at than me. "Seamus. Seamus was part of the Bunaidh."

I gasp.

Of course. Aubree told me months ago that Seamus' death had a bigger impact than I could possibly know.

This would make sense. He must've held a position of honor to be a Bunaidh.

I swing my legs back and forth. "What...what does it mean, that he's not...*here?*"

She exhales. "I have no idea. I'm sure my mother does, though. She'll have some sort of plan to have his lineage present during the spell."

"But..." I shake my head. "Doesn't he have any family? Is there no one to take his place?"

"Unfortunately, no. His parents died many years ago. They never had any other children." She pauses. "Seamus knew he needed to settle down, to commit to a faerie so he could produce offspring. To preserve his lineage. But he was not one to be tamed. That boy would have joined the Wild Hunt if he had the chance."

I blink. "The Wild what?"

She laughs, melancholy lacing the timbre of it. "They're sort of like a group of faerie renegades. A bunch of fae who don't belong to either of the fae realms and ride around creating havoc. You know, kidnapping innocent mortals on All Hallows' Eve, bringing war and destruction, that kind of thing. Think mortal teens but on faerie steroids.

"But really, you knew the boy." She attempts a smile. "He was not one to be controlled. My mother warned him many times to secure his place within the history of the fae, but he wouldn't have it." She rubs her hands together. "He just always thought he'd have more time. Sure, he was way over two hundred years old, but that's fairly young for the fae." Her voice drops to a whisper. "He should've had more time."

I nod. She's right. Seamus' light was snuffed far too early for such a pure soul. My throat tightens. Of all the deaths I've ever lamented, his will always be the most painful.

"I miss him," I say softly.

"Me, too." Aubree's cheeks are wet.

Guilt niggles along my insides. Not the way I'd planned on spending our time regrouping here in the Mortal Realm.

Before I can think of anything else to say, she shifts her attention back to the open drawer at my desk. "What's this?" She grabs a small metal figurine from the corner, flipping it over in her palm so I can see it.

"Oh. That's a lucky elephant that belonged to my mom. Elephants were her favorite animal. Dad bought it for her when they were first married. Apparently, she never let it leave her possession, while she was alive."

Aubree winces when I refer to it as lucky. Probably memories of the *unlucky* rabbit's foot she bought months ago flitting through her mind. She flashes a fake smile and hands it to me.

I stifle a laugh. The small figure barely fills the middle of my palm, its weight surprisingly heavier than it appears. The metal is slightly tarnished from years of wear. The simple etching of tusks, a trunk, and thick legs add to its inviting quality.

I'd forgotten I even had this. Warmth floods my fingers as I slip it into my jeans pocket.

"Can I ask you something?" I ask.

"Yeah?"

"Aibell somehow glamoured herself to appear as Laoise. How

did she do that? Does it have anything to do with the necklace she wore?"

Aubree's mouth falls open. "She wore a necklace? What kind?"

I shake my head. "I don't know. Just a silver one...like a medallion. It was big and round."

She nods. "Sounds about right."

"What does?"

"There are objects that are spelled to do things like what you just described. No doubt the king spelled the necklace to allow her to transform into whoever she needed to be, to trick us. My guess is she was planning to deliver you to the king's doorstep. No fight needed."

I scowl. "Why do I keep falling for these tricks? Everything is so confusing."

My friend turns an empathetic look toward me. "Don't let your guard down now, love. Our journey has just begun. There will be more deception to come. And don't be hard on yourself. Any one of us can be tricked, if we're not careful."

I open my mouth to respond but stop. *What is that sound?*

Uncertain, I freeze. But Aubree just shakes her head, turning back to sift through the echoes of my life. I glance around. Nothing is out of place. Guess it was nothing.

My journal sits on my nightstand. I reach for my pen, ready to jot down a few lines that have been floating through my head for days, when I hear it again.

Aubree's head snaps up. We race to the window together. My jaw drops open at the sight.

Just as an ear-splitting crash thunders outside my house.

Chapter Twenty-Four

An orange flash fills my bedroom and the windows rattle so hard I hear a *crack*.

Flames engulf a tree on the next street over, the roof of a nearby house perilously close. Neighbors flood from the surrounding houses. Familiar faces run, cries of panic on their lips, grasping for one another.

Aubree scans the street below. "What was *that*?"

I shake my head, my eyes glued to the scene beneath us.

Our answer comes a second later.

A flash streaks across the sky, a half mile farther away than the first one. It lands with the same impact as the first. Something explodes, a cloud of smoke filling the sky. It's too far away for me to make out, but my heart skips at the idea that a house with people inside just dissolved into nothing.

From a meteor asteroid.

"Oh man...I knew it," Aubree whispers.

I place one hand over my mouth. "Whoa, this is bad."

"I knew I had a weird feeling. This is a consequence of the plagues." She turns to me. "Do you have a basement?"

I nod, just as another black streak races through the sky, crashing somewhere to our left. I scream, involuntarily throwing my hands over my head. Another plume of dark smoke tumbles through the air.

"Run!" I yell.

Aubree and I fall into the hallway—and right into Eric's chest.

He heaves a breath, his hair wet from his shower, his t-shirt stuck to his body. "What's going on?"

Nym bounces at his feet, rubbing his hands together.

I grab him by the elbow. "Asteroid shower. Move!"

By the time we hit the stairs, Oliver stumbles from the guest bedroom. "Caoine?"

"Downstairs!" I order.

By the time we're on the first floor, my dad and Laoise are already gone. Killian stands at the door to the basement, motioning us down. My feet barely graze each step as I descend. Another *boom* rocks our house, the walls shaking. I grab onto them with a shriek.

That one was *so* much closer.

"Dad!" I yell as I race to his side.

He's wrapped in his blanket, that dumb box of tissues in one hand. The cat curls her tail as she prances behind him on our way down the steps.

He puts an arm around me. "I'm fine."

I look at the group. All seven of us have made it to the basement, including the cat. She continues to rub her body up against my dad's leg and a puff of cat hair flies in the air. It tickles my nose but I refrain from sneezing. "Any ideas on how to survive this?" I ask Aubree.

She shakes her head. "You think I've got a constant line to my mother or something? I'm as helpless as you are."

Boom. Dust falls from the ceiling and a few audible gasps fill the space around us.

Oliver has his phone in his hand. "Let's see how widespread this thing is."

His fingers fly over the screen as he pulls up the live news broadcast. Eric stands over his shoulder, reading right along with him.

Oliver shakes his head. "Nothing on any asteroid shower. It's either an isolated event or none of the news outlets have gotten wind of it yet."

Eric points to the screen. "Click on that."

Oliver does as he's asked.

The prince's face falls. "Oh no."

Aubree crosses her arms. "Speak. Don't just make frightened noises, please."

Eric continues to stare at the screen, reading, as he gives an update. "Plane crashes...somewhere in Eastern Europe. A few countries, actually. They started a few hours ago. Not just planes, but cars, too. It looks like whole populations of people are falling asleep without reason." He looks up at us. "Like entire countries are going dark all at once."

I shake my head. "That doesn't make sense. People falling asleep isn't one of the plagues, right?"

He frowns. "No, it's not."

Boom. The cement floor quakes beneath my feet.

Killian taps his chin, glancing at Laoise, who nods back at him. "I believe we might have some insight into this matter."

Aubree huffs. "And?" She clearly has zero patience for male fae right now.

"Days ago we heard rumors...whispers of an urgent matter that the silence had to tend to. We saw a large decrease in their ranks from what we had before."

I click my nails together in thought. "So, a significant number of the silence left the Unseelie Realm? And you think they came here?"

Laoise turns her silver eyes on me. "Indeed."

Oliver slips his phone in his pocket. "Why? What would be their purpose in the Mortal Realm?"

Killian reaches to his side to rest his hand on his bow but

blinks when he realizes it isn't there anymore. "To aid the human population."

Eric puts his hands on his hips. "Aid them how?"

The elf exhales. "By putting them to sleep."

I raise a hand. "Whoa. Come again? How is putting the human race to sleep going to aid us?"

Laoise tilts her head. "The silence sees the plagues as impossible to stop. They are a peaceful kind, ever looking to show compassion on those that are suffering."

I glance between the two of them. "Okay."

"They believe that by putting humans to sleep before they meet a painful death at the hand of the plagues...they are granting them mercy."

Oliver practically jumps out of his skin. "What? How can that possibly be merciful? Putting us to sleep will literally cause more death and destruction. Nothing about any society on earth is prepared for entire populations to suddenly fall asleep!"

Killian's voice is steady. "I understand this, son of Earth. However, the logic of the silence is different from yours. They believe this is the most compassionate course of action."

Oliver crosses his arms and taps his foot. "Great. So if the plagues don't kill our entire population, the silence will be sure to finish us off."

Laoise sighs. "They do not mean to end life. This is how they hope to fix the problem."

"Yeah, but why start now?" I ask. "Don't they realize the queen is actively trying to fix the Seals?"

Killian nods. "Of course. But this is a precaution since they believe our chance of success is small."

Awesome. Even the faerie with the Gift of Faith thinks we're about to fail.

"Fine." I huff. "Even so, once the plagues destroy the Mortal Realm, they'll move on to the Faerie Realms. Are they going to put all of you to sleep, too? Don't they care they're about to die?"

Laoise shakes her head. "They believe the queen will be

successful in fixing the Seals. They are confident our realms will be restored. They're just not sure of yours."

"That doesn't seem very nice." I cross my arms.

Killian stills. "This is not an insult to your kind, daughter of Earth. It is simply the way we think."

I curl my fingers into my hands.

Oliver throws his hands up. "Great. So what do we do about it?"

My dad speaks for the first time since we've been in the basement. "We go."

Every single head turns in his direction.

Eric braves the question we're all thinking. "Go where?"

My dad looks right at him. "We go to the Seelie Realm. We find the queen. So she can do the spell." His gaze turns into flint. "We end this thing now. Before the silence finishes their quest."

Chapter Twenty-Five

The next two hours are agony. We wait in the basement for another thirty minutes, to ensure no more asteroids make impact outside my front door.

When we emerge from the house, my street looks like a war zone. Debris is all around us, plumes of smoke dancing into the bright blue sky from seven different locations. Cries of mourning and loss ring through the air. The sound is the polar opposite of my own banshee song, yet it carries the same weight of loss and agony.

Not a single resident of my development is inside their house. Groups of ten or more are gathered together as they animatedly discuss what they saw.

I push past the urge to puke, my hands shaking. Instead, I snake my arms around my waist, hoping to keep myself safe from the outside world. From the things of magic that my fellow humans know nothing about.

This is not okay.

Nothing about this is okay.

We kick into high gear, heading back into the house to prep for our trip into the Seelie Realm. Aubree and Laoise work on packing food and water, Killian and Eric retrieve the weapons to clean and create make-shift waistbands to hold them while we hike. No one is worried about a few guys carrying around weapons right now, anyway.

Oliver and I care for my dad, who needs a large amount of TLC. He hasn't showered in a couple of days but there's no time for that now. The best we can do is find clothing appropriate for our journey and locate enough meds that should be able to keep him awake, just in case Eric's idea about the Seelie Realm helping our sickness doesn't pan out.

I hand the box of tissues to my dad. "You sure you'll be okay going with us? This isn't going to be easy."

He nods. "Of course. I ran track in high school, remember? I've got mad endurance." My dad gives me a wink.

I scowl. "Yeah. Twenty years ago. Won't help you much now."

He recoils. "Hey! I'm not that old."

"Dad, you graduated twenty-two years ago."

He pauses. "Did I?" His shoulders fall. "Huh."

I wrap my arms around his neck and squeeze him in a hug. "I still love you, old man!"

"Hey, now."

Oliver chuckles and pats my dad on the shoulder. "I don't think you're old, Mr. Roberts."

My dad grumbles. "At least I've got someone on my side."

He stomps out of his bedroom while Oliver and I attempt to hide our laughter.

Once he's gone, Oliver turns to me, taking my hand in his. "Hey."

My heart races away from me. "Hey."

We're quiet for a minute. We need to talk but I'm not sure where to begin.

"This mind reading thing you have with Eric," Oliver says, running a thumb along my hairline. "Why him?"

"Huh?"

"Why do you have a special connection with him and no one else? Like Aubree?"

"I—" My throat closes. "I don't know." Guilt floods through me.

His face clouds. "Feels like it might be because you have feelings for the guy."

"Wait, what?" I jerk back. "No. It isn't like that. Not at all."

Oliver's jaw flexes. "It sounds like you might be trying to convince yourself of that."

Heat crawls up my neck and across my face. "It's *not* like that. Eric...he's like a brother to me. He—" I huff. "You weren't there when I was in the Unseelie Realm with him. You didn't go through what we did."

His posture turns stony. "Yeah, thanks for the reminder. I'm aware that I couldn't be there with you."

"That's not fair, Oliver." My tone is sharp but I do my best to keep my voice low. "It wasn't my choice to go there. But once I was...Eric and I had to work together. To get me home. And once we did, I realized we're more alike than I ever knew. He's my best friend."

"Is he?" His nostrils flare. "I thought I was supposed to be that."

"You're my boyfriend."

"Am I?"

The earth drops out from beneath me, my head whirling at his anger. I sigh. "I don't know why we have the connection. We just do. Please try not to be jealous."

Oliver doesn't say anything more. He simply leans in, kisses me on the forehead, and walks out of the room. At least I'm still his girlfriend, I guess.

I fight back tears as I rearrange my face into something normal —as normal as the apocalypse-life can be—and head back out.

By the time the eight of us are ready to leave the house, it's close to midnight. The scene outside my door hasn't changed a bit, other than the fact that the sky is black. Every neighbor is still outside watching the clean-up efforts and giving eyewitness accounts to police. At least five news station vans are scattered along my road. Reporters lit by cameramen stand before various points of devastation as they update the town of Lincoln about the destruction caused by the asteroid storm.

My heart slams inside my chest. Is this the best time to be leaving our community? What if we're needed here?

But I already know the answer. Of course, we need to leave. Or this kind of chaos will only grow worse. I swallow against my parched throat.

As we stand in my front yard, Aubree glances up and down the street. "We'll need to walk. There's zero chance my car will get through this mess."

Oliver scratches his head. "Can't you just use your faerie charm and worm your way out of it?"

Aubree tosses her aqua-toned hair over her shoulder. "Certainly. But it's easier to play the part of a human if I practice not using my charm, don't you think?"

I lift a shoulder. I honestly never thought of it that way.

We set off on a steady walk down my street. None of us say a word. Not only because our attention is constantly drawn to the destruction around us, but also because this is it. This journey will determine if we're actually able to fix the Seven Seals. If we're able to save the Mortal Realm from extinction.

A somber mood hangs among each of us, like old tinsel on a Christmas tree left up past the New Year.

As soon as we're out of my housing development Oliver whips out his phone.

I glance over his shoulder. "What's up?"

"Just a last-minute check on current events. Since we won't have cell reception once we cross the Veil."

I nod. "Good thinking."

Oliver's face crumbles.

Eric steps closer. "Oh man, what is it this time?"

Oliver grits his teeth. "More death and destruction because of the mysterious *sleeping sickness*, as the news outlets are now referring to it."

Killian looks up. "Which location on Earth has been affected this time?"

"It looks like a few countries in Western Europe and part of the Middle East now."

Aubree shakes her head. "Dude, those guys have got to stop their vigilante crusade. Every human in the Mortal Realm will be dead before the plagues even finish their job."

I give her a glare that says *shut up*. Oliver looks crushed. Although my dad and I may not have a ton of people we're close to in this realm, Oliver is a regular guy. With family and friends and all the things that would be devastating to lose in one blow. Especially if he's one of the few humans to survive because we've escaped to the Seelie Realm.

Aubree winces. "Sorry, Oliver. I didn't mean to be so blunt."

Eric snorts. "Yeah, you did."

She scowls but doesn't defend herself.

I shrug. "Okay. So we walk faster. We get this thing done, like, *yesterday*. And we won't have to worry about any more sleeping sickness problems."

Killian blinks at me. "You truly think it's possible to go back in time to accomplish such a task?"

Laoise pats him on the shoulder. "I believe it is simply an expression of their kind. I do not expect we will time travel."

The elf nods as if he's learned the most fascinating fact.

We walk in silence. A water tower in the distance is on its side. Plumes of smoke rise into the obsidian sky from a dozen spots just in front of me. Every few minutes a shout or scream trickles along the night air, sending chills across my arms and through my soul.

By the time we've reached the entrance to the Veils, the chaos around us is a memory. A full white moon hangs above, crickets welcoming us with their nightly song.

A chill runs down my spine as we stand before the Seelie Veil. I can't help but glance in the direction of the Unseelie Veil. Although it's invisible, I know it's there. Waiting for me. Ready to swallow me as it's done twice before.

My blood pounds inside my veins, my head full and fragile. I draw in a long breath.

This is different. The Seelie Realm has nicer faeries. And it's warm, so much warmer than the Winter Realm. Also, we've got the daughter of the queen to help guide us. It's a plus that she's on good terms with her mother, as opposed to the Unseelie king's son escorting me on my first trip into the place. Eric was just as much a wanted criminal as I was.

Aubree directs us into a line. "Come, stand here. We will need to cross quickly. Once we're inside, we'll move as one. Although the Seelie Realm is friendly, there are always enemies no matter which realm you're in."

No truer words have ever been said. I whisper a grateful prayer to the Creator that I have such allies this time around.

Oliver looks at me as if he wants to say something. But he never gets the chance.

Before I can doubt myself again, Aubree pushes me through the Veil.

Chapter Twenty-Six

Pleasant emotions fill every fiber of my body, pulsing deep within my veins.

Memories of my childhood course through my brain: Hot summer days spent on the beach chasing after seagulls. Lazy evenings catching fireflies with a thousand stars scattered across the night sky. Crisp apple pie consumed with abandon on an afternoon in autumn. Building a snow cave after the first heavy snowfall of the season.

The Seelie Realm is the complete opposite of the Unseelie. The second I step inside I sense a source of welcome, of worthiness. As if I'm meant to be here. Like I was always meant to be here.

Fields of flowers roll in every direction, filled with every color of the rainbow along with a few I never knew existed. The flowers grow as high as my knees, my waist, and even my neck, in some spots. A million gentle butterflies with wings that span the length of my forearm flutter from one blossom to the next.

One butterfly stops and hovers mid-air, glancing our way. I swear I see a smile on its small face, its antenna waving in welcome. I blink. A tinkle of a giggle vibrates around us and then the butterfly disappears to the next flower.

My fingers quiver with excitement.

A large magenta body of water sits to our left, soft waves cresting and rolling along the surface, even though the source of the waves is nonexistent. The azure beachy sand along the edge of it glitters. I squint.

Diamonds. The sand around the pond is made up of diamonds.

A laugh bubbles up from inside me and I can't help but let it spill out.

"Coming?" Aubree asks from over her shoulder.

Everyone from our group except for Oliver, my dad, and me have begun walking ahead. Clearly, the other fae aren't nearly as impressed with the landscape as the humans.

I nod and flash a huge smile at Oliver and my dad as we begin walking. There are literally no words right now. Killian and Laoise speak softly as they move ahead. Aubree leads the way, Eric close behind her. Nym, of course, bounces at the prince's legs.

I place a hand on my dad's elbow to give him support as we walk and nod for us to walk a bit faster to catch up. This realm is far safer than the Unseelie, but faeries are tricksters. I'd rather not fall into another trap.

My belly shifts as I remember how I was poisoned in the name of *fun* while in the Unseelie Realm.

I raise my voice so Aubree can hear me. "Any idea how long this journey might take?"

She doesn't look back for her reply. "Less than a day. But we're stopping somewhere first."

"Oh?"

None of the other fae appear surprised by this.

She nods but doesn't elaborate. And I don't feel like shouting anymore.

So we walk between shivering flowers in impossible colors. I fight the urge to lie down and fall asleep for a few hours. At least Oliver got a little rest before we left.

I continue to marvel at the colorful canvas sprawled before us.

Field after field of flowers dancing in the sunlight. The sky is ever-shifting, from pink to golden to mauve and back again. Clouds that look like indigo marshmallows clutter the expanse overhead.

I literally could live here forever.

Hey.

I jump, drawing odd looks from Oliver and my dad.

My eyes immediately land on Eric. He wears a smirk as he looks over his shoulder at me.

Our telepathic connection is still strong. He hasn't spoken to me this way since before we broke him from prison. Is he embarrassed?

Nym spins around and steps in line with my dad, taking him by the hand. "Shall we walk together?" The small man gives my dad a yellow-toothed grin.

My dad attempts to laugh but ends up in a fit of coughs. Nym pats his back, directing him forward, muffled conversation echoing back to me. I don't miss the way my dad stumbles over his steps as they move away. He's clearly exhausted already.

Eric slows his gait, coming in line with Oliver and I. Oliver tenses.

Hey, I say back to Eric.

He stiffens but continues walking. **Wasn't sure if you'd remember how to do this.**

I smirk. **I had a good teacher.**

Eric just laughs.

Oliver glances between us, his brows scrunched together.

Right. We should probably talk out loud.

I clear my throat and look at the prince. "Uh, so, you've still got your magic touch."

He smacks a large flower out of his way. "I wasn't sure if you even heard me, to be honest. Not until Aubree and Laoise showed up in the castle."

Oliver frowns deeper.

I look at him. "The talking inside our heads thing?"

He pulls in a quick breath like I've slapped him. He slowly nods but won't look at me.

I turn back to Eric. "Well, to be honest, if the queen hadn't sent us on an errand to save your butt, I'm not sure I would've believed it was you. I seriously thought I was just suffering from trauma."

Eric ponders this. "But isn't that why you came to the Unseelie in the first place? Because she sent you?"

"Yeah, of course. But I heard you before we met with her, too."

He stops walking. "Wait, what? You heard me talking to you while you were in the Mortal Realm?"

I glance uncomfortably between the prince and my boyfriend. "Um, yeah?"

Anticipation stirs deep in my gut.

This again. Why does everyone keep bringing up the fact that this shouldn't be possible?

Oliver notices how far the others are ahead of us and motions for us to keep walking.

Eric scratches a hand through his long hair. "I...I had no idea. I mean, I was wishing you could hear me. But the fact that you did? That's *crazy*."

I shrug. "So I've been told."

"No Caoine, you don't understand...it shouldn't be possible."

"And yet it is. Are you upset that I heard you? I mean, if anything, it only made our journey to get you out all the faster."

He exhales. "Sure, it's just...surprising."

"Well, you should be happy I could hear you. It convinced me of your true loyalty. Otherwise, I might've let you stay beat up while we escaped the realm."

His mouth curls up in a goofy grin. "Thanks?"

Oliver huffs but doesn't say anything.

I shake my head. "Really, Eric. I can't tell you why we've got a stronger connection, telepathically, than most. But we do." I stumble to find words that won't cut Oliver any deeper than he already is. "And it helped us save you from the king and eliminated all doubts in our minds of where your allegiance lies. You should be happy."

"I am." Eric's expression turns wary. "I mean, you believe me? That I didn't betray you when you escaped the Unseelie the first time?"

I smile. "I do."

His shoulders fall. "I wasn't under my father's powers once we were caught. But I also knew we were toast if he thought I'd been helping you. So I led him on to believe it was all part of my master plan to bring you to him." Eric's face turns dark. "I thought it worked, too, until that run-in with Aibell back there. I guess my dad was never fooled. Maybe his plan was always to imprison me."

"I'm sorry." I give him a weak smile.

"Doesn't matter. At least I was in a position to help get the others inside the castle."

My jaw drops. "You did that?"

He nods. "Of course. They didn't know it, but I caught sight of them as they gained ground on the castle wall. I sent the guards from that section to another area of the castle so our guys could enter without resistance."

"Wow. Thanks." Guilt riddles my exhale.

"And, I told Laoise how to get you out of the castle, once my father was out cold."

I nod. "I do remember that. I wasn't sure what your game was, but now I see that you were loyal. *Are* loyal. I'm sorry for ever doubting you." I smile at him. "We appreciate all you've sacrificed to help us."

Oliver clears his throat. "Yeah. Uh, it was cool that you took care of Caoine and all. Helped her get back home." He pauses, his jaw tensing before his next words. "I...guess I owe you."

"You owe me nothing, brother. I will likely spend a lifetime making up for what I did to you." Eric swallows. "I am sorry, Oliver. Truly."

A hollowness blooms in my stomach. Faeries never apologize.

Like, ever. Somehow I know this isn't just a human trait Eric's picked up from spending so much time in the Mortal Realm. He truly cares for his old friend.

Oliver pulls in a long breath and looks away.

And we continue to walk. We travel another few minutes.

Then Aubree spins like a whirlwind. "Laoise. Help?"

Without another word, Laoise grabs hold of Killian and Aubree, who are closest to her, motioning to the rest of us to take hold, as well.

We disappear.

Chapter Twenty-Seven

Not a single one of us breathes. Still as statues, as we listen.

All is quiet for a full thirty seconds. Then...

Soft steps, barely audible. In fact, Oliver and my dad don't even look in the direction the barely-there footfalls come from. Is my fae hearing growing now that I'm in a faerie realm again?

I stifle a gasp as they come into view.

The *silence*.

Three of them. They trudge slowly but steadily along. Not a creature stirs around us. All sound has been sucked into an unseen void.

They shuffle past us with determination. Their half-goat, half-fae bodies are covered in hair, pointed ears on top of their heads. Cloven hooves are crossed in front of their chests as if in prayer. Just before they're out of sight, the one in the back turns his head and looks right at me. I swear I see a smile spread across his face.

Can he see us? It felt like they could when I saw them in the Unseelie Realm. Is it possible that no amount of faerie magic can trick them?

I gulp but they keep moving until they're out of sight.

Laoise keeps us hidden for another sixty seconds after they're gone. Finally, we dare to breathe.

"Whoa." Aubree tugs a hand through her silver hair. "That was close."

Killian taps his chin. "What are they doing here? I believed them to be preoccupied within the Mortal Realm, if not at the castle defending the work of the allies there."

Eric shifts. "All the more reason for us to get to the queen."

Aubree nods. "Let's rest first since we're stopped." She glances at my dad. "I don't want to push us too hard."

I give her a silent smile of thanks and lead my dad to a nearby area cleared of flowers where we can cop a squat. Nym follows. I pull bottles of water and snacks from my pack and pass them to Oliver and my dad.

We're only seated for a minute before Aubree motions me over. I stand and join her to the side, leaving the three others to talk.

She takes a swig from her water bottle, nodding toward my dad. "How's he doing? Any improvement?"

I lift a shoulder. "I mean, he's still wheezing but he hasn't seen any illusions since we arrived so...that's a win?"

"I'd say so."

"Besides, he's definitely standing straighter. He could barely walk without stumbling when we left."

She nods, her gaze resting on him for a beat.

We eat our granola bars quietly and watch Killian and Laoise fall in beside my dad. They strike up a conversation much more easily than they ever did with me. My chest squeezes. My dad is like that though, far more extroverted than me. Friendly. Disarming.

Eric comes to stand beside me and Aubree. "I've got a theory on why the silence are here."

Aubree sighs. "Do I want to hear this?"

He shakes his head. "Maybe not, but it makes sense." He pulls in another gulp of water before going on. "They're scouts."

I frown. "Scouts?"

He nods. "For the plagues. They're here to check to see if they've entered the Seelie Realm yet."

Aubree scowls and looks away.

He crosses his arms. "Think about it. It's common knowledge that the Mortal Realm is the first to go, once the spell is enacted. Then they'll move on to the Seelie Realm before the Unseelie. My father—" He winces. "*King Raghnall* created it that way so he would have time to stop the plagues before our realm was wiped out."

My friend doesn't hide her sarcasm. "Nice guy."

"Are you surprised?" Eric finishes his water. "It's always been about him, hasn't it?"

I chew my fingernail in thought. "So, the silence are here to gauge how long they've got left to try to stop the plagues?"

He fishes through his pack for a snack. "That's what I surmise."

I snort. "Surmise? All right, old man."

"Haha. No, seriously. It makes sense. There weren't that many of them. The rest are all in the Mortal or Unseelie Realms. They're doing recon in this realm."

Aubree sighs. "So the question is, have they seen anything? Have the plagues hit the Seelie yet?"

I look at her. "The only way to know is to find your mother. Quick."

She nods.

The three of us start to pack away our food. I glance at my dad. He's belly laughing at something Oliver and Killian have just said.

He's breathing deeper than since before he was sick, his cheeks almost a healthy pink. Maybe Eric is right. Or at least his sickness isn't getting worse. I certainly haven't felt any twinges of yuck since we've gotten here.

Aubree approaches the group and informs them it's time to leave. We all gather our packs and fall back into line again. This time, my dad, Killian, and Nym take the front along with Aubree. Laoise and Oliver take the middle, still deep in conversation from whatever they were discussing over our rest.

Eric walks beside me in the back.

He doesn't look at me, but his voice suddenly fills my mind. *Stay alert.*

I look at him out of the corner of my eye. *What do you think might happen?*

Not necessarily what might happen, but what might not be happening.

Wait, what?

The plagues. There isn't any evidence of what they might look like in the faerie realms. It's possible they aren't chaos that arrives, but chaos left behind in the wake of nothing. The absence of order.

Holy guacamole, what does that even mean?

Eric shakes his head. *I can't explain it. I don't know what it might be. Only that it might not be the same as what we saw in the Mortal Realm. Just be prepared for anything. Anything out of the ordinary is* not *a good thing. Remember, the Mortal Realm and the Faerie Realms work entirely differently.*

I pull in a ragged breath. *Great. More good news.*

He shrugs. *I could be wrong, but we should be prepared.*
Noted.

Eric turns and finally looks at me. *One thing I do know...I didn't come this far just to let my father succeed. If we go down, he goes down. That's a promise.*

<h1 style="text-align:center">Chapter Twenty-Eight</h1>

The stone cottage sits dead center of the only patch of land without flowers. Rust-colored grass forms the foundation of the property with several wooden fences scattered around the house, each filled with a different species of animal. An empty wagon sits on the edge of the property, although there is no defined road that leads away.

I glance at Aubree. "What are we doing here again?"

"There's something I need to grab from Nan before we get to my mother's castle." She winks at me. "Trust me, you'll like her. We can even stop for supper."

Oliver walks toward the small abode. "As long as she doesn't plan on having *us* for supper, then I'm down." He chuckles.

I glare at him. "Apologies for my boyfriend's lack of tact."

Killian frowns. "How can this Nan have us for supper if she cannot have us for supper? I do not understand."

My dad pats the elf on the shoulder and looks at me. "I've got this one." The two walk away in the direction of the stone house.

When Aubree knocks on the door, the first thing I notice is how incredibly short it is. The top of the entrance barely reaches the top of my head and I'm only above average height for a female human. Many of the fae in the realms are far above average, in comparison.

A high-pitched squeal comes from somewhere inside and I wince at the sound of glass shattering.

I give Aubree a side-eye but she doesn't respond.

"Coming!" that same treble voice replies.

Heavy footsteps echo from within, the distinct commotion of a chair toppling over and the screech of a cat resonating before the door finally swings open.

When it does, we're greeted with a faerie woman no bigger than an eight-year-old human child. She's plump and rosy, with violet irises trimmed in gold, and shimmery gold ringlets that capture her jolly face.

Oh, and she's got wings. Like, real ones.

The translucent champagne-hued wings flutter behind her, the top edge of each curling around her shoulders slightly.

"The Creator of the Realms smiles upon me!" She bounces with each word. "Aubree, daughter of the most high queen, it's so good to see you!"

She embraces Aubree tighter than I've seen anyone hug her before. Before I can wonder what it must feel like, I'm yanked into that same hug. Intense and jarring, I'm wrapped in a feeling of deep love, compassion, and joy. My chest fills with warmth, my skin suddenly cold and weepy once her touch is gone. Ravenous for the faerie's touch.

How can I want to be held by a complete stranger?

Nan continues around the circle, giving each of our group a snug embrace before finally stepping back.

"Come, come!" She waves us in. "Come in and have a rest. I've got a special brew I think you'll enjoy."

Aubree laughs. "Thanks, Nan. That sounds perfect."

The inside of the cottage is one large room, three times bigger than what it appeared to be on the outside. Every inch of the wood-paneled walls is covered with various objects hanging at odd angles, some that I recognize, some I don't. But all are related to farming or animals or cooking. A sieve, a hoe, the leather circlet of a harness for oxen.

The far left wall is lined with beds, each made of straw and covered in a hand-quilted blanket. On our right is a fireplace that fills more than half the wall. Several pots hang inside, boiling liquid sending plumes of smoke up and out of a couple of different small holes in the roof. The rest of the wall is lined with shelves of bottles and jars of herbs in what looks to be the kitchen.

Aubree smiles at Nan as we each take a seat at a wooden table that seats twelve that fills the remainder of the room., dropping our packs at our feet. "Nan is an old friend of my family. And she's the best healer in all the realms."

Nan scoffs with a giggle. "Oh, Aubree." She chuckles again.

"It's true, Nan." Aubree can't help but laugh. "Where would the Seelie Realm be without you?"

Nan moves to the fireplace in the kitchen to stir one of the pots. "It would have a lot less mischief, I'd say!" Her hearty laugh booms around the room.

I tip my head to the side, taking in the full scene. She's got to be the most eccentric being I've ever met. A giggle blossoms from within my core. I adore her. "Is that what all those beds are for then? Because you're a healer?"

The faerie's wings flutter. "You'd be surprised how often every single one of them has been filled at the same time."

I blink and count eight beds. That *is* surprising.

Oliver squints in thought. "Wait, I thought the fae could heal themselves. Why would they need a healer?"

Eric sits back in his chair. "Most ailments, yes, the fae can take care of those. But some can only be fixed with the aid of a healer. Certain plants that are toxic to the fae, an attack from an animal." His eyes land on mine. ***An arrow spelled to kill,*** pops in my head.

Visions of Killian working his magic on Eric to save his life flow through my head. Is Killian a trained healer?

I wrinkle my nose. The memory of Aibell attempting to kill Eric the last time I was here makes my belly flip.

Hadn't it been obvious at our very first encounter with her that she wasn't an ally?

Nan retrieves a fabric pouch from a cabinet and begins mixing a boiling liquid in a large black cauldron that sits smack in the middle of the kitchen counter. "So what brings you to these parts? Did the day accidentally flip and flow backward again?"

Oliver and I toss Aubree a confused look but she shakes her head.

She looks back to Nan. "Nope. I'm here on request of my mother."

"Ah. Of course. The wise queen will have something juicy for me to concoct, will she not?" Nan rumbles with more laughter. Before Aubree can answer she sets a clay cup of steaming liquid before her. "First, let's catch up. I want to hear all about your time in the Mortal Realm. What was it like? Are you back to stay?"

Aubree passes the first cup down the table to Killian, who sits at the far end. "I'd love to catch up, Nan. But mind if I say hello to Corky first?"

Nan's cheeks grow a deeper scarlet with her grin. "Aye, my dear. She's right out back." She nods in the direction of the back wall which has no door.

I expect Aubree to hop up and head to the front door. Instead, she walks directly to the spot where Nan just pointed out. And disappears through the wall.

I jump.

I forgot my best friend has strange faerie powers, too. This will take a little getting used to.

I step to the right to get a look out the window. Aubree strides across an area devoid of grass, into a small animal pen constructed of wood that glows yellow. My jaw drops when the creature comes into view.

It's a dog the size of a small horse, entirely alabaster save for the crimson ears that rise from the top of its head. A rope is tied around his neck to keep him settled in his pen. He leaps in the air as soon as he sees Aubree's approach, the faint sound of a yelp drifting around us.

Aubree buries her head into the thick coat of his neck, her arms circling around his body as far as they can go. Which isn't far.

"She's a *Cŵn Annwn*." Nan's voice startles me.

I twirl to face her.

She continues to ladle the liquid into more cups. "She's a hound of The Wild Hunt."

"Hellhounds," Laoise says.

Nan has a mythical hellhound as a pet? I side-eye my friends.

Nan chuckles. "She was orphaned as a youngling. I've raised her as my own. She takes no part in the Hunt, neither do they know where to search for her." She gives me a wink. "She's as gentle as a newborn babe."

I go still in wonder. The Faerie Realms will never cease to amaze me.

Nan turns to set cups of her special brew before the rest of us. "And what are your names, friends of Aubree?"

Laoise takes the lead in Aubree's stead. "I am Laoise and this is Killian. We are of the Seelie Realm. It's a pleasure to be here in the Seelie Court, Healer Nan."

Nan nods with a broad smile and looks at Eric.

"I'm Eric." He clears his throat. "Of the Unseelie."

"The king's son, no doubt?" Nan gives him a wink.

He just shifts uncomfortably and points beside him. "This is Nym."

"And a *faen*," Nym says, straightening.

My dad lifts a hand. "I'm Brent, Caoine's dad. Of the..." His forehead wrinkles as he looks at me. "Mortal Realm?"

Nan sets a cup in front of my dad with a wink and a smile.

My dad goes to take a sip but I place a hand on his.

"Drink up." Aubree's voice startles me. "It's safe to drink.

Nan serves only liquids that heal or are beneficial. She's incapable of causing harm to another, even if they're human."

She walks across the room and sits back down. Her shirt is covered in short white hairs, her cheeks blotchy from where Corky the *Cŵn Annwn* has covered her in kisses.

I nod thanks to Aubree as I turn to Nan. "I'm the Caoine he was referring to, Aubree's friend. And this is Oliver, my boyfriend."

He nods at her, as he takes a swig from his mug.

I do the same. And immediately pause. I blink up at Nan. "Hot chocolate?"

She beams. "Divine, is it not? Have you ever tasted such delight?"

I go to speak but Aubree cuts me off. "No. *Never*. This is amazing, Nan. How ever did you come by the recipe?"

Nan glows as she bustles around the kitchen again. "Took me years to concoct. But I'm always glad to share my love of cooking with friends!" She giggles and waddles to the wall of tinctures.

Aubree catches my eye, glancing at what is clearly a woven wastebasket in the corner. Strewn along the top are several white paper packets that have been torn open and discarded. The wording of a popular brand of hot chocolate mix is visible on each one.

I stifle a giggle.

Nan's intention is so pure and sweet. She longs to make others feel at home, to bring joy to others. She is literally *so* adorable. I sort of want to take her home with me.

But I can't. My eyes begin to droop. A quick glance at Oliver and my dad shows they're in the same state as I am.

The warm homey feeling along with hot chocolate has done us in.

Before I can say another word, I'm asleep.

Chapter Twenty-Nine

When I wake, I'm in one of the infirmary beds. I shift into a sitting position and stretch my arms overhead with a crazy huge yawn. Scratch a hand through my hair.

Oliver is on the bed to my left, still out like a light. My dad is asleep to my right, Nym lying beside him. As I glance over, the little man flashes me a bright smile. I give him a weak wave with a quiet chuckle.

That guy hasn't left my dad's side since they met. It isn't lost on me that my dad appears more awake now. Healthier overall.

Killian, Laoise, and Eric are in deep discussion at one end of the table, while Aubree and Nan talk at the opposite end.

I consider laying back down for a few more minutes of sleep but catch a name that twists my heart in two.

Seamus.

I turn my attention to Aubree and Nan. Why are they discussing Seamus? An invisible vice contracts inside me.

I hop out of bed and slide my feet into my shoes, then head over to sit with them. A small pile of acorns sits on the edge of the table. Payment for Nan's provision?

Aubree glances at me. "Good morning, sleeping beauty."

I scratch my head again and glance out the window. "Wouldn't it be good *evening*?"

She shrugs. "Feel better?"

"Much." I nod. "What did you put in that hot chocolate?" I ask Nan.

"Nothing, dear." She laughs. "My home has always put visitors at ease. I'm glad you could rest before the completion of your journey."

I nod in thanks. "Don't let me interrupt. Go back to what you were saying."

Specifically about Seamus.

Aubree avoids looking at me. "I was just talking to Nan about Seamus. She, uh...she hadn't heard about—" She swallows.

Oh. Right.

For the first time since meeting her, Nan's face falls. "My heart is pained at the passing of such an honorable faerie. May the earth be nourished and grateful for the return of his spirit."

I suck in a breath, the middle of my chest burning on fire. My throat closes, hot tears threatening to appear.

Will the loss of my friend ever grow easier?

Aubree glances at me, quiet for a moment. Then, "Did I ever tell you about our friendship? Seamus and me?"

I shake my head.

My friend smiles at a memory. "We were raised together, in my home."

My jaw drops. "You were?"

"Yep. I've known him my entire life. His parents were advisors to mine. Like, literally the closest confidantes to mine. Once his father passed, he and his mother were welcomed to remain with us. Seamus was raised with the same education right alongside me."

"Whoa."

She nods. "He was like a second brother to me. In fact, I wouldn't even have a brother if it weren't for him. He saved my brother Dain when I was very young." She blinks away tears. "Seamus had the biggest heart of any fae I ever knew."

Nan fiddles with her hands. "That boy had a heart of pure gold."

"I'm glad I knew him, even if only for a short while," I say.

The three of us sit in silence, Aubree and I refusing to address the elephant in the room. That Seamus' killer sits at the end of the table right now.

Because Eric isn't truly Seamus' killer. Not when he was brainwashed into being a puppet. King Raghnall is responsible for my friend's death.

I grit my teeth. We *will* stop these stupid plagues and we will fix those Seals. If only to spite that pathetic excuse of a fae.

Aubree recovers from her emotional moment. "Seamus had the Gift of Discernment...did you know that?"

"Wait what?" I look back at her.

"His gift. He could discern right from wrong in a millisecond, while in the Faerie Realms. If he'd been with us while trying to get Eric free, he would've had things figured out long before we all did. It's one reason he was such a people watcher, while in the Mortal Realm. He might not have had use of his gifting while there, but he could always tell so much about a person, just by observing them."

Huh. I can't help but smile.

I wonder what he knew about me? Did he sense my gifting long before I even entered the Unseelie Realm?

Nan stands. "Oh, that reminds me. You're here for the toy." She waddles away before I can figure out what she means.

I tilt my head toward Aubree. "The thing your mother wanted you to do?"

Aubree smiles and grabs hold of my hand. She doesn't use words but I know what she wants to say.

That she's glad she has me by her side. That she couldn't have handled the loss of her closest companion in life if I weren't there to mourn with her. That I'm like a sister to her.

I know this because that's exactly what my heart tells me. In the time when I thought I'd lost my dad, she was there for me. To pick me up and make me feel whole again.

The two of us have been through so much together. I sigh. We just need to get through one more hurdle and maybe we can go back to being normal teenagers again. Albeit, *faeish* teenagers.

My mind wanders to the conversation from the night before. "I have a question." I eye Nan as she stands on her tippy toes, looking through a shelf at the far end of the room. "Last night with the hot chocolate. Nan claimed it was her recipe when she clearly used packaged hot chocolate from the Mortal Realm. How is it that Nan can lie? I thought fae can't lie?"

Aubree shakes her head. "She believes what she says."

I pause.

"Nan is a bit nutty, I'll admit. But she truly believes the crazy things she says. Therefore, it *is* true. That thing with the days running backward is a conspiracy theory she's had for ages. It's easier just to agree with her than to try to talk sense to her." She smiles as she watches the woman. "She means no harm. She's like a second mother to me."

I smile, too. Then we both break into giggles when she accidentally knocks over a broom on her way back to us.

"She's quite clumsy, too," I whisper to Aubree.

"You have no idea," she says under her breath.

Nan returns with a small object in her palm. She sets it on the table. "Found it."

The mood at the table changes again.

She's brought a top.

A literal children's toy top. Like the old-fashioned ones with a pointed end that you spin to see how long you can keep it upright before it falls.

Aubree gasps and takes it in her hands. Tears begin to fall. "Thank you," she whispers.

Which is huge. Along with apologizing, the fae never say thank you. Ever.

Nan nods. "It rightfully belongs to you anyway. You are the closest thing to family that Seamus had."

I look at Aubree. "That belonged to Seamus?"

She swallows. "Yes. His father gave it to him on the day of his birth. In turn, his father's father had given it to him when he was born. It's been a part of his family legacy for thousands of years. He was meant to give it to his son or daughter but—" She pulls in a shaky breath. "It's meant to be mine now."

This is what her mother wanted her to retrieve?

Nan nods. "It's yours now." She sets her hands in her lap. "Is that all your mother wanted? Is there anything else I can get you?"

Aubree shakes her head. "That's all."

I straighten. "I'm curious..."

Nan tilts her head as she looks at me.

"Do you—" I glance at Aubree, then back at Nan. "I mean, would you know any way to break a law, given by the king of the Unseelie Realm?"

Nan's mouth goes round. "Oh dear, no. I wouldn't know about those sorts of things. But there's one thing I always keep in mind. Sometimes the answer is right in front of you. You just need to choose to take hold of it."

I attempt to hide my pout. What does that mean?

Aubree glances over her shoulder to see Oliver and my dad stirring from sleep. "We should get going. We're on a time crunch."

"Yes, of course." Nan brightens. "Does this mean you'll figure out what's wrong with the sky?"

Aubree wavers and glances at me. "The sky?"

"Yes." Nan toddles over to open the door. "I'd like to know who turned off the light switch this morning. It was the strangest thing. The sky went out just like that." She snaps her fingers.

Then she turns and looks right at me. "Someone is messing with our realm."

Chapter Thirty

The sky has darkened to a deep rosewood, streaks of misty rose clouds pulled and stretched in every direction. Echoes of mint blow past me, tossing my hair. The night is comfortable, surrounding me with perfect spring warmth.

I pull my backpack higher on my shoulders and glance around at the fields of flowers leading from Nan's cottage. Every single flower has gone to sleep. Petals are pulled around them like a protective blanket. Even the leaves of each stem have curled around themselves.

The air inside the cottage was too stuffy. A minute by myself in the early night air is just what I need. I'm just about to turn back to the rest of the group when something out of the corner of my eye makes me stop.

Orange and fluffy. My dad's cat.

"Hey, girl. What are you doing here?" I ask.

I bend down as she saunters over, her tail lifted high. She rubs her face and body along my legs and I scratch behind her ears, earning a friendly purr in return.

"How'd you get into the Seelie?" I tilt my head. Does she even realize she's not in the Mortal Realm any longer? I pat her head once more before standing. "You can stick with us. We'll get you home soon."

She meows in response. My heart flutters in an odd way. I totally get why my dad fell in love with her.

I learned months ago that it's not uncommon for household pets to find their way through one Veil or another. Something about cats and dogs not being human or faerie must be their ticket through the doors without having to use magic. Stories of pets going missing without a trace only to return in a month or more, unharmed and seemingly out of nowhere, are common in these parts.

The cat sits patiently at my feet when the door opens, the remainder of the group spilling out. Nan waddles right behind them, her face flushed with excitement at our impending journey. If only I could have as much confidence in us as she has.

She trips over an air current but catches herself. "Travel safe, dearies." She proceeds to shove leftovers from the meal we just consumed into Aubree's pack. "For the road."

Aubree gives the short faerie a hug. "Of course, Nan. Be safe. I'll be back soon to visit."

"You're all welcome to visit anytime! I always need help with Mork and Mindy." Nan laughs.

I glance at Aubree.

My friend smiles. "You never did get to meet the animals. I'll give you a private tour the next time we're here."

I blink. Do I even want to see faerie farmyard animals?

Nan pulls each of us into a hug before sending us off. She reserves an extra hug for me.

My dad jumps when he sees our visitor. "Hey! My cat." He bends down and picks her up, as she shoves her face under his chin, a loud *purr* resounding.

Nan waves goodbye and the nine of us continue on our journey.

"Friendly?" Nym asks my dad, his large orb-like eyes on the cat.

He nods. "She took care of me while I was sick."

Nym's look is curious. "She has name?"

"I call her...well, *cat*. I never got around to anything else."

The little man nods as if this is the most logical answer, ever.

Killian, Laoise, and Eric walk ahead, my dad and Aubree taking the rear of the group. Oliver and I fall somewhere in the middle as we walk through the Seelie forest.

He casually snags my hand, holding it tightly in his. We walk in silence for the first few minutes.

Then, he says, "Have you forgiven him?"

"Who?" I squeeze his hand.

"Eric. I mean, really forgiven him. For what he did to me? To your dad?"

I sigh. "At first, I didn't see that there could ever be a way, in the Mortal Realm or any other, where I would be convinced to forgive him. But like I said, we went through a lot while I was in the Unseelie Realm. I had no choice but to trust him. And he had to trust me, too.

"I know I can't force you to accept that he was under his father's power, that his actions weren't his own, but that's the truth. Once I accepted that, forgiveness came a lot easier." I look up at Oliver. "But I get if it's taking you longer. I mean, I wasn't the one with a knife to my throat last Halloween."

His mouth twists with emotion and he looks away. "I..." He clears his throat. "I want to forgive him. I believe you, when you say it wasn't him doing those things to me. But then I feel like... did I ever really know the real Eric? Like is he even my friend?"

I lay my head against his arm as we walk. "Honestly? I've gone over and over that in my head, since my first feeling of understanding him, while in the Unseelie. And I think, yeah. I do believe that the Eric we got to know in high school was the real him. I think his actions controlled by his father—as nefarious as they were—I think they were few and far between. Maybe like he was possessed at certain points in time or something?"

I shake my head. "I don't know how to explain it. But from

the time I spent with him in the Unseelie, and since we've been together here, I see glimpses of the old Eric." I rub my thumb along Oliver's wrist. "I think he's the same friend you had, Oliver. We just need to believe that. And to forgive."

A notch forms between his brows. We walk for a few more minutes in quiet. Finally, he says, "I think I am. Forgiving him. I don't feel as...angry anymore. I—" He huffs. "I can't guarantee things will go back to what they were, but...I'd like to try."

Oliver looks at me, pulling my hand up to his lips, pressing a kiss along my knuckles. "Especially since he's like a brother to you." He smiles at me, melancholy but filled with hope. "I believe you, Caoine. I know how important it is that you find a family to call your own."

"Thank you, Oliver. I appreciate you at least trying. It means more than you could know."

He leans down and gives me a quick peck on my lips before tilting his chin in front of us. "All right. I'm done with the heavy. I think I'll see what Killian is up to." He chuckles. "That guy is quite the character, isn't he?"

I laugh. "He is."

As Oliver walks away, I slow my walk so my dad can catch up. I give him a once-over. "You look like you're feeling better. Like, a lot."

He brightens. "I do. I haven't coughed since before we were at Nan's. I guess Eric was onto something with this Faerie Realm connection thing. I feel stronger, too. Like maybe I could play a game of football, reliving my glory days of high school." He chuckles and flexes the muscle of the arm not occupied by the cat.

I press a hand over my dad's forehead. "It doesn't appear that you have a fever anymore." Could it really be that simple?

Of course not. My heart sinks. If I've learned anything about the Faerie Realms, it's that nothing is ever that easy.

If my dad and I don't figure out a way to get out of the king's *law* then we'll likely have to live here forever. Not that being in the Seelie Realm would be so bad for me. But there's zero chance

Oliver will want to stay here forever. No part of Faerie is truly ever safe for a human. And what about my dad?

I push against the panic that rises deep in my chest.

Cat—which is apparently the cat's new name—leaps from my dad's arms and begins to trot around his feet. Nym pulls him into a deep conversation. I walk a bit faster to catch up to Eric.

"Any new revelations on your father's law?"

He looks up at my approach. "No. I still have no idea how to break it. I'm anxious to hear what the queen has to say about it. She'll have to know how to undo it." His throat bobs as he swallows.

My chest tightens but I nod. "Makes sense. I mean, maybe she's created the same kind of law at some point or other?"

"That's what I'm hoping." He pauses. "How's your dad doing?"

"Good. Really good, actually. I think you were right. Being here in the Seelie has helped to reverse the sickness. I haven't felt a twinge of anything since I've been here."

Eric runs a hand through his shoulder-length brown hair. "I'm not sure it's permanent. But it will do for now."

We walk in silence for another minute. As if we're back at Lincoln High traversing the hallways on the way to our next class.

As if all the things that have happened between us haven't happened. I sigh. So much awkward.

My shoulders droop. I miss the old Eric. Not the one that tried to kill my dad, of course. But the one I came to know just a few weeks ago, while trapped in the Unseelie Realm.

He aggravated me. Definitely annoyed me like a kid brother. But we also had a connection, a friendship unchallenged by any other I've ever had in my life. Different from what I have with Aubree and even Oliver. Will we ever have that again?

I nudge him with my elbow. "How are *you* doing?"

Eric frowns. "Me? I'm fine. Why?"

"Well, you did spend some time in the king's prison." I purposely neglect to refer to that monster as Eric's father.

Now he's the one to shove me with his arm. "You should know. You're the one who healed me. *Life-giver*. I mean, I should at least have some PTSD, but I don't. I feel...great. You literally healed me in more ways than one."

We haven't had a chance to discuss my surprising faerie gifting.

I nod. "Yeah, about that. Did you know? Like, did you have any idea at all, while we were together?"

He shakes his head. "I had no clue. I figured you'd probably have something, but that?" That was a serious shocker."

I snort. "Tell me about it. But then...well, how did your father know?" I clear my throat. "The king, I mean."

Eric shrugs. "Aibell maybe? I mean, now that we know she was always working undercover for my father, it makes sense that she may have seen something that tipped her off."

"Yeah." I sigh. "I'm sorry I doubted you, by the way. I...I should've known. It would make perfect sense that you would go along with the king, to ensure my safety. I just—wasn't thinking, I guess." I grit my teeth. "I feel like I never make the right decision. I'm sort of doubting everything about myself right now."

He looks at me. "You shouldn't. You're smart, Caoine. Way smarter than me, anyway." He scowls. "I'm the one that should be doubting my decisions." He shakes his head.

I place a hand on his forearm. "Eric, don't beat yourself up. The king...he literally has the Gift of Suggestion. It's no wonder you were brainwashed. That you couldn't think for yourself." I glance back at my dad, who's laughing as Nym uses his magic to levitate Cat in the air. To the cat's utter dismay. "I don't blame you. Oliver doesn't blame you. And I know my dad doesn't blame you."

Eric's face crumbles. "Is that even possible? That you could actually forgive me for what I did? That you all can move past how horrible I was?"

I nod. "Absolutely. I know you're fae, but let's be honest, there's no difference between mortals and fae when it comes to making mistakes. We all make poor choices or follow someone's lead that we shouldn't have. It's what makes us, *us*."

I swallow against a tight throat. Am I preaching to Eric or myself?

Oliver and Aubree pass by as they gather with Killian to watch the spectacle in front of us. My dad and Nym are mesmerized by Laoise, as she melts into a small ball of light, once more appearing whole again. The cat's tail puffs twice its size and she hides between my dad's legs.

I stop and turn to Eric. "Look, I know things have been weird. So, can we just...I don't know, like choose to hit the reset button? I sort of miss the old you. Well, the new old you. The non-brainwashed one, that is. The one that saved my life in the Unseelie."

Eric laughs. "Yeah, I knew what you meant." He crosses his arms. "And yes, I'd like to hit the reset button. Your friendship—" He sucks in a quick breath. "Honestly? Oliver's was the first real friendship I've ever had. But after our time in the Unseelie together, it's like—"

"We could be siblings?"

He startles. "Exactly. I've never known any of my siblings. But I feel like you are the closest thing to one I could have."

I allow a small smile to form. "Yeah, I know what you mean."

Maybe things are salvageable between us after all.

My dad shouts with a laugh and I look to see him running around with Nym. *Running.* I lift a hand to my chest in awe. He really is feeling better.

Nym levitates a rock and begins to make a tall pile, carefully balanced with magic.

I look at Eric. "I believe that. I never had true friends before coming to Lincoln, either." I struggle for the next words. "I think Oliver needs you." I glance over at Oliver who's still deep in conversation with the other faeries. "He hasn't been the same without you. He's lost his joy."

Eric's chin quivers. "I...I'd like that."

I nod.

My dad shouts again.

This time he and Nym have wandered a bit farther away from the group. An oversized ocher-colored vine that stands straight up and reaches into the clouds shivers as my dad scales the leaves and climbs into the unknown. He laughs as he reaches for something tucked tight within the leaves.

Nym remains on the ground, his hands moving in a pattern to show he's the real force behind my dad's ascent.

My jaw drops. I take in a breath, ready to reprimand a man twice my age who should know better than to mess around in a foreign land he knows nothing about.

Instead, my dad falls. Nym squeaks as he loses control of his magic.

My dad plummets towards the ground.

Chapter Thirty-One

Before a scream rips from my throat, Eric leaps forward, his arms raised over his head. A golden leaf the size of a double bed springs from the side of the stalk and wraps itself around my dad, catching him mid-air.

In four long strides, I'm by my dad's side, helping him step down from the pulsating plant that just saved his life. My dad visibly shakes, his arms looped around my shoulders as I usher him to solid ground.

He blinks. "What just happened?"

Nym gathers close to my dad. "My prince save my friend!"

My gaze lingers on the short fae for a second before whipping back to Eric.

He's breathing heavily, sweat gathered along his hairline. His face is lined with concern. "You okay?"

I swallow. "You did that?"

Eric's eyes lock with mine.

"How?" I ask.

Laoise steps from the group that's gathered to the side. "He has truly returned to us." She tilts her head. "He is a woodsprite, Caoine. Remember?"

My jaw drops. Of course. I swing around to look at him again. "But, how? You've never done anything like that before." My voice is far more accusing than I mean it to be.

Eric nods. "I've always had the ability to manipulate physical nature. But—" He pauses. "I lost it when I came to live with my father."

Killian scratches his chin in thought. "Your true nature was lost when you stopped being who you were created to be."

"Something like that." Eric shrugs. "I don't know exactly how it works." He breathes heavily again. "I only know that it went away years ago. I hadn't recovered the ability since returning to the realms."

Aubree smiles. "Another sign that you are out from under the king's power."

"I wish I knew this back then." Eric attempts a smile but it fades just as quickly. "I wish I knew a lot of things. But it's too late, I guess." His unspoken words have meaning to only me.

His mother. Eric speaks of his mother. I know this because we once shared a conversation about our mothers with one another, not that many moons ago.

If Eric is becoming who he truly was before his father's influence, is it possible he could reconnect with his mother? If she's even still alive?

My mind wanders to the thimble he tossed into the magical well in the Unseelie Realm. My chest grows thick with cotton and it's difficult to find air.

If I can save my mom, you can find yours.

He jumps at my intrusion, then nods.

I turn to Killian. "I've been wondering something. How come you and Laoise haven't lost— or traded— your powers when the silence have been close?"

He nods. "My guess is they only borrow, or exchange, power when needed. So far, they have left the wisp and me alone."

"Huh." I consider this for a minute.

Caoine!

My head shoots up. The voice is inside my head, but it's not Eric's. I look around for the one who just spoke to me. My dad and Nym have straggled back to the thick stalk, digging at something in the ground. The cat suddenly skitters away, her hackles raised. The beanstalk quakes, each leaf coming to life.

Before a single one of us can make a move, a hand the size of a dump truck reaches from above and plucks my dad and Nym from the ground before disappearing into the dark clouds above.

"Dad!" I scream.

The six of us race to the stalk as fast as we can, our packs thrown to the side as we run. The cat remains in her safe spot a few dozen feet away.

With a leap, I jump onto the trunk, my hands and feet finding an immediate foothold. Brown arms wrap around my middle, pulling me back to the ground.

"No!" I fight Oliver like a trapped animal. "Let me go! Dad!"

Oliver whispers in my ear. "Not on my watch."

I spin around to smack him but he catches my hand.

"Stop." Adrenaline controls every movement he makes. "Not without me. I'll go first."

"No!" I struggle against his gentle embrace. "I can climb faster."

Killian and Aubree are on the stalk, already two stories up.

Oliver glances up. "Just wait."

"Let me go!" Tears stream down my face now. *Please, Creator. If you're real, please save my dad!*

Eric steps to the base of the trunk, his words for me. "He's right, Caoine. Let the others get a head start." He turns to me. "We'll get him back. That's a promise."

I gasp, my chest splitting in two. Fae don't make promises.

He grabs the lowest branch and begins to climb at breakneck speed.

Oliver releases me. "Now we go." His voice is low.

I swallow back my anger and whip around to start climbing.

Every nerve in my body quivers with rage, my blood pounding a beat of alarm.

I will not kill my boyfriend. I will not kill my boyfriend.

If I chant it enough, maybe I'll succeed. I grind my teeth as I ascend.

Oliver is the last on the stalk. I have no clue where Laoise has gone.

Muscle memory from weeks ago, when I climbed the king's castle, floods my body. I overtake Eric in just a few strides, Aubree's feet now in view.

How high does this beanstalk even go? And how am I climbing so fast?

I suck in another lungful of air, never getting quite enough. My fingers go numb and I see spots. From panic or exhaustion, I can't be sure.

Killian's legs disappear, followed soon after by Aubree's. They've found the top.

Another four footholds and my head pops through a literal hole in the ground where the stalk extends into another universe.

Aubree extends a hand to me, yanking me to my feet before bending to aid Eric. I glance around. The place looks similar to what was below, except without all the flowers. The ground is more hard earth in shades of celadon, sage, and slate. The sky is a deep plum. More clouds?

How does this exist above the dark faerie sky?

A house ten times bigger than any I've ever seen looms before us. The front door is as tall as a small skyscraper, each window the size of a two-story building.

Oliver finally crawls from below. I turn away and ignore him.

He coughs. "Are you kidding me? Did we just climb a real beanstalk? Where's Jack?"

Killian frowns. "I do not know this Jack that you speak of."

Aubree tosses him a sarcastic look. "Where do you think mortal fairytales come from?"

Oliver blinks but stays quiet.

Eric looks around. "Which way did they go?"

A muffled noise from behind the giant door draws our attention.

I stifle a cry.

"Wait!" My dad's voice rings loud and clear from within the house.

<h1 style="text-align:center">Chapter Thirty-Two</h1>

I leap towards the door, my only thought to save my dad before he ends up in a bowl of giant stew. Oliver grabs me around the waist to retrain me. Again.

"Hey!" I elbow Oliver in the ribs as hard as I can. He lifts my feet from the ground and I kick my legs like a wild animal. "Oliver!"

My next shout is muffled beneath his hand.

"Shhh," he whispers in my ear. "Are you trying to get us killed?"

The others in the group bristle, their attention on high alert.

Eric raises a hand, his head tilted as if deep in thought, clearly speaking to Nym. "Wait." He pauses in concentration. "He's fine. They're okay."

I gasp and stop fighting Oliver. "What?"

Eric's gaze collides with mine. He nods.

Oliver releases me. "Can we get inside?"

Eric squints at me. "He's on his way."

Aubree shakes her head. "Who's—"

The massive door in front of us groans, squeaks, clangs open with giant-style fanfare. Dead center stands Nym.

His oversized ears quiver, eyes bulging with delight. "Friends!"

Eric is the first to cross to the little man. "Nym, you're all right?" He glances behind the faen but it's too dark to make out anything. "Is Brent safe?"

Nym waves his spindly arm into the house. "Friends come inside?" He bounces and claps his hands. "Meet Gnait!"

I blink in confusion. "Who's *Nate*?"

"Gnait new friend!" Nym jumps as he backs up to let us through the door.

At the same time, my dad shouts something, immediately followed by laughter.

Nym hoots. "Come! Join fun!"

He sprints away. Killian and Oliver struggle to close the door behind us. Eric and I lead the way into the dark hallway, cautiously following the voices ahead.

Another tumble of laughter from my dad splits the dark. I hesitate. What is going on?

"Friends!" Nym announces. "Got friends!"

We enter a room lit by wall sconces and a fire in a stone pit that sits in the center. The ceiling is as high as a kite on the windiest of days, of course. An immense wooden table is in the middle of the room with four wooden stools that would take me half an hour to climb, spaced around it. On one sits a man ten times the size of The Rock.

My dad stands on another.

I choke back my shock. *Shoot.* If only I had my pack, I could snag the switchblade I brought.

All around him are tiny round bits of fruit that I don't recognize. He's got several in his hand. He winds his throwing arm up and lobs it in the air, in the direction of the giant. The small orange bit lands squarely in the giant's mouth.

My dad throws his hands in the air with a cheer. The ground rumbles with the vibrations from the giant's laughter, as he pounds his leg with his hand in excitement.

"Dad!" I yell.

My dad and the giant finally turn to see what Nym has been chattering about.

"Caoine." My dad brightens. "Hey."

I wince. "Hey?" Is he kidding me?

Killian steps forward and glances at Nym. "This is the Gnait you spoke of?"

Nym nods enthusiastically.

Aubree crosses her arms and glares at my dad. "You're okay? You scared the realms out of us!"

I hide my snigger. The parent is getting reprimanded this time!

My dad's face falls. "I thought Nym told you we were safe?"

Eric scratches a hand through his hair. "He did." His expression is apologetic as he looks at the rest of us. "I didn't exactly have time to tell them, though."

Oliver nods. "We were sort of trying to save you from becoming supper." His distrust is obvious as he gives Gnait a once-over.

My dad reaches a hand towards us as if we can just hop up on the stool without a second thought. "Come! Meet Gnait."

None of us move.

Gnait smiles down at us. His dark skin is smooth and his dark curls stick up a bit in the back. Is he a child?

"Hallo." His accent is thick.

His bulbous nose lifts up with his chunky cheeks and massive smile. Crooked white teeth fill most of his face. His eyes are much too small, practically disappearing behind his happiness. His dirty feet are bare, the bottom edge of his pants halfway up his calf, ripped and tattered.

Does he live here alone? Is there no one to take care of him?

Killian gives a slight bow. "It's a pleasure to meet you, Gnait."

The giant simply giggles.

Aubree and Oliver both nod in *hello*, their expressions tight.

Eric sniffs. "Gnait."

I clear my throat. "Erm, hey Gnait. Uh...thanks for taking care of my dad," sounds way more like a question.

Because, really, why did he even take him in the first place?

Gnait looks at my dad. "I like Brent."

My heart pounds so much faster than needed. "Yeah. I like him, too."

No one else says a word.

"Think maybe we could...have him back?" I ask.

My dad laughs. "Oh, he's not keeping me against my will. We were just getting to know one another."

Right. Because that's always a good idea in the Faerie Realms. I sigh.

"Okay," I say, even though that's a lie.

He gestures towards the giant who gently picks him up and places him on the ground in front of us.

My dad nods in thanks and brushes his clothes of wrinkles. "Gnait heard my scream when I fell and came to help."

I glance between the giant and my dad. "Yeah, but you fell like, minutes before he grabbed you."

He shrugs. "He wanted to help. He thought Nym and I were in trouble and brought us here to save us."

Alarm melts across Eric's face. "He was saving you from us? Did he think we were a threat?"

Nym lifts his palms. "He not know. He want us safe."

I bristle. Am I supposed to thank the giant who stole my dad away from us?

Instead, I say, "Cool."

Gnait smiles brightly, as if I've just told him he's won a prize.

"So...can we go now?" I give a forced smile to my dad.

He jolts into action. "Sure, sure." He turns to the giant. "Can you help us back down? We've got to go now."

Gnait stands. "Of course."

My stomach leaps into my throat.

Without warning, the giant reaches down and begins picking each of us up and placing us on his shoulders. I squeak as he grabs me. I'm slightly surprised by just how tame his hold is. As soon as I rest on his shoulder, I grip his shirt with all my strength.

Eric and Oliver sit with me on one side of Gnait's upper body, my dad, Aubree, Killian, and Nym on the other arm. We have to grip his shirt tightly to stay on his shoulder without sliding off. Each step is like a wild roller coaster ride. But with death at the end of it.

Oliver clears his throat. Eric and I turn to look at him. His cheeks deepen into a muted crimson.

He sighs. "Thanks." This single word is muttered. As if it's a secret.

Eric tilts his head. "For what?"

Oliver won't make eye contact with him but I can sense this apology is only for Eric. "For going after Brent. That was...cool of you."

"Everyone on this journey is important to me."

Oliver's jaw works and he still won't look Eric's way. But he gives a small nod.

I stifle heaving a sigh. Baby steps, Caoine. He'll get there.

In another minute we're out the front door and at the top of the beanstalk again. My breath is literally taken away by each sway of Gnait's steps.

Oliver's look says the same thing as mine. *Is this real?* I'll bet he never thought he'd be doing this six months ago.

I keep hold of Gnait's shirt but lean my head on Oliver's shoulder, my earlier frustration with him gone.

We come to an abrupt stop.

Gnait turns his head in the direction of my dad. "Will you come visit?"

His low voice shakes the leaves of the vine that peak through the hole in the ground.

My dad pats the giant's shoulder. "Of course! We've got an important errand to run, but I'll stop by to say hello on our way out of the realm."

Gnait smiles. "My little man, too?"

Nym bounces with glee. "Yes! I come, too."

The giant gets busy stepping onto the beanstalk and stepping down. "This makes Gnait happy. I will wait to see my friends again."

The ride down is far scarier than the climb up. At least I had control of where I chose to step and how fast to go when I climbed. With each movement the giant makes, my heart leaps into my throat, sinks to my belly, and circles back around once more. I attempt to ignore the extreme height at which I could fall to my death.

As soon as we're on the ground, I exhale, sucking in another lungful of air like it's scarce. The rest of the group gingerly pats their bodies as if to ensure we're all in one piece. We find our packs quickly.

Gnait grabs the vine again. "Be safe, friends. I will see you soon?"

My dad and Nym nod with vigor. This brings another smile to the giant's face.

In four long strides, he disappears through the dim clouds once more.

Chapter Thirty-Three

The cottage is small. Larger than Nan's home, but definitely small for what I'd imagine a queen would reside in. Especially after walking so many hours to get here.

"This is your house?" I ask Aubree.

She nods. "This is my house."

The dwelling consists of mud-caked walls and a roof constructed of twigs and straw. No windows. A single wooden front door.

I pause. "It's...nice. But how is this a castle?" I shrug. "Not to be mean or anything, but this place is small."

Aubree snorts and slaps me on the back. "This isn't the whole thing, silly."

She steps through the door without a knock. Killian, Laoise, and Eric follow her as if this is normal.

I glance at my dad and Oliver. They shrug and wait for me to make a move.

"Am I missing something?" I ask once we're all inside.

The interior of the house is much larger than what it appears to be from the outside. We're standing in a main foyer area, but there's a main sitting area the size of my house to the left, and a kitchen of the same dimensions to the right. A set of stairs that I can't see the ending to go straight up into the ceiling. Along the back wall of the house are books. Just books.

The most substantial bookshelf I've ever seen in my life, if I'm being honest.

Eric crosses his arms. "Not all castles are protected by magic." He smiles.

"What's that supposed to mean?" I frown.

"It means..." Aubree pulls a chair out from the table. "That we don't need magic to hide our home." She takes three different colored books from the shelf and sets them on the table. "We can hide our domain in plain sight." Finally, she walks over and turns on the kitchen faucet.

At first, nothing happens.

Then the stairs that go into the ceiling vibrate, shake, and move like rolling waves of the fiercest storm.

The floor beneath them shifts and they descend directly below. They keep moving until they're no longer above ground at all. The only thing that remains is a compact set of steps that leads beneath us.

Aubree gives me a wink. "After you." She gestures towards the stairs.

Oliver backs up. "I'll follow, thanks."

Eric laughs and claps Oliver on the shoulder. "Where's that no-fear spirit our captain used to exude?"

Oliver holds his hands up. "This isn't a soccer field. I'm not too proud to admit I'm not going down there first."

His eyes glance into the darkness as if we've just entered a haunted house.

Aubree laughs. "I'm kidding. I'll go first."

Killian and Laoise follow obediently after her, not a care in the world. I push my dad to go after them, Nym right by his side. I definitely want him sandwiched between full-blooded fae so he stays as safe as possible. No more run-ins with giants, thanks.

Oliver and I go next, Eric taking the rear. Why am I so

nervous about this? This is the Seelie queen. She's chill. She likes me. I should be all kinds of relaxed right now.

So why do I have a sinking feeling?

Oh, maybe because we're descending into the pits of a realm that's not my home. PTSD from the Unseelie Realm has me paranoid. *Oof.*

The stairs twist and wind at sharp angles, obsidian swallowing us with every step.

"Boo," Eric whispers right by my ear.

"Eep!" I jump but grab the rail to keep from falling. I growl. "Watch it, prince. If I go down, you go down."

Eric chuckles. "Come on, Caoine. Just having a little fun." He leans closer to whisper in my ear again. "It's not every day we're in a haunted house, right?"

I growl again and attempt to elbow him. "Not cool listening in on my thoughts."

He snorts. "You sort of popped it into my head, Caoine. I can't just listen in, remember? Not my fault."

My nerves must truly be on edge if I'm projecting my thoughts now. I sigh.

Oliver laughs from in front of me. I attempt to slap his arm but end up swatting the railing instead since I can't see a thing. Eric and Oliver laugh harder. I pout, even though no one can see my temper tantrum.

Just when I'm about to ask Aubree if we're lost, a light switches on. I wince, squinting.

Aubree is on the ground level. "Once footsteps are detected on this level, the lights automatically come on."

Oliver steps down from the stairs and looks around the open cavern with awe. "Cool."

Without another word, she turns and walks through the closest stone wall.

I huff. "Dude. Could she at least tell us what's going on before disappearing like that?"

Laoise tilts her head. "She will return, Daughter of Saoirse. Why all the worry?"

I sigh. Good question. Why all the worry?

But, of course, the faerie is right. Seconds later Aubree reappears, the wall straight ahead rumbling to life and moving out of the way at the same time.

Eric puts his hands on his hips. "Fun trick."

She fiddles with her hair, to make herself more presentable. "Usually visitors must wait here for a time until they are cleared to enter the queen's domain." She smirks. "My gifting comes in useful in this case. Otherwise, we'd be waiting quite a while."

As she finishes speaking, two royal guards dressed in gold leather and helmets appear in the new darkened doorway.

Aubree catches my eye. "Ready to meet my mother?"

<h1 style="text-align:center">Chapter Thirty-Four</h1>

I've stepped into Downton Abbey. No joke.

I'm not sure why I thought the Seelie royal residence would be a castle just like the Unseelie Realm. Of course, it would be different.

The entire thing is underground. It's as massive and elegant as any estate from early twentieth-century England.

Each room is inlaid with wood flooring and antique trimming. Intricately woven rugs and tapestries. Hand-carved furniture that stands out as not exactly manmade. Ceilings that hang two stories above our heads. We pass through a library packed with wall-to-wall books, a sitting room, a formal dining room, and into another sitting room.

I rock my head back to admire the delicate artwork of fae and nature painted overhead. "All this to keep the queen's home secret?"

Aubree shakes her head. "We live underground for security reasons, sure, but it's more than that. Our kind have always preferred to remain close to nature, to embrace our roots. Dwelling underground reminds us of our heritage and puts us in touch with that which we love most: *creation*."

I nod. "Your home is beautiful."

"It changes every so often. My mother will revamp the place to reflect various mortal cultures." She smirks. "She's stuck in early twentieth-century Western Europe right now."

Oliver runs a hand over the soft cushion of the sofa. "I can see that. Is this stuff real? Like, actual antiques from the Mortal Realm? Or are they recreations?"

She shrugs. "Who knows? It'll be different the next time I come home, anyway."

Aubree plops down on the sofa, my dad and Nym settling in beside her. Killian and Laoise choose two stiff hardback chairs in the corner. Eric walks over to the fireplace, inspecting the tapestry that hangs above it. Oliver and I take the other sofa, the one along the wall with the windows. Windows without glass panes but with what is obviously a manufactured scene of a waterfall outside.

I allow the view to sink in. Living underground does have its drawbacks.

My dad leans forward, elbows on his knees. "So, is there anything we need to know about the queen? Or, how to interact with royalty?"

Aubree blinks. "Just treat her like you would anyone else. She won't bite."

Eric snorts. "I think he means, does he need to bow or say *Yes, your beloved majesty,* or something like that. Life with my father isn't quite the same as it is elsewhere."

She frowns. "No, my mother isn't particular."

Killian shifts in his seat. "I look forward to meeting the queen. I've never had the opportunity to do so."

Laoise nods. "Agreed. I have heard of her beauty."

I look at Aubree for a reaction. The queen's beauty is something I haven't quite pegged yet. Her appearance shifted continually each time I saw her. Is it the same for everyone else, or do they settle on a single vision of her?

Aubree only nods.

We sit in silence for a few minutes. Aubree suddenly stands

and all of us jump to our feet in response. A second later, the door swings open and the shifting image of the queen enters the room.

She immediately finds her daughter and embraces her. "Aubree, my love. You have done well."

Aubree beams.

The queen smiles and releases my friend, turning to the rest of us.

Her pale brown skin practically glows, striking aqua eyes finding mine. "Welcome, Daughter of Saoirse." She glances at Eric. "I see you have accomplished the task I requested. Welcome, Unseelie Prince." She gives a slight nod.

Eric returns in reply with a nod of reverence and a bow.

Is he nervous?

She turns to Killian. "Welcome to the Seelie Realm, dear son." Her attention shifts to Laoise. "And Daughter of Light. I welcome your presence and hope you find my accommodations to your liking."

"My queen." Killian drops into a deep bow.

Laoise follows his action.

Queen Faílenn extends a hand towards my dad. "It is an honor to meet you, Brent Roberts."

My dad's jaw drops as he shakes her hand.

She smiles. "Nym, friend to all. You are an inspiration."

His large eyes glaze over in delight. "My queen!" His voice is nothing more than a squeak.

The queen turns her attention to Oliver. "Hello, mortal son. Your presence here means more than you will ever know."

Oliver takes a deep breath.

What does that mean?

"Caoine. You come with a question." She lifts her chin.

I glance at Aubree and back to the queen. How is it that her mother literally knows everything?

"Yes. My dad and I have discovered a...*side effect* from our time in the Unseelie Realm."

"You speak of the decree King Raghnall placed upon you?"

I nod. Swallow.

The queen's face softens. "I believe you know the answer you seek."

I bite my cheek, a quick glance at Eric. His mouth tilts down as if he's known all along, too.

Maybe we all have. We just haven't wanted to admit it.

My heart picks up pace. "We can't get out of it, can we?"

She shakes her head.

I pull in a shaky breath. "Not unless the king reverses the law."

"You are correct, Daughter of Saoirse. By now you have discovered your time in the Seelie Realm has lessened your symptoms." She looks at my dad. "However, your sickness will return with time. Residing within the Seelie Realm is only a temporary solution."

Oliver puts an arm around me. "With respect, Queen Faílenn, there's no way the king will reverse what he's declared over Caoine and Mr. Roberts." He pauses. "Does this mean they will have to live within the Unseelie Realm forever?"

She looks at Oliver with compassion, then turns it toward Eric. "There is only one other way for the law to be broken."

Eric's shoulders fall. "Upon the death of my father."

She nods.

I jump. "King Ragnall must die for us to be free?"

Killian bristles.

Eric's chin trembles.

Oliver grips me tighter. "No. There must be another way." He turns to look at Eric. "No matter what someone's done in the past, no one deserves to die."

Eric's chest rises. He nods at his friend.

Oliver nods at Eric, then looks back to the queen. "What can we do?"

Her smile is empathetic. "There is no other path, my son. Choose what you will but Caoine and Brent cannot change what is done."

My jaw drops. "You can't do something? Like, isn't there a spell or something you can do to reverse his law?"

The queen tilts her chin down. "I am sorry, my child. There is no other way."

I bury my head in Oliver's chest. Heat swells in my chest and I fight back the emotion that rips at my throat.

We've come so far. Delivered the books of Judgment and Discernment to the queen. Broken Eric from faerie jail and gotten him safely to the Seelie Realm.

But even once the Seals are fixed, my dad and I will still be doomed to death. Life within the Unseelie Realm will not be kind to us. In any way.

No. I clench my jaw. That won't happen. We *will* find a way to break the bond.

I swallow my tears, and lift my head, looking at the queen. "When will we do the spell to fix the Seals?"

The queen nods. "As soon as the Bunaidh arrive. Then we can proceed."

"Good. Once that's finished we'll decide what to do about... the other thing." I look at Oliver. "We'll figure this out. Together."

<h1 style="text-align:center">Chapter Thirty-Five</h1>

The swirling pool jumps with two-headed fish and frogs the size of small dogs. Mist floats above the small pond, rising back up to the source of the waterfall. Shades of every color of the rainbow mix together and then separate as the water flows and twirls in its dance. The water is much darker than I imagine it normally is, thanks to the gloomy sky above.

Oliver, Eric, my dad, Nym, and I are seated in the sage-hued grass that surrounds it, not far from the house that hides the castle. Killian and Laoise chose to remain underground in the queen's home. Aubree has already entered into meetings with her mother and other Seelie Council members. Catching a little fresh air before the big ceremony was my suggestion.

Not that we haven't had enough of it. But something about the weight of my impending future is just too heavy to endure while below ground. I glance at my dad. Does he feel the same anvil-type noose around his neck?

Going back to the Unseelie Realm for good is something I could handle. I'm part fae. I'd eventually learn the ways and might even discover new magic to play with. But my dad? He's already lived a lifetime of hell in that prison. Trapping him in that kind of life isn't an option.

My heart pounds as I glance at Oliver. As much as I agree with him about taking the life of another, I'm not sure I can avoid the opportunity if given the chance to set my dad free.

I swallow.

My dad and Oliver are distracted by Nym, who once again amazes them with his newfound powers of levitation and making things hover mid-air. An odd-looking fish lifts from within the swirling water, only to plop back beneath the waves once more.

Oliver laughs.

As long as flying rocks don't endanger us, I guess I'm okay with a little fun.

I turn to Eric. "Got any plans once we're done with this whole thing?"

He shrugs and picks at the grass. "Hadn't thought that far ahead yet."

"Is returning to the Unseelie Realm an option?"

He shakes his head. "I don't see how. My dad will never let things rest. And I can't imagine Aibell giving up her grudge against me. Spending a life always looking over my shoulder isn't something I desire."

His brow pulls together and I sense that he's thinking of his lost mother. Is it possible for him to even find her? We've both lost our mothers, though in different ways.

Invisible needles prick my fingers as I think of my mom, a reminder of what I've missed out on. What would life have been like if she'd been in it? I glance at my dad. Our relationship would never have been what it was. Would I trade my past for a life I've never known?

I watch the water spin around in the air. Down and up. Up and down. "Think maybe the Mortal Realm would be an option?"

Maybe Oliver wouldn't mind having his best friend back again?

He winces. "I'm not sure about that one. What would I do?

It's not my...home. I'd have no choice but to return to the Unseelie, every so often. In stealth, of course."

I force a laugh. "You'd have a banging landscaping business in the Mortal Realm, that's for sure."

His smile doesn't reach his eyes.

I sigh. "Maybe Queen Faílenn would let you stay in the Seelie Realm?"

"Maybe."

I slump. I guess my dad and I aren't the only ones without a true home, once this thing is over.

"Got room for one more?" Oliver slides closer to the two of us, leaving my dad and Nym to their playtime.

I pat the spot next to me with a smile.

Oliver rests a hand along my waist. "I, uh..." He clears his throat. "I'm serious about your father. Killing him isn't an option. There's got to be a way to convince him to change his mind."

Eric smiles, for real this time. "I appreciate your confidence. You've got more faith in him than I do."

Oliver squeezes my waist. "What is it that your father wants? Why put that law on Caoine anyway?"

More stuff I never wanted to tell Oliver. He worries about me too much.

I frown. "He wants to use my *gift* to bring the late queen back to life."

A look of horror envelops Oliver's face. "Oh."

"Yeah, *oh*. I'm not talking about Eric's mom, in case you're wondering."

Eric's shoulders stiffen, pain lacing his features.

I quickly go on to save him the unwanted attention. "The queen died like, a bajillion years ago. The king has had her kept preserved in a glass case in his bedroom ever since. He's convinced I can bring her back to life."

"Whoa. That's heavy."

Eric shakes his head. "It wouldn't stop there, though. I guarantee you that even if Caoine agreed to do what he asked, my father would keep her. He'd want her as close as possible. A gift like hers has never been seen with any of the realms, ever. My father will never lift the law he created. He wants Caoine. To keep her, he knows he'll need to keep her dad under the law, too."

"Does Aibell know this?" I ask. "She'll be livid when she discovers she *doesn't* get to kill me after I've resurrected the queen."

Eric shrugs.

Oliver shakes his head. "So, you've got nothing? Like, to blackmail him or something? Isn't there a way to trick him into reversing the law?"

Eric lifts his brows. "Do you have any ideas?"

Oliver's face drops.

"Because I've known the man for years but don't have a clue where to begin. He will not be easily tricked. And no, I have no idea how I could possibly blackmail him."

"Look," I say. "Let's not worry about this right now. We'll figure something out...eventually. Right now, we just need to stop those plagues. 'Cause if we have nothing left to go back to, then what's the point of all this worry?"

Oliver runs a hand over his head. "That's the truth. I sorta miss my guitar right about now."

Eric smiles. "You never did play me anything. I'd like to hear your mad skills."

I snort.

Olivers queezes my side and makes me squeal. "Hey, now. Do I not have mad skills?"

I fight for breath and playfully bat at him. "Okay, okay. Yes. You've got mad skills."

Eric lifts a hand in explanation. "I mean, I can get you an instrument, if that's what you need."

Oliver looks at his friend. "I'm down for that." He instinctively smiles, but it fades quickly.

Eric pauses, taking a deep breath. "Hey, I wanted to say...I—"

He blows out a breath. "Look, you know that night of Halloween, that...it wasn't me. You know that, right? I'd never hurt you, of my own will."

Oliver plays with the grass. Finally, he nods. "Yeah. I think I get that. Now."

Eric's shoulders visibly slump, an invisible weight rising from his shoulders. Oliver looks at his friend, a small smile finally allowed to show. Without another word, Eric hops up to join my dad and Nym.

Silence settles around Oliver and I, my skin soaking in the beauty of the Seelie Realm. I take a moment to just be. Listening to the sound of my dad and Nym and Eric goofing around. Allowing the echoes of the Seelie creatures to settle into my soul. A light scent of lavender circles around me before moving on.

"Hey."

I turn to see Oliver surveying every inch of my face. I smile. "Yeah?"

"I'm sorry."

"Sorry?" I tilt my head.

He nods. "For being so crabby this whole time. I believe that you and Eric don't have feelings for each other. I'm not sure why I ever thought that."

I laugh. "Yeah, I'm not sure why you'd be jealous of him, either."

Oliver chuckles, places his thumb along my jawline. "I've been crazy not to believe you. Forgive me?"

"Always."

His grin is infectious, the corners of his eyes crinkling with joy. I take in his warmth and presence. The way his crooked tooth plays peek-a-book from between his lips. His beautiful dark skin reflecting beneath the strange ethereal sky.

He leans in to kiss me when I sense the stillness around us. I turn to see what's stopped my dad and Nym from their play and gasp.

Standing on the opposite bank are the silence. Three of them. Just like we saw before.

I grab Oliver's arm. Eric is on his feet before any of us can say a word.

Nym jumps up in a protective stance in front of my dad and I know Eric has just spoken to him inside his head.

"Caoine?" my dad says softly.

Eric holds a hand to the side, toward my dad. "Don't move."

Oliver and I slowly rise.

My dad's voice is steady. "What do you think they want?"

The prince shakes his head. "Not sure. But I have a feeling it can't be good."

The words are barely out when it happens.

My dad collapses. Right where he's standing.

"Dad!" I scream and run to his side.

Nym already stands over him, his spindly fingers touching his face and hands.

I look at Eric. "What's wrong with him?"

Eric swallows, glances at the silence, and then back again.

No.

Oliver's eyes are panicked. Then he falls, too, lost in a dreamless sleep.

My dad and boyfriend lie asleep at our feet.

"Eric!" My voice is strained and childlike.

"No!" he shouts at the silence on the other side of the bank. "Stop! Reverse what you've done!"

But they're gone.

The silence leave in the same way they appeared.

"This can only mean one thing." Eric's chest rises and falls with passion. "The silence are almost done with the Mortal Realm. They're searching for every human alive. It doesn't matter if we do the spell. The Mortal Realm is about to be lost forever."

Chapter Thirty-Six

Oliver looks dead. So does my dad.

They appear to rest as if in the deepest of slumbers. Their skin sags with gravity. Their bodies are stiff, frozen in this one moment in time. It's almost impossible to convince my brain that they're alive. That they're merely sleeping forever.

Forever until death takes them.

Before I can vocalize my worries, Nym reaches out, pulling each of us together so we're touching. I blink. And we're back inside the castle, in the same sitting room as before.

Eric grunts in surprise, I simply gasp, from where we kneel on the floor around the bodies of my dad and Oliver. I don't have time to ask what just happened.

Aubree rips into the room. "What's going on?"

I struggle to my feet. "The silence. They're here."

"They—they spelled them?"

I nod.

She wipes both her hands down her face and slumps into a chair. "This is not good."

I look down at Oliver, my arms snaking around my midsection. "Eric thinks this means their work in the Mortal Realm is done." My tears increase tenfold. "Are we too late?"

Aubree pulls in a strained breath. "Let me go ask my mother. She'll know what to do."

Tears flood my cheeks, heat pulsing through my veins. My hands shake as I help Eric and Nym set each of them onto the sofas.

I run my fingers over my dad's forehead and double-check Oliver's pulse.

They're fine. I know this. Only sleeping. Still...

Eric looks at Nym. "How did you do that? I thought you couldn't teleport like that anymore?"

I blink. Oh, right. I spin on the little man. "Yeah. How did you do that?"

Nym shrugs. "The silence come near, they take powers and give." He lifts a hand and directs it towards the fireplace. Nothing happens. He shrugs again. "Powers taken. Powers given."

Eric settles into a nearby chair. "Whoa. Okay. So they did that shifting power thing while they were here. Along with putting the only humans in our group to sleep. What else did they do?"

I shake my head. Fear rattles my chest as I lean against the sofa, my head on Oliver's shoulder. We sit in stillness for several minutes. When Aubree returns she brings Killian and Laoise with her.

Killian frowns and goes straight to my dad's side. He places a hand on his forehead. "They are merely sleeping." He says this with authority, as if we haven't figured that out yet. The elf turns to us. "We must work quickly."

Eric stands and looks at Aubree. "Do we have time? What did the queen say?"

Aubree's bottom lip trembles as she refocuses. "There is time. But not much." She looks at me. "More than half the population in the Mortal Realm has been put to sleep. Destruction is wide-spread. Whole communities are gone." She blinks away tears.

I jump to my feet and look at Laoise. "Have the rest of the Bunaidh arrived?"

She tilts her head, her silver eyes solemn. "Not quite yet. But they should be soon."

Eric asks what I'm thinking. "How much longer?"

Laoise looks at my dad. "She expects the last of them to arrive by the end of the day. Until that time, she requests that we retrieve a necessary component for the spell."

Killian nods. "We need to find a talisman. One unique to you. Nearby, in the direction of the waterfall. She says Caoine will know how to find it, to trust her judgment. She hopes to have the group of Bunaidh assembled by the time we return."

I squeeze my hands into fists. "But, I can't do this. Every time I try to help, something goes wrong."

Aubree approaches slowly. "Nonsense. There's a reason my mother believes only you can find your talisman. I'm guessing it has to do with your banshee side."

"But Eric's a wood sprite. I'm sure he can find it without me."

Eric screws his face up. "What? Why wouldn't you come? Don't you want this to be over?"

"Of course I do. But all I do is fail." I look at the sofa and my chest clenches. Eric's right. I do want this to be over. I *need* it to be.

Aubree crosses her arms. "Come on, Caoine. If my mother says you're the one to find the talisman then you need to do it. She wouldn't have suggested you lead the way if she wasn't entirely trusting in your abilities."

I swallow against the sick feeling in my stomach. "I—I have no idea what I'm doing. I trust those that I shouldn't—" My gaze falls to Eric. "I don't trust those that I should."

His face falls from frustration to compassion.

I hiccup. "I'm not fully fae. I wasn't made for this."

Killian lifts his chin. "Caoine Roberts, Daughter of the Faerie Realm. Accept your fate as both human and fae and do what you were meant to do."

I still. Killian has never referred to me in such a way. Nor has he ever acknowledged that I'm truly fae.

The Gift of Faith.

If Killian believes I can do this then...

I fall back to my knees, my hand smoothing Oliver's hair, my eyes trickling over the beloved figure of my dad. I'll do anything to save the two most important men in my life. *Anything.* It's time I shove aside my self-doubt.

My entire body trembles, breath hitching in my throat as I look back to my faerie friends. "What do I need to do?"

Chapter Thirty-Seven

You will know what you seek once you find it.

Right. I scowl and push past a low-hanging branch in the forest beside the castle.

How is it that a queen who barely knows me trusts me with this much responsibility? And *why*?

I've been wandering through trees and under the murky sky for the better part of an hour. I've seen strange woodland creatures definitely not native to the Mortal Realm. I've glimpsed ethereal foliage unlike anything most humans will ever see in their lifetime.

And all I've found are dead ends.

At least, I think they are. Nothing has jumped out at me as being *the thing* the queen wants me to find. This mysterious object that will somehow save the realms.

My stomach clenches tight. I'm barely an adult. I don't need this pressure.

I close my eyes and concentrate on *not* having a panic attack. And I hear it.

Water. Trickling. Like, maybe it's similar to the waterfall I visited earlier, where we saw the silence, except I know it's not because I walked in the exact opposite direction. This can't be *that* waterfall.

Or can it? I push through more forest, intent on finding the source of the sound. Sure enough, another few dozen feet deeper into the woods reveals a small pond with an even smaller waterfall feeding it.

The water is a light teal, crystal clear. Perfectly rounded rocks line the bottom, making the surface below uneven. Unending. Eventually, the rocks turn obsidian, hiding secrets only the Seelie Realm is prepared to tell.

I gasp at the beauty of it. At the way tangerine grass grows in lovely patches all around the sides, like pillows awaiting the next unsuspecting fae to lay his or her head for an afternoon nap. The trees here are all the same. They resemble something of pussy willows, with large tufts of lime green blossoms at the end of each branch.

My feet move of their own accord. I slide down a few large rocks that make up the entrance to the cove. Finally, I find the inviting grass.

I can't help myself. I slip off my shoes, fall to my bottom, and stick my toes into the water. A feeling of childhood overwhelms me, slithers deep under my skin. I laugh at this thought.

What is wrong with me?

Then I freeze. Faerie magic. Something isn't right here.

I shouldn't have come out here all alone. Not without the protection of another faerie. But the queen told me to. Why would she send me into trouble knowing the fate of the realms relies on my shoulders?

The breath stalls in my chest as I yank my feet from the water, skitter to shove my shoes back on—

And then I hear it. A song.

Not just any song. The most beautiful music I've ever heard. Including my own banshee song.

A trap! This must be a faerie trap, just like I suspected.

I turn to run, to put as much distance between myself and this luring place of seduction. My shoe catches on a small rock and I tumble onto my face. A whimper hides in my throat, masking the fear that so desperately wants to tumble out of me.

My fingers grasp the orange-hued grass as I struggle to my feet. But I slip back down. Onto my chest. Into the most vulnerable position possible.

"Hello."

The voice comes from behind me. I have no choice.

I turn around to face the creature that has found me.

Chapter Thirty-Eight

Her smile is everything.

My heart slams into the sides of my ribcage as I take in her sheer beauty. The girl emerges from the water. Only her shoulders and head are visible, but I sense the rest of her is just as breathtaking as what I can see.

And what I sense is that she isn't human. She isn't even fae.

She's a mermaid. I don't need to see her tail to know this.

"Hello." I can't stop myself from replying to her.

She's captivating, drawing me in, fogging my brain with all sorts of ideas. Thoughts that I should join her, that maybe life below the water is exactly what I've been seeking my whole life. That the urgency of the quest the queen sent me on is nothing compared to this desire, this carnal wanting to become a part of that pond. Of that world.

"Who are you?" Her question snaps me out of it.

I blink and pull in a quick breath. Look around. I'm still leaning on one elbow, in my very precarious position. I'm sure to avoid eye contact as I push myself up, dusting my pants off. "I—I was just—"

What was I *just* doing?

"Are you here for the song?" The mermaid tilts her head to the side.

And I can't help it. Can't help but marvel at this elegant creature.

Her hair is as dark as night, blades of royal blue slicing through it. It splays out in the water around her, a life-giving blanket. Her skin is a deep brown, a glittering canvas of walnut and cinnamon and tawny. My brain can't decide on just one.

She laughs. Her wheel-spoked eyes shift in color. First pale pink, then a medium amber. "Are you going to answer me?"

"I—" I huff. Why do I feel the need to apologize? "I didn't mean to disturb you."

"Who said you're disturbing me?" Her question is pleasant. Unassuming.

Jealousy snakes along my core. Her song is beautiful. Beckoning, filled with desire. How I wish I could release my own banshee song. The pride and joy I've been hiding deep inside for so many weeks.

"I just..." Her previous words suddenly register with me. I frown. "What did you mean, am I here for the song?"

The corner of her mouth pulls up. "Queen Faílenn has many connections in her Realm. She told me to expect you."

"She...told you I would be visiting you?" I shake my head.

The mermaid nods.

I sigh, my jaw clenching. Of course, she did. It would be far too easy for the queen to tell me who I need to find, but of course, she'd go so far as to alert the party I'm to visit of my impending appearance.

I want to growl in frustration but I restrain myself.

"Fine. Yes. I suppose I'm here to see you. But what's this about a song? Are you talking about my banshee song?"

She giggles again. "Of course not. I'm speaking of the mermaid song."

All the puzzle pieces fall into place. Banshees aren't the only creatures to inhabit a song of importance. Mermaids have long been legendary for their anthems of beauty.

I scrub a hand through my hair and plop back on the ground, criss-cross-applesauce. I've found my objective. Now, to figure out *what* I'm to do with a mermaid?

"Um, okay." I pick at the orange grass, unsure how this conversation is even supposed to go. "Why does Queen Faílenn want me to bring back a mermaid song?"

She laughs once more, music lilting over the water, bouncing between the rocks. "For the spell, of course."

"Oh. Right." Of course. That *is* what I'm here for. "Okay, so do you just sing me a song, or what?"

She shakes her head. "No, silly. I need to give you the song."

I remain mute, waiting for her to elaborate.

Instead, she turns and makes a chirping noise similar to what a dolphin would make. She's focused on a section of rocks just beneath where the waterfall connects with the water.

At first, I see nothing. My brows draw together in confusion.

Then bubbles rise to the surface. Just a few at first, then a whole slew of them, making the small pond resemble the inside of a pot of boiling water. I squint at the bubbles.

Two figures twirl up from the depths of the pool. Their tails glint in the daylight, one a pale lavender, the other fuschia. When their heads break the surface, a grown mermaid and a mermaid that appears no older than five years old look at me.

I jump in my seat. It never occurred to me that mermaids could be children.

The other female smiles at her companion who rests at my feet. Her skin is bronzed, her hair as white as mine. I blink rapidly at how jarring it is to see someone with hair that lacks color. This must be what it's been like for others to view me my entire life. No wonder the kids at school avoided me.

As she draws near, her eyes reflect a solid plum. I try not to stare.

The smaller mermaid swims right alongside her older counterpart. Her skin is white, although not quite as white as my own. Her chestnut brown hair and eyes look almost normal, as if she were just a human child out for a swim. Will her features change as she grows?

"Yara, Cordelia. Come meet my new friend." The mermaid before me speaks enthusiastically, like we're old acquaintances.

I look between her and the other two, as they close the distance.

"Muriel," the older mermaid says. "Is this the one?"

Muriel nods, her smile deepening. "The time has come."

The time? How long ago did Queen Faílenn predict that I'd need this mermaid song? When did she alert them to my impending visit?

A wave of dizziness sweeps over me and I touch my head.

"Are you all right?" The littlest mermaid comes right to the edge of the pool, resting her arms on the soil. She notices my missing pinky finger, worry etched across her face.

I quickly shove my hand beneath me, but I can't help but smile at her. Her every feature is delicate, perfect. A china doll waiting to be held.

"I'm fine." I glance at the other two mermaids. "Muriel told me I need a song."

The tiny mermaid nods vigorously. "That's right. It's my song you need."

I tilt my head. "Your song? Why, it's very kind of you to offer me such a gift."

She giggles, her chubby hand covering her mouth. Her cheeks go pink as she laughs.

The other mermaid puts a hand on the little mermaid's shoulder. "Go on, Cordelia. You know what to do."

Cordelia swirls to face her. "Did you bring the shell, Auntie Yara?"

Yara bops Cordelia on the nose, pulling a hidden hand from beneath the water. "Of course, I did."

She opens her palm to reveal an intricately detailed clamshell, pearlesque cerulean sparkling in the light.

Cordelia gasps and takes the shell into her small palm. She looks at Muriel. "It's exactly right."

Muriel laughs. "It is. Are you ready?"

Cordelia nods again. Taking a deep breath, she gently opens the shell. Seconds later, her mouth falls open, the most mesmerizing sound I've ever heard filling the cove.

The song twirls around me, lifting my hair and kissing my skin. It ruffles the grass and pokes holes in the falling water to her back. Yara and Muriel stay back a few feet, allowing the small mermaid to find her way.

I don't understand the words but they speak to my soul, all the same. I'm filled with warmth and joy and a sense of home. Images fill my mind. Pictures of Oliver playing guitar, and my father cooking Mexican food, and Aubree ruffling Seamus' hair. Wet coats my lashes despite the smile that's plastered on my face.

All at once, the song ends. The cove goes silent.

I exhale in disappointment.

Cordelia is giddy as she closes the seashell. Her cheeks go an even deeper shade of red. She holds a single hand toward me, the shell sitting right in the center.

I reach out and take it from her. "That was the most beautiful song I've ever heard."

Her smile radiates life.

"The song she sang was for you, Caoine, Daughter of Saoirse." Yara swims over and circles an arm around Cordelia's waist.

I look back to the young mermaid. "I'm honored."

Cordelia opens her mouth, as if to reply, but stops. She simply nods again.

A red flag arises inside my core as I look at Muriel. "Is there something wrong with her voice?"

Muriel leans her head on her arms as she rests along the grass. "You're holding it."

Fear stabs deep in my belly. I look down at the shell in horror. "This...this is her *voice*?"

"Of course." Yara squeezes a smiling Cordelia tight.

I scramble to my feet, holding the shell from my body. "But...*why* did she give me her voice? I thought I was here for her song?"

"A mermaid's song is her voice," Muriel says as if everyone knows this fact.

"But—but..." My jaw wags open.

"Do not fret, human." Yara strokes Cordelia's hair. "Her voice will return in time, just as it does with all mermaids."

My fingers finally curl around the shell. "You mean, you give your songs away often?"

Muriel laughs. "Not often, but certainly a handful of times throughout our lifespan. It is the journey of a mermaid. Our voices are used for many things. They are powerful, able to cause destruction and to bring new life."

"It is a rite of passage." Yara takes over the explanation. "This is Cordelia's first Giving. You should be honored. A mermaid does not give her song to just anyone."

I huff in amazement. "Th—thank you. Again. I...I don't know what to say."

Is it all right that I thanked a fae? Her demeanor didn't change when I said the words.

Cordelia smiles and waves me over. Tears prick my eyes as I lower myself back to the ground. I lean in as close as I can without falling into the pool.

The small mermaid pushes herself onto her hands, popping out of the water. She places a gentle kiss on my cheek before allowing the water to swallow her back again.

Tingles flow across my face and down my neck, down my arms. "I am honored to have your song, Cordelia. I'll never forget this kindness."

Her cheeks go scarlet once more. Then she waves, swiftly

turning to kiss Yara before flipping tailside up and diving beneath the water.

Yara gives me a short wave, as well, before joining her young family member.

Muriel looks at me. "Go, fae-human. Time is short. You have what you came for. Return to Queen Faílenn. If the Creator allows, we will cross paths again."

Before I can thank her again, she disappears under the water.

Chapter Thirty-Nine

My trek back to the queen's castle takes far less time than I remember. I'm just rounding a bend of unusually large plum-shaded bushes when I hear voices.

I gasp and hide back at first.

"It's not like I have her on a ball and chain." I recognize the sarcasm of that voice.

I step out to greet Killian and Eric as they pad towards me. Only Eric appears to be surprised. Probably too distracted by his conversation to listen intently. It's obvious Killian knew of my approach.

"Hey guys." I slip the precious seashell into my pocket. "Where are you going?"

Eric scowls. "We're looking for you. Where have you been?"

It's my turn to frown. "I've been on the queen's quest."

"It's been far longer than necessary." Killian gives me a look of disdain.

"How long have I been gone?"

"Like, hours." Eric shoves his hands on his hips.

It's now that I notice a sword slung across his back. Killian sports one, too.

I nod toward them. "What's with the metal?"

"Like I said, it's been hours." Eric reaches back to pat his sword. "We assumed the worst, of course."

My jaw drops. "Uh! Excuse me. You don't think I can take care of myself?"

Eric smirks. "I've seen you trip over air, back at West Lincoln High."

"Ugh. Rude! Have you forgotten I'm a banshee? Many fae here fear me, you know." I prop my hands on my hips.

Eric rolls his eyes. "Yeah, yeah. I'd still feel better if you'd let me give you a few sword fighting lessons."

I raise a brow at him. "I just might take you up on that."

He smiles. "Mind if we escort you back, now that we know you're safe?"

I pinch the edges of an imaginary dress and curtsey. "But of course, kind sirs."

Killian stares at me, clearly confused by the whole interaction.

Eric throws an arm around my neck and scrubs his knuckles into the top of my head. "Come on, Pipsqueak."

"Hey!" I yell, but he doesn't stop. "You're like the brother I never wanted."

"Ha." He's laughing now. "I'd be the best brother you ever had. Especially if it means I get to annoy Oliver, too."

I playfully shove him off. Before I can banter further, Killian and Eric both come to a halt.

We're at a point where I recognize the foliage surrounding the hidden castle. Neither of them speaks but their bodies immediately display tension. Eric cranes his neck behind us.

"Caoine." Killian growls this so quietly that I almost miss it. "Get inside the castle. Now."

I glance at the small house in the distance. How fast can I run? Would it be safer to just stay with them?

I swallow. "What's going on? Who's coming?"

Eric leaps into action, shoving me behind him and pulling his sword out in one swift motion. Killian pulls his weapon free of its holster, too.

"Eric?" My voice shakes.

I hide behind the breadth of him, like a coward.

On second thought, don't move. Eric's voice is panicked inside my head.

Eric?

Don't. Move.

Killian comes to stand shoulder-to-shoulder with Eric, both of them holding the hilt of their swords with both hands, their metal ready to fly.

The bush in front of us rustles, and bends. A slender figure that is all too familiar steps from the shadows.

"Hello, friends."

Aibell flashes us a perfectly evil grin.

Chapter Forty

Aibell stands angled towards Eric, her sword at the ready. She wears a smirk that says she intends to win this battle. Killian squeezes his sword tighter. "Aibell. I'm not surprised to see you."

She snorts. "Quiet, elf. I'm here to slay the pathetic prince. Then I'll bring my king the human."

Even from behind him, I can sense Eric grinding his teeth. "Bring it, *traitor*. Let's see who the true *marfóir* is. Which one of us is the king's true assassin?"

"So eager to repeat our last meeting, when you so nearly lost your head?" Aibell swipes her sword in a circle, laughing.

Killian leans toward Eric. "Are you sure? I am ready to fight alongside you."

Eric shakes his head. "This is my fight. It always has been."

Killian nods, relaxing his posture, and sliding his sword back into its sheath. He gives Eric a quick pat on the back before stepping back.

I blink. What just happened? Why would Killian not help protect Eric against Aibell? What if he's injured?

My mouth wobbles in uncertainty but Killian simply nudges me back to stand beside him. Away from danger.

Eric? My heart beats wildly.

He doesn't answer.

Instead, he shakes out his shoulders and cracks his neck, bouncing on his toes.

Now my heart is in my throat. Literally. *Is this for real, Creator? This is your plan?*

I don't want my friend to die. And I'd also like *not* to become the hostage of my frenemy.

Aibell gives a surprise attack by leaping forward and smashing her blade into his. Eric flinches but holds his own, blocking her attack and stepping to the side.

They circle one another.

I swallow and pat my pocket, assuring the shell is still safe. Killian's warm presence is close by my side. Something furry rubs up against my leg. I look down to find the orange cat purring and smiling up at me.

Cat! I gasp and pick her up, terrified she might jump in between Aibell and Eric, taking a fatal blow. She purrs against my chin as I snuggle her and scratch behind her ears. The distraction is brief. I refocus on the fight, my heart pounding faster than ever.

Aibell swipes again, Eric easily defending himself. She laughs. He scowls. It's obvious she's playing with him.

In a flash she rushes him with multiple swings of the sword, pushing him back toward the waterfall. He stumbles but regains his footing, getting one more stab of the sword in her direction before she backs off.

I suck in a breath.

Aibell laughs again as she swings her sword in a circle, walking around Eric once more. Treating this like a game.

I growl under my breath.

Eric steps forward with a slash but she easily dodges his attack. He jumps to the side, ready for her next move, barely blocking the stab to his side.

She arcs the sword around to his other side. Block. Again, she swings. Block. Swing. Block.

Eric is out of breath already, yet she doesn't relent.

She shouts this time, bringing the sword from overhead, down hard. He uses both hands to hold his sword steady, the blade shaking with his weary muscles.

She stalks her prey in a circle again. "Ready to give up, Princeling?"

He pants, wiping his sweaty hands on his pants. "You'll have to kill me first."

"Oh good. Exactly what I plan to do." Aibell steps on a nearby rock and leaps into the air, once more bringing her blade down on his head.

He throws his sword up just in time to catch her strike, although his is off-kilter. His sword tilts, allowing her blade to graze his shoulder. The fabric of his shirt tears minutely and he stumbles to the side.

Eric grunts as he regains his composure. Aibell attacks again. And again.

Her sword is like lightning, flashing so quickly I can barely keep track of it. Echoes of clanging metal rings between the flowers, tumbling over the water.

The prince's grunts grow louder with each block. Aibell only laughs.

She's in a rhythm now. She doesn't allow Eric to recover, with barely enough time to block her next swing. He stumbles to one knee, pushing off the ground with his free hand as his sword feebly keeps her blade from piercing his skin.

He jumps to his feet and bounces to the side, regaining his footing. She charges him like a bull. She stabs right, left, right.

Clank! Their swords are a musical ballad, a lament for the impending blood to be spilled.

I grip Cat tighter. Killian stands as still as a statue. Won't he help?

Eric screams in pain. My heart jumps to my throat.

Aibell has broken through his defense, her sword slicing clean through his left side. His shirt plumes cobalt blue. He winces and favors that side, lifting his sword hand in defense once more.

Her eyes glisten with desire, a hunger that says she's ready for this to be over.

Eric attacks, catching her off guard. She growls as she blocks his move, stepping to the side easily.

He huffs, attempting to attack again. But she's ready for him. She lifts her sword, pushing his aside and circling back around for a better angle.

Except, she hasn't been paying attention. She hasn't realized his feeble defense had nothing to do with barely-there sword skills and everything to do with position.

His position.

Aibell's back is to the waterfall. Her feet are precariously close to the edge of the ground that ends so abruptly. Her face is filled with an arrogant smile. She leaps forward, putting distance between her and the edge. I hold my breath. Eric counters her attack, slamming his blade into hers over and over again.

He becomes a madman, slicing the air, and crushing her with the weight of his attack. Her jaw drops as she steps back.

I blink. He's been holding back. Was this his plan the entire time?

Again, he charges, his blade swinging overhead, from the side, straight in. She blocks, but just barely.

She steps back.

He attacks. She grunts and leaps to the side. He's ready, throwing another swing from that angle to put her back where he wants her.

She steps back.

He attacks.

Step back. Attack. Step—

Aibell screams as her right foot misses the ground, sliding down the soft embankment. The swirling pool behind her sends tendrils of mist towards her, begging her to join the fun below the surface level.

Come to us, it pleads.

Her good hand grabs for something solid to hang onto, her sword flying into the water beneath her dangling feet. Her lame hand is no good in the situation, the impairment she always feared would be her undoing.

Unarmed, she hangs from the side by one hand, her body pressed tightly to the muddy earth.

Eric points his sword right at her face. "Do you concede?"

Aibell snarls. "Never."

He presses the tip of his sword to her throat. "Are you sure about that?"

Her eyes dart to the side. She scowls. In a blink she flips around, pushing off from a rock jutting from the side of the wall. She grabs another rock, yanking herself up and over the side before Eric can get a grasp on what she's even done.

She jumps to her feet and runs toward a copse of trees.

I yelp as the cat in my arms sticks its claws into my arms and breaks free. The thing runs faster than I've seen any animal travel.

With a hiss, the cat flies into the air and lands on Aibell's back, bringing her to the ground. Immediately, vines pop from the ground, wrapping themselves around Aibell's wrists and legs to keep her down. I side-eye Eric. Now that the fight is over, he's allowed to use magic.

The cat rolls off the faerie. Before I can form a thought the animal morphs, changing, growing into a full-sized being.

Pasty skin. Dark curly hair.

Aibell gasps from her position on the ground.

The two are identical.

Except the one standing isn't Aibell.

The cat is Catherine.

$$\textit{Chapter Forty-One}$$

"Cat?" My voice is barely a whisper.

She looks at me, her brown eyes glimmering with mischief. Her dark curls tumble over her shoulders and down her back. Her glasses are long gone. A white gown flows to the ground, her feet bare.

She smiles. "Hello, dear friend."

I blink. "What—what are you doing here?"

She laughs and I swear I see beams of light encircle her head, the sound of bells chiming in the distance. "I live in the Faerie Realms. Where else would I be?"

I balk. "Oh, I don't know. West Lincoln High? With me?"

She gives me a wink. "But you're not there, either."

"True." I pause and give her a once-over. "Why didn't you tell me who you were when I got to Lincoln?"

Her skin shimmers. "The time wasn't right."

"And the time is right, *now*?"

She glances at Eric. "It was made to be."

Aibell grunts from where she sits on the ground, as she tugs at her restraints.

I look from the prince back to Cat. "Did you know what would happen? The night of our double date?"

Her visage grows sad. "No. I was aware that something might happen soon. One reason why I was all too eager to spend time with you. But by the time I got to the Veils, you were already gone. My heart is vexed about that, friend."

I want to agree but wait. Am I sorry? If Eric hadn't stolen me into the Unseelie Realm—even against my wishes—I never would have learned his true nature. Never would've become friends with him.

The very journey we're on right now might never have been possible.

Can I wish away the fact that I am now part of a plan to save not only the Mortal Realm but the Faerie Realms, as well?

I pull in a slow breath. "I'm not sorry." I look at Eric and smile.

His chest still heaves from his fight with Aibell, sweat gathered along his hairline, dripping down his cheeks.

I nod to him. "What has happened, happened. We're here now. And I wouldn't change a thing."

Eric's face grows pink and he swallows, one hand staunching the flow of blue blood dripping down his left side.

"I mean it," I say to Cat. "I'm thankful for all that has happened, no matter the struggle. But what now? What will become of the Mortal Realm? What about the Seals?"

Her face is grave as she glances from me to the prince, and then to Killian. "There is hope yet, Daughter of Saoirse. Never give up. Especially when it comes to your mother."

Saoirse.

I gasp. She's been with us all this way. She's heard us talk.

"Can you help me save my mom?"

She smiles. "I don't need to, Caoine." She steps forward and places a hand on my shoulder. "You already know how."

I scowl. "No. No, I don't."

"All will become clear in time. Only you can save her, Caoine."

"What?" My voice is too high-pitched.

"Enough." Aibell finally decides to join the conversation. Her gaze is nothing but daggers aimed at her sister.

Eric flicks a wrist, removing all the vines that held her down. Aibell grumbles as she rubs at her wrists and stands.

Cat nods at her sibling. "It is good to see you, sister."

Aibell scoffs. "Is it? Or are you bothered by my presence? The reject faerie that tainted our family line?" She snorts. "Don't pretend like I don't know your true thoughts of me, *Sister*. I've always been the outcast."

Catherine tilts her head. "By some, yes. But isn't this the way it always is? There is never a way to be liked by everyone around you. We are all created differently. We hold different values." She glances at Aibell's withered hand. "Some will place value on the wrong things. But not everyone is against you."

Aibell scowls. "I doubt that." She steps back. "It was made clear to me just how different I was. How I didn't belong."

My heart pounds. Aibell has always felt the same way as me. Like she didn't belong.

Cat shakes her head. "Is it others that make you feel this way? Or is this a view of yourself you refuse to release? How we view ourselves can be more powerful than how others see us."

Aibell's brow pulls tight. "No. Everyone hated me. Because of this." She lifts her left arm. "They hated me because I wasn't normal. Like them."

"I never did." Cat steps closer. "I always accepted you for who you are. You pushed me away."

Aibell jumps back. "No! No, you didn't. You—" She shakes her head. "You couldn't have."

"There were others who stood by your side, as well. You just refused to see it."

Silence rolls around us as Aibell takes this in, her mind calculating behind those blue eyes.

Cat steps toward her again. "There's still time to choose the right path, sister. I believe there is still good in you."

Aibell growls, her face burning crimson. "Stay away! I'm not like you. I'll never be like you!"

Finally, I find my voice. "Like her how, Aibell?"

The faerie's eyes flash red in my direction. "Like *you*. Normal. Accepted."

I huff. "I'm *not* normal. I've never been normal. I'm a mutt. Never fully human, never fully fae. Aibell, I was like you for years. Always believing I could never have any friends. That no one would accept me for who I am." I glance at Eric. At Cat. "But I was wrong. It was all in my head. I was the one who never allowed anyone in. I couldn't accept that while some would hate me for looking different, others wanted to know me for who I am."

Aibell snarls. "Easy for you to say. You've got powers." She yanks a necklace from beneath her shirt. "I have to rely on the magic of others to do anything remotely fae."

I sigh. "I didn't even know I had those until a week ago. My friends helped me see past the fact that I was stubborn for far too long. I was the only one who stood in the way of being *normal*."

Seconds pass in quiet. Finally, Aibell looks at me. "I don't buy it. I was born a *neamini*. I'll always be a neamini. The Creator hates me. Made sure I would always be an outcast."

I shake my head. "You were created exactly the way you were meant to be. Never forget that."

Anger erupts from her like fireworks. "Then I hate the Creator even more for making me this way! And I hate *you*!"

Before any of us can react, she runs.

Her feet are swift, carrying her so much farther than I thought in those short few seconds.

"Aibell!" Cat yells after her.

But before she can get away, a foot appears in the trees. A large one.

Then a hand reaches from the shadowed sky and picks Aibell up.

Chapter Forty-Two

Aibell shrieks as she's lifted into the air.

"Where are you off to, mischief maker?" Gnait grips Aibell tighter than necessary and she fights against his beefy fist.

"Gnait!" I shout. "Stop. You can put her down."

His face crumples in confusion. "The traitor is attempting to escape, isn't she?"

Aibell's face falls at his use of the word *traitor*, the very thing she so often accused Eric of being.

Cat nods as if this type of thing happens all the time. "She was, but please do not harm her. She is my sister, after all."

Gnait shrugs. "She will remain in one piece."

Aibell looks horrified, even as he sets her back on the ground. With nowhere to run, she shifts uncomfortably. Gnait crosses his arms and stands above her.

Cat looks at her sister. "I implore you to please listen to reason. Turn from this path you have chosen to take. Your life can be filled with much joy if only you choose to take hold of it."

Aibell spits on the ground at Cat's feet. "That will never be my life. Do with me what you will, but I will never be anything other than a neamini."

"You leave me no choice, then." Cat's shoulders fall. "I must take the very thing which you despise. You will no longer be fae."

I gasp.

Cat goes on. "You blame your problems on the fact that you weren't made truly fae, and so it shall be. From this day forward you are no longer a faerie." She lifts a hand and waves it before Aibell. The space between the two of them glows a bright yellow before fading away. "You are now mortal. Once you leave the Faerie Realms, you will not be able to return. You shall age as any mortal and will be afflicted in the same way as mortals."

Aibell flinches minutely but otherwise, she doesn't appear to care about her new life sentence.

Cat nods. "I am vexed it has come to this, sister. May your days be filled with joy in your new life."

With a grunt, Aibell steps back, looking at each of us. Cat glances at Gnait who immediately picks Aibell back up—gently, this time. Aibell fights for only a minute before accepting her fate.

As the giant carries her towards the Veil to the Mortal Realm, her attention never turns from Cat.

Does she regret the choice she's made? Or is this what she's always wanted? To be a part of a people just like her?

We stand in silence after they've gone. Killian watches the spot where they disappeared. Eric puts his blade away, hands on his hips as he recovers from his physical exertion.

I turn to Cat. "Tell me...who are you?"

"Have you not guessed?" She smiles. "I am Clíodhna, Queen of the Banshees."

My jaw drops.

She shakes her head. "As my twin, Aibell should've shared the same rights as I. However, she was born without equal power to me. This never sat well with her. She made the choice to separate herself from us." She sighs. "This is why she was always so jealous of you, Caoine. You have power that she never had access to. And this is why I am sure you possess the power to save your mother."

"What must I do?"

"All things are connected. You see life as many different paths, many choices that lead apart from one another. Divided. But unity exists in all. You will find that the solution to one can be the solution to many."

I glance at Eric and back again. What's that supposed to mean? "So, if you're Queen of the Banshees, does that mean you can tell me more about who I am? What I'm meant to do?"

The corners of Cat's mouth tilt up. "You already know who you are, what you were meant to do. You have found your true identity, Caoine Roberts. Nothing can take that from you now."

My throat tightens. Except that I *haven't*. Each time I think I know the answer, that I know what to do, it turns out wrong. I'm not as strong as she believes I am. I'm not who others believe me to be.

I exhale. "But there must be more. Can you train me to be better? Can I become a better banshee?"

"Do you truly feel you need this?"

Before I can speak, Eric catches my eye, his look questioning.

Do I?

Killian raises a hand. "With all due respect, we should consider moving on. I believe the time has come to complete the spell."

I nod. "Of course." I look at Eric, and his bloodied shirt. "You okay to head back?"

He gives an affirmative. My belly clenches.

Oliver and my dad need to wake up. Soon.

We travel back to the secret cottage in the woods in quiet reflection. So much has happened in such a short time. My brain can barely wrap itself around all of it. There are a million questions I want to bombard Cat with. But now is not the time. It's time to focus on saving the world.

Just before we enter the small house, I turn to Eric. "You sure you're okay?"

He nods. "I'm good."

I shake my head and motion for him to come closer. I place

one hand on his sliced shoulder, the other over the gash along his left rib cage. He winces at my touch.

Heat pulses through my hands and I close my eyes to concentrate, to focus on mending his skin, muscles, and tendons. Restoring his body to what it once was.

He sighs and I know the healing has taken effect. I step back. Eric gives me a sheepish smile.

I look at him out of the corner of my eye. "I wasn't so sure if you were going to win that fight."

He stops, placing a hand on his chest in mock hurt. "You doubted my abilities?"

"No. I overestimated Aibell's."

He shrugs. "Same thing. I had everything under control, Caoine." He nudges me with his elbow. "Didn't I tell you that you could trust me?"

I snort. "Yeah, but so did Aibell."

"Hey, now. Don't compare me to her. Them's fightin' words."

I laugh as we descend the spiral staircase underground. "Well, I'm glad you're okay. I would've been...*sad* if the outcome had been anything else."

Eric laughs. "Aww. Caoine would've missed me if I died? Can't wait to tell Oliver about that one." He gathers me in his arms and gives me a noogie on my head, playing the part of the big brother. He clearly has regained his full strength.

I fight my way out of his grasp and smack him on the chest with a laugh. We walk the rest of the way with the others until we're safely in the sitting room again. I cannot wait to see Oliver and Dad again.

Except what I find is not them. It's something altogether different.

The sleeping figures of my loved ones are gone.

Chapter Forty-Three

Queen Faílenn stands before the fireplace, Laoise across from her. "Welcome Clíodhna, Queen of the Banshees. It is an honor to have you here."

Cat tilts her chin in greeting and my brain is flooded with confusion over this regal being that pretends to be my friend. Where did the awkward teenager who knew nothing about boys and spent all her time reading go?

The queen looks at me. "We have moved your father and Oliver to a more comfortable resting spot until the spell is completed. It may take some time for the silence's hold to release them from their slumber."

I exhale, my heart rate slowing for the first time in hours.

Safe. They're safe. That's all I need to know.

Queen Faílenn scrutinizes each of us. Aubree and Nym, who sit in the corner, Eric, Killian, and Cat. Myself. "The Bunaidh have arrived in full. The ceremony will begin in just a few moments." Her eyes settle firmly on her daughter. "Aubree, may I have a word?"

Aubree's chest rises slightly and she nods. The two step from the room, leaving the rest of us alone.

A question that's been at the back of my mind ever since Cat showed herself demands my attention. The rest of the group settles onto the sofa, awaiting the event we're all eager to see to completion.

"Can I ask you something?" I keep my voice low.

She nods and directs us to step to the corner.

So, if you're the Queen of the Banshees does that mean...I mean, you've got, like, power, right?" I huff. "Like, are you as powerful as the queen or king of the Faerie Realms?"

Her face softens. "In some ways, yes. But not in others. It's complicated." She smiles. "I do hold more power over you, specifically, since you are of my kind."

My heart stirs at these words. I'm of her *kind*. I belong.

Emotion clouds my throat and all I want to do is throw my arms around her neck and break down into a messy puddle of tears.

But now isn't the time.

I blink away tears. "Can you help me reverse a law? One that King Raghnall declared over my dad and me?" I swallow. "So that I can go back to the Mortal Realm and do what I was created to do as a banshee? To give peace to those as they enter the afterlife?"

"There is an obvious answer to what you seek, Caoine."

I shake my head. "No, we've already gone over the obvious choices. I know deep in my bones that the king will never undo what he's declared over my dad and me. And I think I'm fully on Oliver's side when it comes to death. I'm a banshee. I aid and I soothe. I do not kill."

Her cheeks glow with pride. "Took you long enough to figure that one out."

Those words echo a faint reflection of my old friend, Catherine. My heart warms.

Now I do hug my old friend. This beautiful creature before me can be both a mentor and a friend. Layers of intimidation melt from between us.

She pulls back. "The option I speak of isn't one that you've given."

I freeze. "There's another way that we can be free?"

"You are a banshee. The most powerful of all the fae."

I startle. Banshees are the most powerful? Aubree and Seamus had alluded to this, but I thought they meant we were *some* of the most powerful. Not *the* most powerful.

"Using your banshee nature, you can transfer your curse to the one who created it."

"What? That doesn't make sense. My song is meant for nothing other than to announce the end of life. I'm not able to do anything beyond that."

She shrugs. "There is much you do not know, Caoine. Your song is meant for so much more than that."

"Whoa, whoa, whoa." I hold my hands. "Are you telling me I just need to sing to him and the curse will be broken?"

She shakes her head. "It's never that simple. But your scream is not only for ushering others into death. It is a beacon of light, as well. A summoning for those of your kind. You must use it as it was intended to be used."

I freeze. What?

Cat goes on. "Banshees live in the Mortal Realm, not the Faerie Realms. We are the only fae tasked with such a life, never able to return to our true homes for the sake of others. We are spread far and wide around the amazing world of the mortals. We've always been able to use our song to call to our sisters."

An invisible fist punches me in the gut. I have the ability to speak to other banshees? At any time?

I've *never* truly been alone. I've always been part of a community exactly like me. One that I can access at any time.

Warmth floods my entire being. Acceptance by the fae and humans had already taken place in my heart. And now I have another family. Eighteen years of loneliness is so far gone I can't even see it anymore.

I will never be alone again. *Ever.*

Tears flow down my cheeks and I fall into Cat in another

embrace before I can stop myself. We hold one another for minutes, every molecule in my body refusing to let her go.

When I finally pull back, I can't help but ask, "If banshees are the most powerful of the fae, is that why I have such a strong telepathic connection with Eric? Why I could hear him between realms?"

"Um-hm," she says, nodding.

Adrenaline tumbles through my chest. The answer is so simple! My connection with Eric is stronger because of who I am. Not because I secretly have feelings for him, not because he's still under his father's spell. Because of *me*.

I have a million more questions for her: How do I summon other banshees? Will I gain the same telepathic connection with Aubree now that we're in the Faerie Realms?

But her focus shifts over my shoulder, toward the door. The queen and Aubree have returned from their secret talk. Aubree's brow pulls together when she sees me.

I wipe the tears from my face. With my eyes, I tell her I'll fill her in later. She gives me a small smile in reply.

My chest swells with pride and love and friendship.

Queen Faílenn steps forward. "It is time. The Seven Seals must now be repaired."

Chapter Forty-Four

The room is made entirely of a strange faerie slate, every surface shining and glimmery. The queen has led us down another hidden set of stairs, into the deepest part of her home.

There is no furniture. There aren't even any corners.

The walls continue in a single circle, the ceiling much higher than seems possible, being this far underground. There are no rugs or wall hangings or anything that would suggest this could be a living space. The entire area could fit an Olympic-sized swimming pool.

In the very center of the floor are two familiar objects: the Book of Judgment and the Book of Discernment.

Both lie open, neatly placed inside a circle of faerie symbols carved into the hard stone floor. A metal bowl filled with dried leaves sits to one side, a large flask with amber liquid on the other. Otherwise, there aren't any other objects in the room.

Queen Faílenn stands to the far side of the circle. Immediately, several other fae that I don't know follow her. These must be the remaining Bunaidh that we were waiting for.

It becomes clear that each of the faerie symbols that are carved into the floor aren't just any symbols. They're the symbols for each bloodline. Each faerie stands on a particular spot, meant only for them. Even Cat finds her place among the Bunaidh.

Eric steps around to fill the spot where his bloodline is to stand. His hands shake. Is he nervous?

I swallow and look over my shoulder. Killian, Laoise, and Nym were asked to remain above, separate from the room, since their bloodlines aren't part of the spell. Aubree is the only other fae that remains with me. I assume she tagged along because the queen is her mother.

But then she does something unexpected. Aubree walks around and steps into line right beside Eric.

I frown. Why would they need two from the same bloodline present?

The queen nods for me to take my spot. The very last space has a symbol I've never seen before. It's two figure-eight knots flanked with a Celtic spiral on either side. Does this signify my place among the fae? My bloodline? Some fae thing I've never learned about?

I suck in a long breath and step to my place. It sits directly across from the queen. Eric and Aubree are to my left, and Cat is to my right, along with four other faeries, I don't know.

My heart races.

Queen Faílenn lifts her hands. "Welcome fellow Bunaidh. We gather here to secure the Seven Seals created long ago. To end the destruction of all the realms." She gestures to her left. "Aenghus, son of the Tuatha Dè Danann bloodline. Rhiannon, daughter of the Mabinogi bloodline. Bran, son of the Lyr bloodline. Clíodhna, Queen of the Banshees."

She turns to me. My body goes as still as a statue.

"Caoine, daughter of Saoirse."

She shifts to Eric and I release my breath.

"Eric, son of Raghnall, King of the Unseelie Realm. Aubree, mediator for Seamus, son of the Cliste bloodline."

I gasp.

Aubree pulls a small object from her pocket. Seamus' toy top.

I swallow. That's what the queen needed to speak to her about. They needed someone to represent Seamus' bloodline.

Considering their friendship, it makes perfect sense that it would be Aubree.

I give her an encouraging smile. She pulls in a shaky breath, her attention back on her mother.

"Diarmuid, son of the Donn line. Brighid, daughter of the Lasairfhíona line." The queen lifts her hands again. "Welcome all. Let us begin by placing your talisman inside the circle."

Each member around the circle silently steps forward, placing a small object inside the faerie symbols. A tinder box, two small crossed spears, a mirror, a figurine of a white horse, a bird. Is that thing alive? There's also what strikes me as a dragon scale, and a single holed flute. Aubree places Seamus' toy top in the center.

I pull the seashell free from my pocket. As a banshee, I need to give a song. But it's too dangerous to sing my song while in the fae realms. I learned that on my first trip to the Unseelie Realm. The queen must've known what she was doing, in directing me to provide a different kind of song. I'm to give the mermaid's song as my talisman. Our songs—those of the banshee and mermaid— call to humans in the same way, captivating them.

With a breath of courage, I step forward. My gaze rests on the seashell as I give it one last squeeze before letting it go. I'm the last to take my place back on my symbol.

Queen Faílenn bows her head and all the other fae follow. I dip mine in return but quickly glance around to be sure I'm not missing anything.

"Creator of the universe, the realms, the mortal and the fae, come into our presence. Blessed are you, eternal Creator who brings light, joy, and peace. We zimvite you here to aid us in our quest to bring healing to our worlds."

She steps forward and picks up the bowl. She lifts it overhead. "Accept our offering of earth. Let this be an aroma pleasing to you. A symbol of our unwavering faith and adoration for all you have done for us."

The queen bends down and replaces the bowl, picking up the flask of liquid. "Accept our offering of sacrifice. Let it be pleasing to you. A symbol of our love and dedication to you."

Once again, she returns the item to the floor and comes to a standing position. She holds her hands to the side. "Let us unite, an act of solidarity that all realms are connected through the Creator."

Each of the faeries takes the hand of the person beside them. My left hand slides neatly into Eric's, my right grasping Cat's. Their hands are warm. So warm.

Is it my imagination or are my hands freezing? Like, super cold? A jolt of electricity zips from the core and my chin quivers involuntarily.

What is happening to me? Am I really this scared?

Nothing bad is going to happen, Caoine. This is what we've wanted for so long. The whole nightmare will be over in a matter of minutes.

So why do I sense something is off? Like this is too good to be true?

Queen Faílenn closes her eyes and begins whispering words I don't understand. None of the other fae join in, but they close their eyes, as well.

I close mine, too. Then I open them. I can't relax, not knowing what is going on around us.

At first, nothing happens but the repeated words of the queen. Then the books on the ground begin to glow, words spread across each page lighting and darkening in succession.

I'm just about to close my eyes again when I hear it. A *whooshing* sound. Translucent white smoke circles around our heads, going around, and around, and around. The edges of my clothes are picked up by the rush of air as it passes by, faster and faster.

Eric blinks in surprise. He nods at me with assurance.

This is it. We're doing it! The spell will fix the Seals and life will go back to normal.

The queen's voice grows louder, the pages of each book flashing so brightly and quickly that the entire center of the floor is lit almost as brightly as the sun. The wind whips around us so fast I can barely catch my breath.

No wonder everyone has their eyes closed.

I pull in a breath, lifting my chin. Ready to end this thing. Joy fills my core. Elation that I can finally be a normal teenager.

The spell is almost over. I can feel it. This thing will be done in seconds.

"Don't move." The voice growls next to my ear, a sharp object pressed tightly to my throat.

I gasp.

"It's time you die, Caoine Roberts."

Chapter Forty-Five

Hot breath coats my neck. A beefy hand is wrapped around my body, pinning my arms down. The voice is male, the figure massively tall.

King Raghnall.

Eric takes a single step toward us before the blade of the dagger is pressed deeper into my neck.

"Stop right there!" The king has drawn the attention of all in the circle now. "No one moves or the girl dies."

Caoine. Don't move. Eric's words bounce inside my head.

Despite the fact that the queen no longer chants, the spell continues around us. Wind whips at our hair, drowning out the king's words. The dimmed room is lit brightly by the flashing of the symbols in the books.

Aubree's entire being is nothing short of terrified. Clíodhna's face is masked but I sense a deep anger rising from within.

The queen doesn't bother to hide her distaste. "Why have you come?"

The question goes deeper. We all know this is far more than merely stopping the reparation of the Seals.

King Raghnall's grip on me tightens, his breath stinking of garlic and rotten eggs. "Caoine knows why I'm here." The timbre of his voice drips with sultry desire. "She has something I need. She has a Gift that I need to bring my beloved Queen Mairéad back to me."

"You mean back from the grave." I bravely growl the words.

His grip on the knife at my throat tightens. I tense.

Cat turns fully to face us. "There is no controlling a banshee. You of all fae should know this, *king*."

I can hear his sneer behind his words. "There is always a way. A law declared by the king is unbreakable. Even for a one such as your kind."

My friend's blue eyes flash red. "You are mistaken. The power of a banshee cannot be tamed."

The king takes two steps backward, dragging me along with him. "Watch me." I feel his head turn to the side. "Faen! Where are you faen?"

A squeak echoes from behind us. Nym.

"Take us out of here. Now. Take us back to the Unseelie castle."

Nym comes into sight, just off to the side of us, glancing at Eric.

Eric looks at me. ***Be still. I'm working on a plan.***

A little faster please? I grit my teeth at how whiny my voice sounds, even inside my head.

Distract him. Say something.

What am I supposed to say? Nice to see you again? We really should do this more often, Raghnall?

Eric huffs.

"Faen!" Raghnall shouts again.

Nym jumps in place, his eyes on Eric again. He freezes. Oh crud. What are they planning?

"Stop!" I scream. "Stop." My voice is softer this time. "I'll come with you. Just...don't hurt my friends."

What? Eric's voice shouts inside my head.

You told me to say something. I glare at him.

Yeah but not that.

Raghnall's hold loosens just slightly. "The books. I need both books." He looks at Nym, his tone commanding. "Faen."

Nym takes two steps towards the circle. Stops.

Caoine.

I jump. This voice doesn't belong to Eric.

Caoine. You know what to do.

Cat lifts her chin toward me. I suck in a breath.

The wind around us picks up, turning more fierce.

The queen lifts her chin. "You have failed, King Raghnall. The spell is almost complete."

He growls. "Stupid faen! Get the books. Now."

I look at Cat, pleading. ***I don't. I don't know what to do. Tell me.***

You already know. Believe in yourself.

I freeze. ***Are you kidding? I haven't done anything right so far. Why can't you just tell me?***

You are a banshee, Caoine. Seek your true nature. You will find the answer there.

I grind my teeth together. Is she serious? I've got a madman at my back and a knife at my throat! How am I supposed to focus on something I don't even know how to control?

"Move!" The king is seething. Bits of spittle fleck the back of my neck and I cringe.

Nym hops over to the circle but stops. He looks from Eric to the books back to Eric.

The queen's face hardens. "You cannot stop this, Raghnall."

The wind is as fierce as a hurricane.

Cat stares at me. ***Believe in yourself, Caoine. The solution you seek can solve many problems.***

Believe in myself? Is she serious?

I release my breath, trying to settle my nerves. What did Cat say about banshees and our connection? My throat tightens as I swallow. The blade digs deeper into my skin.

A memory flashes in my mind. *Your scream is not only for ushering others into death. It is a beacon of light, as well. A summoning for those of your kind. You must use it as it was intended to be used.*

Summoning.

Can I summon another banshee to help? How would I do that?

Eric's voice pops in my head. ***Caoine. Keep him talking. I can't do this without your help.***

I shake my head. ***I—I don't know what to do. I need help.***

Help. Summoning.

My mother.

I can summon my mother to help. That's how I can find her. That's how I'll be able to save her from her fate as a bean-nighe.

My scream. Cat said I could use my scream as a beacon of light. Is that how I can summon another banshee? Is it possible my song isn't only intended for a time of death?

T'm suddenly filled with the desire to sing the most beautiful of banshee songs I've ever sung. It's been too long since I've sung. It's a physical weight I can't shake.

But what if I scream and instead it ushers death? What if someone dies, right here, right now? What if my scream announces the death of my dad or Oliver?

Caoine. Cat's voice is stronger now.

"The books, faen." The king steps closer to the circle. "Or I start killing each of your friends one by one."

Eric's face falls. ***There's no way I can do this without you, Caoine. Someone is going to die.***

Tears tumble down my cheeks. Who will I kill? Who will die today?

I have no choice. I need to summon my mother.

In a heartbeat, I know exactly what to do, as if the answer has been in my head all along.

Without drawing attention, I slip my hand into my pocket,

pulling the carved elephant Aubree found in my desk just days ago.

The one that belonged to my mother.

I slip it from my pocket, prepare to scream.

A beefy hand closes around my fingers. "No more tricks, banshee."

The king rips the elephant figurine from my hand and flings it to the floor.

Chapter Forty-Six

"Nice try." The king's hot breath is back on my neck. "I know all about your plan to summon your *mother*."

I gag, pulling against his blade. How does he know that?

"No one is coming to save the day, human." He lifts his chin, gesturing toward the summoning circle. "Get the books now, faen. Or the first one to die is my son."

Eric tenses. Nym worries his hands, slumping toward the circle with his head down. He picks the books up silently. No one in the circle dares to stop him.

"You're bluffing." This comes from Aubree.

I blink in her direction.

"You won't hurt Caoine. She's too powerful. You need her power. And you can't kill one of us without letting go of her."

"There's no way out of this," the queen says softly. "Let the girl go."

"No." Raghnall grumbles. "I guess you'll never know if I'm bluffing or not."

In a single swift motion he turns toward Nym, shoving his knife under the creature's chin. His other arm still holds me in place. "Take us to my castle. Now!"

Nym looks from Eric, back to me. He squeezes both books against his chest with one arm, grabbing hold of Raghnall's hand with the other. He closes his eyes.

I close mine in preparation for the trip through the void.

Nothing happens.

My exhale is sharp. Nym's face is in a panic, his attention once more darting back to Eric.

Raghnall grunts in anger.

Eric's face is stoic. "Looks like Nym's powers don't work down here."

Raghnall's face turns crimson. "That...that's impossible!"

Eric shrugs. "It doesn't appear to be impossible. *Father.*"

The king drops his hold on me, shoving me to the ground. He snatches the books from Nym, shifting his dagger back to its sheath. He wraps a single beefy hand around Nym's throat and squeezes.

Nym makes a choking noise, both his hands flailing to grab at the king's arms, fighting for air.

"Take us away from here. Now, faen!"

"Stop it! You're hurting him." I fight to get back on my feet but the king sends a kick into my side, sending me back down.

My head cracks against the hard, stone floor. Spots float across my vision.

"Try again, faen!" Raghnall's eyes are blood-shot, wild like the Hunt.

Nym gasps for air again. Nothing happens.

"It won't work, Raghnall." Eric goes to take a step forward but thinks better of it. "You've lost."

King Raghnall releases a lion's roar. He tosses Nym to the side like a ragdoll. Nym's body slams against the stone wall with a crack. He slumps to the ground, a trickle of blue blood flowing from his head.

I stifle a shriek.

The king's sight is set on his son. He begins stomping toward the circle, malice reflected in his every move.

Sometimes the answer is right in front of you. You just need to choose to take hold of it.

Nan's words echo through my mind.

I glance between Nym who slowly opens his eyes, wheezing on the ground, then at my circle of friends who are frozen in fear.

The answer is right in front of you.

I look down. The only thing in front of me are my legs, as I lie pathetically on the floor of the castle.

The king takes another step.

Stop him. Eric begs.

The answer.

I suck in a breath. *Creator, be with me!*

Leaning onto my side, I swing my leg toward the king, hooking it around his ankle just as he takes one more step.

The king flies forward with a hefty *umph*. Both books fall from his arms. His face smacks the floor with a solid crack.

He howls in anger and pain. As he lifts his head, blood drips from his nose, running over his lips and across his chin.

I scramble across the floor and find the elephant figurine that belonged to my mother.

It's warm between my fingers. I squeeze the object in my hand, pull in a breath. Think of my mother.

And I scream.

Chapter Forty-Seven

I release the scream that could shatter eardrums. It's piercing and shocking and all the things it always possesses. But for one thing.

Hope. This time my scream is pregnant with the light of hope.

I focus on bringing my mother to my side, on her restoration, on ending the curse from the king.

None of the other fae seem bothered by the release of my banshee song, not even Nym. Except for King Raghnall. He howls from his spot on the floor, pressing his hands against his ears.

Ribbons of wind continue to swirl around our heads, move in and out of our arms and legs. This scream is to call my mother. But deep inside, I know it does more.

Those bright lights still reflecting the hope we have of fixing the Seven Seals. Of ending the plagues. This scream is for life.

A flood of energy shoots through my body, giving me the sensation that my feet are actually lifting from the ground. Am I flying? I can't tell. Every cell in my body feels like it's pulsing, beating, dancing to the music of my melody.

Nym disappears from where he stands, suddenly appearing right beside me. He has the king's dagger in his hand. I blink. He *can* use his powers down here. The faen staggers, his eyelids wavering. Blood still drips along his head.

I need to heal my friend but there's no time! Eric nods at me.

And then the use of my powers catches up with me. Blackness surrounds my vision. I sway on my feet. Eric runs the few short steps to catch me before I fall. A headache like a freight train slams into my temples. I'm shaking, a most unattractive moan coming from deep inside me.

The king shouts as he continues covering his ears. Royal blue blood now drips from his ears, as well, coating the sides of his face and running between his fingers. His wails are pure agony.

I gasp.What have I done? Why are none of the other fae affected?

And then I see her. *My mother.*

Saoirse.

She's beauty and light and chaos all wrapped into one. She hovers close to the wall, her specter form not truly human.

She looks like...*me.*

White hair, mismatched eyes, a waif-like figure. Even her skin is almost translucent, just like mine. The differences are obvious, too.

Her hair is wild and unkempt. A white dress, ripped and tattered. Her eyes, as beautiful as they are, are lined in red, as if she's missed a hundred nights of sleep.

She freezes, her face contorting into confusion.

Caoine, do it now. Cat's voice is once again inside my head.

I glance at Raghnall and back to my mom.

"Help." It's the only word I can think to say.

Is it enough?

Before I can conjure anything else to say, my mom turns her attention to the pathetic figure cowering on the ground.

She floats closer. Her inhuman eyes are now locked on the king.

He wants me dead. He's placed a curse on me and dad. I don't know why, but I know she'll be able to hear me.

She doesn't bother to look at me but the way her eyes glow with malice convinces me that she understands perfectly.

Before I can blink, she's closed the distance between her and the king, her movement supernaturally fast. Her hands cup the king's head, his blood smearing across her fingers, dripping from her wrists.

Her gaze turns crimson, her disheveled hair lifting around her from the wind that's still whipping around us.

She lowers her mouth to his, her lips hovering an inch away from his. As if she's about to give him a kiss.

A kiss of death. Then she screams.

The painful shattering of glass I'm expecting doesn't happen. Instead, I hear a song. A beautiful lament, laced with love and hope and joy.

Is this what the other fae heard me scream when I summoned her? Is it possible I no longer need my silver cloak to control my banshee song?

Her song is the most beautiful thing I've ever heard. I don't want it to end. Ever. I want to fall asleep and live inside its melody for eternity.

This is what those who are destined for death hear when I sing to them. My song really is a comfort. A thing that leads them into the afterlife in the most beautiful way possible.

My chest explodes with warmth. Pride.

My mom gave me this. I couldn't be more grateful.

The king's face goes limp and he slumps to the ground in a state of paralysis. Unmoving. At the same time, the wind around us comes to a sudden halt, every flash of the light from within the books now extinguished.

Silence fills the room. A silence unlike any other I've ever experienced.

No one moves or dares to breathe. Seconds pass. No, eternities pass.

Queen Faílenn lifts her chin. "It is finished."

Finally, I turn to look at the circle. Each of the fae are touching their heads, stumbling back as if coming out of a dream.

Eric looks at me. I push to stand on my own and nod at him.

The books on the ground are just that. Books. They don't glow, the pages aren't flapping back and forth from the wind. The air is still once more.

I look at the queen. "Are they fixed? Are the Seals whole again?"

Her mouth twitches into a smile. She lifts her chin in affirmation.

I can't contain the flood of relief that pours down my cheeks. Elation is my only friend as I leap into Eric's arms and hug him more fiercely than I ever thought possible. A second later I'm embracing Aubree—my sister in so many ways—like I'll never let go.

Cat is beside me, hugging me and laughing right along with the joyous celebration that all the fae are experiencing at the moment. Even the queen steps around the circle to give me a hug of thanks.

She pulls back, wiping tears from my cheeks. "You've done well, Daughter of the Realms. You've done well."

The tears are immediately replaced by a storm of even more, but I don't care. I'll cry until there isn't any liquid left inside my body. I deserve it.

I turn to find Nym but he's gone.

Of course. Why would I think he'd ever stick around? I hope he's okay after that hit on the head. I find Eric and Aubree for another round of hugs.

Then I gasp and grab Eric by the arm. "Oliver. My dad! Are they awake?"

But before I even finish the thought, I whirl around. My mom. She's here. The only thing I've wanted in life is right before me.

Her face is still filled with confusion. She tilts her head as if she's trying to remember a dream that's just out of reach.

I swallow, stepping forward. "Hello...mom."

She stares at me.

"Do you...do you know who I am?"

Her brow pulls together, her face softening.

We stand like this for minutes, the sound of celebration echoing around us. The king still lies slumped on the ground.

She floats a few feet closer to me. I hold my breath. She lifts a hand, placing it on my cheek.

I expect it to feel cold as ice, like the way people always refer to an encounter with a ghost. But her touch isn't cold. It's warm. Filled with love and curiosity.

The gentle touch of a mother. *Thank you, Creator. Thank you.*

I never get the chance to speak.

Instead, a voice comes from behind me. My dad's voice.

"Saoirse?"

Chapter Forty-Eight

Everything comes to a standstill.

My mom's gaze falls just over my shoulder. I slowly turn. My dad is inches from my back, Oliver lingering by the door that leads from the stairs.

My dad's face is drained of color, the pulse in his neck pounding a visual drumbeat. "Saoirse?" His voice is barely a whisper.

I swallow and step to the side to join the others who stand in awe.

My mom tilts her head as she stares at my dad. Her pupils grow larger and smaller like a camera lens fighting to focus.

With a stumble, my dad closes the distance between them. "Saoirse honey, it's me. Brent."

She flinches with a quick intake of breath.

Tears fall down my dad's cheeks. He lifts a single shaking hand to place on her cheek.

Her whimper is more of a shriek as she shoots backward, her eyes now red. Her face grows dark, her hands clenched at her sides.

"Saoirse." Cat's voice is hard.

My mom turns quickly.

Cat steps forward. "Saoirse." Her voice is softer now. "You're safe. Do not fear."

A low moan creeps from my mom. Her breathing is panicked, her chest rising and falling in quick succession as she pants. She looks around from my dad to me to Cat and back again.

I fight the terror that's blossoming deep in my belly. She doesn't recognize us?

My dad goes to plead with her again, but I lift my hand to stop him. "Mom?" Her focus lands on me. "Mom. It's me, your daughter. Caoine."

Her breathing continues in huffs. Another moan slips free, her eyes still scarlet.

My dad takes a small step forward. "Please, Saoirse."

Her whine is louder this time, like a feral cat cornered in an alleyway. She floats further backward.

I look at Catherine. "Is there something we can do?"

"Once again, you hold the power to heal all wounds. Even those that extend beyond reason," she says.

I shake my head. "What do I do?"

Cat smiles. "You are a healer, Caoine."

Healer.

I swallow. The Gift of Life.

I gasp, glancing at my mom. She still hovers against the wall, her breathing unsteady.

She died on the night I was given to the world of the fae as a banshee. Her body didn't fully pass into the afterlife. She was cursed to stay in the Mortal Realm as a wild banshee, with no memory of her prior life, her banshee screams creating chaos.

Warmth tickles my fingers. I look around the room, finding Oliver. He nods at me, a small smile that says he believes in me.

Aubree gives me the same encouraging look as she mouths the words, *You've got this.*

My heart stumbles over my doubt.

Eric's voice echoes in my head. ***You saved your dad. Now***

go save your mom. He dips his chin, his hazel eyes locked on mine.

I grab my dad's hand and give it a quick squeeze, then turn back to my mom, sucking in a slow lungful of air. I *can* save my mom.

With a few tentative steps, I cross to her. She jolts, flinching toward the wall. I hold up my hands and smile.

She frowns and watches me as I approach.

I keep my palms up. "Hey, Mom. It's just me, your daughter. I promise not to hurt you."

She trembles, as I slowly reach toward her.

I freeze. "I—I love you. I would never hurt you."

Her scowl relaxes, her face softening for an instant before it resumes its distrust.

A minute passes as I stand there, smiling at her, internally begging her to believe me.

I turn my hand so it's palm up. "May I...touch you?"

My mom's mouth falls open and she blinks rapidly. She watches intently as my hand closes the gap.

I still once more. "It's just a touch."

She inhales sharply as my fingers connect with her arm but she doesn't move away. Her only response is a deep moan.

I clear my throat. What do I do now? When I saved my dad I just wanted him to be alive again. Do I simply wish for her to be healed?

Terror floods my chest but I close my eyes anyway. Swallow. Concentrate.

I love you, mom. Please come back to me. I give you life.

Nothing happens. I suck in a breath and concentrate harder. Still, I feel nothing.

I crack an eye open. My mom simply stares at me, her head tilted in confusion.

Please, please. I need you to be alive, Mom. Please.

The longer nothing happens the more I'm choked by my helplessness.

Please.

That familiar doubt taking residence deep in my chest.

No. I can do this. I've always been able to. I just never believed in myself.

I gasp and let go internally, even though my hand still holds my mom's arm.

Love. I love her. I miss her. This is the only thing I've ever wanted.

Vertigo sinks its claws into my head, heat pulsing along my arms and hands. I don't open my eyes, simply allow it to happen.

Warmth. Dizziness. A heartbeat so fast I fear it might leap from my chest.

And then it fades, fades, fades. Until it's gone.

I release the breath I've been holding, releasing my grip on my mom.

Everything is still.

Chapter Forty-Nine

My mom is whole. She's not the broken, wild creature from just moments before.

She's clean and healed. And *alive.*

My mom is alive!

And she looks so much like me. Or I look like her. Or whatever. I don't care anymore.

I throw myself into her arms before she can speak.

Tears stain my cheeks and creep along my neck and soil my shirt. Sobs wrack my chest and I know I sound like a silly little girl.

And I couldn't care less. I don't care about anything in this world other than the fact that my mom is holding me and hugging me and kissing me all at the same time.

"Caoine?" she breathes into my hair.

I nod against her shoulder, too busy crying to form words.

"Saoirse." My dad joins our small reunion with a hug from behind.

"Brent?" Her voice is the most beautiful song I've ever heard.

Minutes pass before I finally allow myself to let her go, to step back. My mom and dad continue to hold one another, tears and words of love filling the space between them.

I hold my elbows, my arms around my waist as I stand and cry. Aubree steps forward, her arms around my middle. Then another someone is there. Cat. My old friend—and apparently, queen—hugs me from the other side.

The three of us laugh and hug in joy and astonishment.

Suddenly, Oliver is beside me. Tears spill over his cheeks as he watches my parents express their love in kisses and whispers.

Eric is watching me, his expression filled with gratitude. Once again, he nods at me. I nod back.

I couldn't have done any of this without him. He may have brought hell on earth and into my life just months ago, but I wouldn't change a thing about it.

Even with the loss—so much loss. Seamus. Gar. So many others that go unnamed—I still wouldn't change it. Without Eric, the king would never have been stopped. Our worlds would no longer be safe.

I wouldn't have my Gift. Wouldn't have my mom back.

Thank you, is all I can think to say to him. If he feels safe saying those words to me, I should be honored to say them to him.

He smiles.

We stand like this for minutes, hours. I'm vaguely aware of the other fae from the spell shifting around me, exiting the room. Whispers echo from the stairwell and Killian and Laoise appear.

The wisp's face practically glows with excitement. My elf friend smiles at me and I can sense the message he attempts to send to me. *Well done* and *You are truly fae* and *You do belong*.

No more doubts.

The pair step over to where King Raghnall remains in a slump on the floor, standing guard over him.

Oliver crosses the room and pulls Eric into a fierce hug, tears now on both their cheeks. Aubree's mother simply stands to the side, taking in each of the groups as we celebrate and process our new world.

Old prejudices set aside. Forgiveness for even the most heinous of sins. Restoration from the clutches of death.

I squeeze Aubree and Cat once more before throwing myself back into my mom's arms, my dad still holding onto her.

"Mom," I whisper. A single word I never thought I would utter.

She kisses my forehead and pulls me back. "Hello, darling."

My eyes swallow every part of her face. Her skin is renewed, her hair shiny and curled. Her youth has been restored and she barely looks older than me.

She wipes away the tears that fall from my cheeks. "You are so beautiful."

I suck in a breath.

My dad rubs my back. "She's exactly like you. Just as stubborn and selfless. This girl has more compassion and grace than I've ever known."

My mom places her palm on my dad's face. "You think all of that is from me?"

Brand new tears stream along my dad's cheeks and they lean in to kiss once more.

"I've missed you," he whispers to her.

She strokes his cheek. "And I, you." My mom turns to me. "Thank you, Caoine, for saving me. For bringing me back to who I am, so I can be with the Creator."

I blink. "Be with the Creator?"

Queen Faílenn glides closer to our little huddle. "Saoirse's time is almost up."

My jaw drops and I look at my dad who appears just as shocked as I am. I whip back around to the queen. "What do you mean?"

My mom squeezes my hand. "She means you've saved me from a life of death as a monster within the Mortal Realm. But the night Nia visited and bestowed your banshee song upon you, that was my last night alive as you know it."

I shake my head. "But...but I have the Gift of Life. I brought you back again. You're alive."

The queen nods. "You saved her from a life in the underworld, this is true. But she must now pass on to the fate that was meant for her long ago. She must become one with creation."

"But...but—" I step back, my head bobbing between the queen and my mom. "I don't understand."

My dad pulls in a shaky breath. "I think I do." His gaze is meant only for my mom. "Caoine has the ability to see a person's true destiny for continued life or their time to pass on while in her banshee state. It wasn't time for my life to end, which is why her Gift worked to bring me back." Another tear falls down his cheek. "But your time came to an end the night of her birth. It didn't matter if Nia showed up and changed Caoine's life, you were going to die regardless."

A smile envelopes my mom's face, the deepest love on her face as she looks at my dad. "I never wanted to leave you." She glances at me. "Either of you. But my time to return to the Creator has come." She pulls both of us into a hug. "I love you both so much." She kisses the top of my head. "Know that I will always be with you. Always."

Sobs wrack my chest again, snot dripping from my nose. I don't care. I squeeze my mom so tightly that I might never let go.

I won't let go.

I don't want to let go.

My dad whimpers as he cries, too, his lips once again on hers. I don't even feel weird that my parents are kissing with me inches away.

This is the only thing I've wanted in my life.

This is not the end, Caoine. Do not lose heart. I pull back and make eye contact with the queen.

It's not the end. I swallow. Of course, it isn't. I have my dad back. I got the one desire I've always had—to be held and kissed by my mom. Our lives will go back to normal. And I will always be connected with my mom, through nature or each time I talk to the Creator.

I glance at my dad. And every time we share memories, she'll be right beside us, in spirit.

Warmth floods my core and I gather my mom in one more hug, stepping back. "I understand this now. I didn't before but..." I glance at my dad. He nods. "I think I do, now."

He looks at me and I know it's time. He's still holding her hands.

I wrap my arms around my mom's waist and look at the queen. "We're ready."

She smiles.

"I love you," my dad says to her. "Even beyond death. You are my soulmate."

"And you are mine." My mom is crying, too. "I love you, Brent Roberts. And I wouldn't change a thing. You make me human."

I stifle a cry. "I love you, Mom. So, so much."

Tears trickle along her chin and neck now. "I love you too, sweetheart." She places a hand on my face. "Remember, I'll always be with you." She looks at my dad. "You just need to look."

He smiles. I can't keep the tears at bay. We both fall back into a hug. I close my eyes tight. I sense the queen doing something beside us.

Then all I feel in my arms is air.

Chapter Fifty

My mom is gone. Disappeared in much the same way that Seamus did.

I pull my hands down my face to wipe away the tears and lean into my dad's chest for another hug. I thought I would have more time with her. Why did she have to leave so soon?

Heat pulses deep inside my chest, an agony spreading across my limbs. A pain unlike any I've felt before.

I never had a mother. But seeing her in person opened a hole in my spirit. Gave me hope for a future that cannot be. I cry into my dad's shoulder until the tears stop coming.

Pulling back, I wipe my face, turning to Aubree and Cat. Eric and Oliver. All my friends that have been waiting patiently. They collectively close in for hugs. Even Nym joins us, the bleeding on his head having come to a stop. The queen stands to the side and watches with interest. Killian and Laoise continue to take their post as guardians.

Finally, I turn to Queen Faílenn. "So, is this it? The spell worked?" I pull in a ragged breath and take my dad's hand in mine. "Can we...can we go home now?"

The queen nods. "You have done well, my child. You may

return to the Mortal Realm, which has been restored to its former glory."

I blink. Whatever that means.

Eric shifts in his spot. "What about my father?" He looks down at the slumped form of the king on the ground. "What will become of him once he wakes?"

The queen's face turns grave. "He will no longer have a memory of being your father. Or of being king. Saoirse turned his own law against him. He is already deep in the throes of insanity. There is no restoring him to the position of king."

Eric jolts. "He's no longer king? What does that mean? Who will lead the Unseelie Realm?"

Queen Faílenn smiles. "You will."

"No." Eric shakes his head. "That's impossible. I can't be king. I—I haven't been raised to lead. I know nothing about leading an entire realm."

The queen nods. "Which makes you the perfect candidate for such a position. You were raised away from royalty. You've lived among the people and know what it is to be common. Power is not something that controls your life."

"But, no. This doesn't make sense. I have brothers. One of them should be king."

She dips her chin. "And where are they? Where were they when their father began the descent of leading his people into bondage? Where are they now, when all the realms need them most, to restore the Seals?"

Eric swallows.

"You're the only one who was willing to come, *Rohan*."

I gasp at the use of his formal name. Something Eric gave up long ago to be something other than that simple wood sprite trapped in a life in the forests.

"I—" He hesitates. "What must I do?"

She smiles. "Kneel before me."

Eric does so.

The queen places her hands on top of his head. "Rohan, son

of Raghnall, former king of the Unseelie Realm, I bestow upon you the role of king of the Unseelie people. To honor and lead them justly and wisely. To show compassion in times of mourning and to show might in times of war. May your reign be long and prosperous."

I release the breath I've been holding.

Dude. Eric is the freaking *king* of the Unseelie Realm?

He pulls in a full breath, coming to his feet. His shoulders sit much higher than before. The way in which he stands is...kingly.

Eric smirks and glances at Nym. Most likely an inside joke they share.

I fidget with the edge of my shirt. ***Congrats?***

He laughs. ***Don't worry. I won't force you to call me King Rohan. Your Majesty will do.***

Now I laugh. Oliver side-eyes us but I just shake my head.

Eric looks at Queen Faílenn. "What will be done with my father?"

Her smile fades. "Take him back to the Unseelie. Give him care as you would any other who can no longer tell reality from fiction. He is no longer a threat to us or the Mortal Realm." She pauses. "Effective immediately, the Laws of Necessity are banished. As long as you and I can work together for the good of all the realms, there is no need for any of the fae to be held captive."

Eric bows a head. "Of course, Queen Faílenn. The Unseelie fae are grateful for the chance to prove themselves once again. We will strive to live in harmony with all those around us."

I frown. I'm not so sure I like this new kingly Eric. What happened to my sarcastic friend?

As if he can read my mind, Eric turns to look at me. ***You're not off the hook, Roberts. You and soccer boy over there will have to put up with me when I visit.***

I sigh and smile. ***Deal.*** I give him a wink and mouth to Oliver that I'll tell him about it later.

A thought occurs to me and I whip around to face Cat. "Wait.

You're fae. Like, the Queen of the Banshees. Does this mean you're leaving school now?"

Cat gives me a sad smile. "I'm sorry but I will have to get back to my role as queen. I promise to visit when I can. But it may not be very often."

My face falls. I look at Aubree. "And you?"

She snorts. "Are you kidding? We can't all disappear from school at the same time or it will be super suspicious." She hugs me. "Sorry kid. You're stuck with me." She glances at her mother. "As long as I'm not needed here, I think I'll stick around the Mortal Realm for a bit longer."

I shrug. I'm crying again. "Okay, I guess."

Aubree laughs.

"Me, too." The tiny voice comes from Nym, who stands by my dad, holding his hand. "I stay, too."

I glance at my dad and back at the faen. "You're staying in the Mortal Realm?" I look at Eric. "Are you okay with this?"

He grins. "Sure. How else will I keep tabs on you while I'm being kingly?"

I narrow my eyes at him. "We don't need a babysitter, thanks."

My dad clears his throat. "Uh, are you sure about that?" His smile is weak. "We don't have a great track record, you know."

"Haha." I stick my tongue out at him.

Everyone laughs.

I look around. "Okay, so things will go back to normal and I'll see my fae friends semi-often." I glance at Killian and Laoise. "What about you two?"

Killian nods. "You might see us once in a while if it suits you."

I smile. "It does."

He glances at Laoise with a smirk. "Just keep your kids away from the forest and warn them not to follow any bright lights."

"Did you just make a joke?" My brows jump up.

Killian's cheeks go scarlet.

Laoise giggles, melting into a small ball of light, then becoming whole again.

I laugh and walk over to give them each a hug.

Finally, I fall into Oliver's arms. He's the one person I haven't connected with yet. The one person my heart has been longing for since this whole journey began.

I look back to my circle of friends. "I suppose I could always come visit you guys, too."

Queen Faílenn shakes her head. "I'm sorry, Caoine. But you cannot return to either of the Faerie Realms until you are ready to leave the Mortal Realm for good. Once you return you will be a part of the Faerie Realms forever."

My jaw drops. "I'm stuck in the Mortal Realm for good?"

She smiles. "A banshee's song does not belong in the Faerie Realms. It is meant for mortals, to comfort. To bring peace. When you return to us, your song will be no more. When you choose to join us, we will be waiting." The queen tilts her head. "Take all the time you need. There is no rush."

My people. I've got people. I'm not simply human. I'm not merely fae. I'm a banshee.

Chapter Fifty-One

The moon hovers in the night sky, a shiny alabaster. Normal.

I sigh and lean my head on Oliver's shoulder. We're seated on my front porch, the warm almost-summer night welcoming.

Despite the world experiencing Armageddon, school has somehow reopened, becoming a safe haven for so many students. Communities worldwide continue to recover from the unexplained bouts of "sleeping sickness" and the problems it caused, along with the freak natural disasters that were unleashed. I guess opening the doors of West Lincoln High was the closest they could get to making life normal for our generation, even if we would have years of rebuilding ahead of us.

He weaves his fingers through mine. "Ready for tomorrow?"

"Graduation?" I frown. "Yes. No. Maybe?"

Oliver chuckles.

I tilt my head to look at him. "You?"

He nods. "Absolutely." His smile is only for me. "We'll have an entire summer together before I leave for college."

I groan. "Don't remind me of our impending separation."

He pulls me close, his lips on mine. I sigh again.

He brushes hair from my forehead and reaches down to pull my right hand up. "You've got this to look at, for when you miss me."

His fingers brush over the ring that graces my right ring finger. The one he gave me soon after we returned to the Mortal Realm.

The ring I saw in the vision from the well, all those months ago while in the Unseelie Realm. Not an engagement ring. But a ring that says he promises to be faithful. That we have a future together.

I twist my hand to look at the small glittery stone, silver sparkling in the moonlight. "So you mean I'll have to stare at it all day?"

He laughs again and pulls me into a hug. "My only worry is who will follow you on your nightly excursions while I'm away."

I tip my head to the side. "Pretty sure my dad can handle it. He *did* do it for like, my entire life before you came along."

He shrugs. "I know. I just worry."

"Have you forgotten? I survived not one, but *two* trips into the Unseelie Realm. I may be part human, but I'm not fragile. I've got a feisty bit of a fae-side, you know."

Oliver settles his forehead against mine. "I know how strong you are, Caoine. I just like to be needed sometimes, too."

I pop a kiss on his lips before pulling back. "I'll be fine while you're gone. I mean, we're heavy another family member, right?"

Nym did exactly what he said he would. He followed my dad home and hasn't left his side since. I still can't figure out their connection but sometimes I get the feeling that Nym has figured out a way to plant thoughts in my dad's mind, even though my dad has no magical connection. They're that close.

Which makes me happy. My dad needs someone in his life other than me. I've always known he'd never remarry. My mom was his true love from the beginning. He's never had any interest in going down that road again.

And I'm okay with that. Nym has a heart of gold and my dad clearly enjoys having him around. The little guy even glamours himself to appear human when they go in public. Short, but human.

I sniff. "Think Aubree will do something psycho at the ceremony?"

"Why wouldn't she?" He winks at me. "This is her first graduation after all."

"First?"

He shrugs. "Who knows what she'll do after school's done? Maybe she'll decide to go back and annoy another group of teenagers."

I giggle and lean my head on his shoulder again. He lifts my left hand, kissing the spot where my pinky is missing. Warmth swells in my chest.

"Speaking of which, you never told me what you've decided to do. I know college is out of the question. But what did Cat want when she visited the other day?"

"Oh, right. I forgot to tell you." I lift my head. "I think I'll snag a job at a local retailer or something, just to pass the time. But..."

"But?"

I stifle a grin. "Well, I think I've found my calling. Like, other than my whole being a banshee each night."

I pause.

Oliver shakes my hand. "And?"

"I'm going to be a teacher."

"Come again?"

"To other banshees. Young fae who are just coming into their gift. Fae who have no clue what to expect and need help learning the ropes. I mean, they're fae, so at least they've got that much on their side. But there is no training in the Unseelie Realm for banshees. They'll need guidance. The thing I so badly wanted when I was a kid, but my dad couldn't provide for me." My smile is genuine, even if laced with sadness. "I told Cat I want to help, I want to be there for others in a way no one could be for me."

"And she's down for that?"

I nod. "She thinks it's a great idea. She's going to direct the banshees my way when they first cross over the Veil."

"Wow. That's so cool." He tucks a piece of hair behind my ear. "Proud of you."

I smile. "Thanks." I lean in and place a kiss on his lips. "I'm kinda proud of you, too."

"Me?" His fingers weave through mine again. "What did I do?"

"Ummm, everything? You went where no other mortal would want to go, just to help me. To save the world."

He lifts his chest. "Well, I do what I can."

I laugh and smack his arm. "Uh-huh."

Oliver embraces me tighter. "By the way, Eric promised to be there tomorrow. To cheer the three of us on."

I snort. "As long as he remembers to keep his King Eric form, and not slip back into his red-headed appearance. I'm pretty sure a few teachers would notice if he showed up like that."

"Oh, he's fully aware of that."

I sigh. "I'm glad you two are talking again." I tilt my head. "Maybe...friends?"

The grin falls from his face, but not completely. "Yeah. I think we are. I mean, we can be. If he's willing to, that is."

I kiss his shoulder. "I'm sure he'd be good with that." I breathe him in.

Thankful for Oliver, for friendships. Thankful that our Creator is always with us.

Oliver gives me another kiss and we sink into a few moments of silence. Memories of the past school year flood my mind.

My first day of school, trying my hardest to keep Aubree, Oliver, and Seamus out of my life. Being totally unsuccessful. All the drama of Halloween and the Unseelie and the Seals.

I sigh. I wouldn't trade this for the world.

And then a niggle, a tickle at the back of my mind, the familiar sensation I've come to know over the past eighteen years.

I pull in a breath and soak in another few seconds of my time with Oliver before I spoil it for him. Then I lean back and give him that telltale look that says it's time.

He nods and gives me one more kiss before he stands, ready to follow me wherever I go.

Excitement fills my core. A longing to share my banshee song, to help others in the only way I know how. Oliver holds up my familiar cloak.

I shake my head. "I don't need that anymore to control my song."

His smiles. "I know. But it becomes you."

My cheeks heat as he slips the silver sheath of fabric over my shoulders. Then I step out into the night.

Ready to share my banshee song with those in need of comfort and compassion.

I share my banshee song one more time as a high schooler. I share it with the man that I love.

Epilogue

Forty-two years later

No one is ever truly prepared for the end.

In high school, we focus on football games and prom and end-of-the-year parties, blind-sided when graduation day appears. A bride plans for months or years for her big day, dreams of cakes and dances and dresses, only to have that purpose stolen with a single kiss.

And then there's death.

The end of a life can be tragic or expected or even a cause for celebration, for those ready to be free of earthly pain and headed to see their Creator. Yet, I have no idea how to feel about *his* death.

Oliver's.

I kneel in the hard dirt of his grave, the cold of autumn seeping into my jeans and bathing my skin. The day is bright, the sun shining unusually intense in the sky above. A slight breeze tosses leaves on the ground and tumbles a scent of crisp spice my way. There are no birds left to chirp. All of those have gone south for the approaching winter.

And here I sit. Staring at the headstone of the only human man I will ever love. *Could* ever love. I had four glorious decades with my partner, ones I wouldn't change for the world. He stood by me through thick and thin, literally. The day we found out I could never have children, due to my...unusual design. Of course, the doctors went on about fertility and statistics and gave hope with different methods of conception. But we never went down that road. Oliver accepted the truth and never looked back. Our life was just him and me. And neither of us ever wanted it to be different than that.

A lifetime filled with trips to Europe, mourning the loss of his parents, traveling the country with his music career, mourning the loss of my dad. At least he got to visit Gnait a handful of times. Aubree gladly accompanied him in so he could see his old friend.

When my dad passed, Nym stopped coming around, too. Another empty space in my heart.

But Oliver and I spent time on beaches and in the mountains and skiing down impossibly high mountains. Every minute with him. Every minute, worth it.

Thank you, Creator. For the time I had with him.

Eric came around as often as he could, always eager to be with his best friend. He would stay for months, only to disappear one morning, an urgent matter in the Unseelie Realm needing his attention. But he'd always breeze back into our lives in some way or another. Ready to take Oliver to a football game, or to celebrate a birthday, or sometimes to just sit and reminisce of days past. He couldn't be here much the past few years, though. Kingly duties, and all.

Just as I knew I wouldn't see Cat again, Aibell and I never crossed paths again. I assume her time on earth aged her as any normal human.

Aubree warned that she wouldn't be able to come around much, once everything with the Unseelie King was finished. Her place was the Seelie Realm, beside her mother. But it still left a hole in my life that could never be replaced. She did visit every so often. She even brought Nan a few times, on her visits. But they were never often enough. I miss her. I haven't seen her in over two years.

Oliver's been gone for one.

I squeeze my eyes tight but no more tears are to be found.

Alone. I've been alone for almost a year. No children or friends to pick me up, to care for me when my banshee side awoke at night. Yet...that was okay. I've been fine with that. My whole life I had either a dad who protected me or a partner who would give his life for mine. I have no bitterness for the fact that I've had to do my job alone recently.

Leaves crunch behind me. I smile. Breathe.

He's here.

For months now I've expected this moment to arrive, but also hoped it wouldn't. For the sake of my heart. The one that was ripped open, bleeding across memories, begging for one more day with the love of my life.

Yet, here I am. Ready. Finally. It's as if Eric was waiting for a cue from my heart, a beacon to let him know when I would be ready. When he could come.

And I'm ready. Now I'm ready.

I slowly stand, brushing soil from my legs as I tuck a loose strand of white hair behind my ear. I turn to face him.

He stands just in front of the invisible Veil. Beside him is a woman. She appears to be the same age as Eric and I, but then again, so do all the fae. Deep in my gut, I sense that she's much older.

Eric has chosen the tall and lanky form from when I first met him, at the beginning of our senior year of high school.

His red hair is striking against his pale skin. It's grown out and tousled. He resembles every bit of the high school soccer player that I remember. An homage to his oldest and best friend?

I glance over my shoulder at Oliver's grave, another wave of emotion filling my core.

Eric is dressed as a royal faerie would dress: leather boots, a vested tunic, gloves. The only thing he lacks is a crown on his head.

With a step forward, I nod at him, my attention settling on the breathtaking woman standing before me.

His smile overtakes his face. "Caoine, meet my mother. Shaylah."

I gasp. He's searched for her for so many years. His search is finally over.

Her large brown curls frame a round face, her honeyed skin flawless. Violet eyes draw me in, welcome me. *Home.*

She's a full foot shorter than Eric but is somehow more commanding.

Shaylah nods toward me. "Caoine. I've heard so much about you."

The breath catches in my throat. "And I, you. Shaylah."

Tears spill free and I laugh. Eric's serious facade breaks. He crosses to me in a few strides, grabbing me into a hug. I laugh as he swings me around in a circle before settling me on my feet, digging his knuckles into the top of my head like the kid-sister that I've become to him.

My blood pulses through my veins and my head buzzes with emotion—elation, melancholy, fear.

He pauses, his smile fading slowly. He notices Oliver's grave behind me. He swallows hard, his jaw tensing.

Emotion clouds his face. "He was my best friend. Even though I hadn't seen him in so long he—he was still the best friend I ever had."

"I know, Eric. I know. And you were his."

These words are true. There was never any jealousy within Oliver when we spoke of Eric, even though he knew Eric would always have a part of my heart.

He reaches back to beckon his mother to join us by the grave.

"Mother, I'd like you to meet Oliver, the best friend I ever had." His tears fall freely now.

Shaylah gives a melancholy smile, holding Eric's hand with both of hers. She looks back to the grave. "It's an honor to meet you, Oliver."

The three of us stand in silence, letting the moment be. Healing and hurting.

Eric doesn't look at me when he says the next words. "I've come here so often over the last year. So many times."

I gasp and turn to look at him. "But—"

Eric shakes his head, his gaze still on that grave. "It wasn't time. You needed space to mourn, to let go of him." He looks down at his mother, wrapping an arm around her before finally looking at me. "I could never interfere with that."

Now I'm the one crying. Fat, hot tears that drip from my chin and melt into my skin. "You waited for me to be ready?"

"Of course. That's what brothers do, Caoine."

I nod. We look back toward Oliver for one last look before our journey.

Finally, he pats my back. "You ready?"

I swallow and glance over my shoulder at the grave of my late husband.

Am I ready?

Ready to leave behind my human existence? To give up my banshee song once and for all? Ready to begin life anew in the Unseelie Realm, the realm I was meant to join since the day of my birth?

Instead of answering, I turn back to Eric and nod. I lean up on my toes and give his mother a tight hug. She returns the gesture with a warm smile.

"Yes. I'm ready."

He sighs. "You sure you won't miss singing at night?"

"Of course, I will." The words are out of my mouth before I can consider them.

That breeze picks back up, whipping another loose lock of

hair across my face, a faint scent of lavender passing by. I tuck it behind my ear.

This is the truth. Somewhere over the years, I've not only come to accept my banshee side, I've come to adore it.

I love myself for who I am and how I was made by the Creator. For what I was created to be. And I will miss it.

I will miss singing my song.

My banshee song.

"I'm ready, Eric," I whisper.

He takes his mother's hand before taking mine in his other hand. "I'm glad you're coming. I've got someone I'd like you to meet." He gives me a wink.

"A...*queen?*"

This time Shaylah laughs. "You will adore her, Caoine. She and Eric are a perfect fit."

He shakes his mother's hand. "She was the one who helped me find my mother. That's how I knew she was the one. She cared about what I cared about. Deeply."

We walk toward the Veil. "You've found your Oliver."

Another tear falls down his cheek, despite his smile. "I have."

Just before the three of us step over the Veil, Eric turns to me, his joyful demeanor now serious. "Can I ask one favor of you?"

"Of course. What do you need?"

"Would you still sing to me sometimes, when we get home? I know it might not be your banshee song but...I love it when you sing. It reminds me of Oliver."

Warmth builds in my belly and bubbles through my limbs, bringing a wide smile to my face. I take Shaylah's other hand in mine so the three of us are in a circle.

I squeeze their hands. "Yes, Eric. I will sing to you. I will sing to anyone who wants to hear. As often as they want. I will sing my song. Because that's what I do.

"I sing."

<h1 style="text-align:center">Pronunciation Guide</h1>

Caoine—keyn
    Saoirse—SEER·shuh
    Clíodhna—KLEE·uh·nuh
    Aibell—ee·BOOL
    Laoise—LEE·shuh
    Raghnall—RAHY·nuhl
    Faílenn—FEE·luhn
    Eithne—ahy·NUH
    Einin—ahy·NEEN
    Elan—EE·luhn
    Marfóir—mahr·FYA·ruh
    Mairéad—muh·RED
    Oísin—oh·SHEEN
    Neamini—nuh·MEE·nee
    Seamus—SHEY·muhs
    Bean-nighe—ben·NEE·yuh
    Bunaidh—bun·NEE

Acknowledgments

It's finished! Reader, I can't express how grateful I am that you stuck with me through this series. It took longer to release the final book in Caoine's journey than I originally anticipated. For those of you that have read this far, thank you a thousand times over!

To my family, thank you for everything you've done to help me make this series a reality. Tim, I couldn't have asked God for a better partner to do life with than you. You are amazing and I count my lucky stars each time you give me the encouragement I need or urge me to go somewhere quiet to write while you take care of the family. Gabby, Grace, and Scar, thank you for being you. Never change who you are to please anyone. God made you the perfect version of you. Each of you inspires me to be a better person, daily. I love all of you so much.

Gloria, this book wouldn't be half of what it is without your input. You are truly gifted as a writer and an editor. Thank you for your unending support and friendship.

Brandy, where would I be without you? Oh, probably not writing at all. And without so many things that you've helped me figure out or accomplish. I'm not exaggerating when I say I wouldn't be able to do this author thing without you by my side. Thank you, friend!

Carrie, my addicted-texter-bestie/#WBCE partner in crime. Thank you for encouraging me to dry my tears each time something didn't go right. I wouldn't want to do anything in the writing universe if you weren't with me!

My beta readers, Jill, Cory, Andi, and Gloria. Your feedback for this book was invaluable. Thank you for helping me make this shiny and ready for release!

Avery, once again, you make my writing so much better. Thank you for always being so much more than "just" a line editor. You are truly a wonderful friend!

Travis, thank you for this final and most beautiful cover! You understood my vision and ran with it. Thank you so much!

Thank you, Jesus. For the words to write and the direction you lead. Life is always an adventure with you! Proverbs 3:5-6.

Never forget, Reader, You Belong.

Laura

About the Author

Laura L. Zimmerman lives in a tiny rural town in south-central Pennsylvania with her husband, daughters, and her four adorable kitties. Besides writing, she is passionate about loving Jesus, singing loudly, and staying active with yoga.

She's an avid coffee drinker and is a sucker for anything Jane Austen related. Thanks to a certain boy wizard, she may or may not be convinced she's the long-lost twin of Luna Lovegood. Laura has been married to her Mr. Darcy for 24 years.

She loves to read and write YA sci-fi/fantasy and middle-grade mysteries. Her favorite tropes are enemies-to-lovers and grumpy/sunshine.

She's the author of the award winning YA fantasy *Banshee Song Series*, and middle-grade mystery novels *The Curse of Ozpa Springs* and *R.A.D. Detectives: The Case of the Missing Robot*! Find her books on Amazon and other major retailers.

Leave a Review!

I love to hear from my readers!

Follow me on social media for all my latest bookish news or to drop me a line!

www.lauralzimmerman.org

If you enjoyed this book, please consider leaving a review on all major retailers, including Amazon, Barnes & Noble, and Goodreads. I would really appreciate it!